SO

by
R.D.HALL

SILVER MINK BOOKS
PO Box CR25 Leeds LS7 3TN
and
PO Box 1614 New York NY 10156

New authors welcome

Printed and bound in Great Britain

SILVER MINK is an imprint of SILVER MOON BOOKS
of LEEDS

Silver Mink books are written for women, Silver Moon
books are written for men; but the themes are similar.

*[Silver Moon Books of Leeds and Silver Moon Books of London
are in no way connected]*

**If you like one of our books you will probably like
them all!**
To order other titles see details and extracts on back
pages

**For free 20 page booklet of extracts from previous books
(and, if you wish to be on our confidential mailing list,
from forthcoming monthly titles as they are published)
please write to:-**
Silver Moon Reader Services

PO Box CR 25 LEEDS LS7 3TN
or
PO Box 1614 NEW YORK NY 10156

Surely the most erotic freebie ever!!

SONIA first published 1995
Copyright R.D.Hall

SONIA

This is fiction - in real life, practice safe sex

CHAPTER 1.

She was a Filipino, with Spanish blood I thought, young and far from home and very nubile, and I suppose I was hooked from that first moment when we brushed past each other in the passageway. Her dark eyes wandered over me, just a little apprehensive perhaps, and the way she put her hands together at her slender throat with such a submissive sort of a curtsey involved my thoughts and dreams and unfortunately the contents of my pants so that in my confusion she was gone before I could speak.

And then those sounds, in a few days that is, and only when nobody but the two us us were in the house - could it be leather smacking onto bare flesh? It sounded so, but could that really be what it was? Was she really flagellating herself? Surely not, but one can imagine the stimulation it gave to my eager imagination!

I licked my lips and dreamed of her upended and wriggling about naked on my lap and did nothing.

Then, one quiet afternoon, the intriguing sounds manifested themselves more clearly than ever before. Surely someone was being beaten, it had to be that, and the little gasps and gurgles that came with it did nothing to dispel the thrill of it! I sat on the landing and pondered in some considerable excitement I can tell you; trying hard to restrain my mounting lust.

Then I heard Sonia's bedroom door open.

"Oh Sir," she said when she saw me - had she known those sounds would bring me out? - and what a sweetly seductive little voice she had and how revealingly she was attired, though I cannot now describe it. She made that erotic little hands-together-at-the-throat submission, or whatever it was.

"Oh Mr Collett, can you help me a moment? Please, oh please?"

Please she said! And how much significance she invested in that one little word and the demure look that shone from those glorious dark eyes! Did I say they were dark? Probably, but I cannot have done justice to them, or to those perfect white pearls of teeth that kept appearing. How beautifully that 'please' sounded in my ears, connecting with all my manly feelings and plucking at them unerringly! And it went all the way to my heart as well, I'm telling you, all the way!

She was Filipino, as I have said, and the Spanish ancestry I deduced from one of her surnames, which was Barros or Barracos - something like that.

She lived on the ground floor next to our landlady, Mrs Keech. The granny-annexe didn't have a granny but a young Irish family temporarily between more permanent homes... I was upstairs - a couple of attic-rooms and a landing. Peaceful by today's standards.

The four little households quite filled the house. There were no vacancies though there was one guest room, used occasionally by a visiting grand-daughter.

I was in foreign parts those days, border country between Camden Town and St John's Wood. And Sonia was in this country training for nursing qualifications and not intending to return home for a jolly good length of time: and from what I learned over the next months, I can't say I blamed her. The old lady, Mrs Keech, gave her a room and full run of facilities because a friend of hers had asked her if she could take in Sonia for a while. But I think she was exasperated by her: she was opportunistic all right and more-or-less pleased herself... Mind you, after I took her on, the

6

two of them got on better and I heard fewer complaints from the old lady.

Sonia and I were sole occupants of the house at that time. It was warm summer weather and so I had my living-room door ajar. Mrs Keech was out visiting relatives - something she did a lot, I was glad to realize later - and the young family was out also, I knew not where.

Sonia had been in residence, oh, for less than a fort-night. We had met, passing to and from the bathroom which had an adjoining toilet which six? Yes, six - and occasion-ally seven - of us all told had to use between us. I had said hello to her already but even before that I knew there was a newcomer - and a female at that - because different undies had turned up for drying-off in the bathroom.

Even those years ago, transparent nylon briefs were favoured by some and I guessed their owner might be a young miss. They weren't so mini in those days and lined and wide gussets were 'de rigeur'.

I noticed also the favoured stockings, suspenders etc, and to myself I awarded her a mark or two of approval.

Well, that day was the beginning of an adventure: I wasn't all that much more than a young person myself. I wasn't green, yet I certainly wasn't mellow. I had appetite and curiosity that went with a zing - like you are at the age I was then.

Consequently, my ears had gone up when I heard those sounds downstairs. Another part of my anatomy also came to life when I recognized what exactly it was I was listen-ing to!

It was afternoon, the quietest and warmest time of the day. I'd abandoned shirt and trousers for sports shorts and sandals and thin, summer-weight pullover only. And the shorts were ones that didn't leave much for the imagina-tion either: they were opaque, but not so opaque a good stare couldn't see what was in 'em. And they were close-

7

fitting, the shape of everything they contained was quite apparent.

Then she raised her eyes to mine, and it was a look of some significance. She was fully dressed by the way, though bare-legged and only sandalled feet: the bodice of her shortish dress hinted at the presence of a soft lacy bra.

Could I help her, the darling! Her English was good, taught to her back home I supposed, and needed mostly polishing over here. She meant really. please come down to me. And I did, though what to essay next I hadn't the faintest idea. Firstly, I had to determine if she was alone or wanted me to believe she wasn't alone.

"Would you like an orange juice from the fridge? It's hot now isn't it?"

I hardly dared breathe.

"There are no visitors with me or I would not ask you for help."

She wandered into the bathroom and I called, remaining outside being the gentleman.

"What's the problem?"

"I cannot hear you, Mr Collett".

So I ventured in..."Oh!" she exclaimed and straightened up but, as she intended, I saw enough: she had pulled her dress and underslip to her waist and was twisting to try to see her rear. I got a view of one of those pairs of transparent briefs, the pink ones with narrow lacy frills at waistband and legs - nates rather: underneath their thin tight smoothness - underneath mainly, those days before mini kinds came in - were a few broken lengths of red at angles, weals that would hardly last the day, I would judge now.

"Oh!" she smiled in surprise, and her hands went theatrically to her mouth. "I was not thinking, I am so sorry."

I regret madam, I thought, I am unable to share your sorrow!

8

She moved the tip of a foot in a half-circle upon the tiled floor, bent her head - her dark hair fell forward covering much of her pale and pretty face - then clasped her hands behind her back. "I expect you have seen punishing before?" She smiled again and this time trustfully - she had made up her mind about me quickly, I guessed.

"Of course," I said. "What can I do for you?"

"A jar of healing cream I have here that I cannot open. It is for my stripes though sadly today they are not many..."

"Surely a small punishment is a - er - desirable thing?" I had become pedantic of speech to match hers and gain a fuller comprehension from her.

"It is not good however to escape a part of a correction Mr Collett and I will be - uneasy."

"If I can help you in other ways - er - Sonia - may I call you Sonia?"

"Please. You understand I am a long way from my home and my parents they worry about my behaviour. It is just to them that I continue if I am bad to have punishment."

"You have been bad Sonia? You have a boyfriend?"

"Oh no, not now... It is in other things I transgress and feel wicked."

It was obviously the moment to dare, and I did so though it transpired - looking back - most of my daring was uncalled for. "Come then," I murmured. "Permit your new friend and neighbour to complete your chastisement." She did not answer so, still bold, I took her hand as if she were my disobedient child and walked her along to her room. On the way she turned her face to me more than once and each time it expressed a gentle acquiescence and almost a quiet triumph of some kind.

"Your shorts," she offered, "are very enhancing. The young men of my town wear similar when they are sporting and fishing." Do they By George, I thought. "Well it's very warm today"

9

I led her across the threshold of her room whereupon she queried with a genuine doubt: "Are you content to correct me, Mr Collett? It is perhaps an unusual request."

"Call me Will. A friend, even I hope a new friend, is for stormy times as well as for fine weather."

"Then I shall obey with confidence my friend. Where do I go now? Shall I bend over in the English manner? Oh, one moment, you will need an instrument of correction: I have three -" Three! I thought and I must say a puzzlement, indeed a consternation crept in upon me. "Three to choose from in order that you can become the stern father." She went to a chest of drawers and opened one. "See?" And three there were.

One was a short leather whip, and well-used I judged, but I disliked it immediately. Though it was obviously meant for children or - I shuddered - small animals, I could not bear the thought of using it: to my European mind it bore connotations of slave punishment or 19th century floggings of prisoners and so forth. The second was a junior-school cane, new in appearance, thin and very flexible, the third a light-coloured strap of leather, two-tongued towards its end, for children again, rather than adults.

I chose the last and she showed disappointment slightly before handing it to me and closing the drawer.

"What's the matter?" I queried. "Where have I gone wrong?"

"The whip is my parents," she answered quietly. "Often I have felt its bite."

"I'm sorry Sonia... perhaps next time you are naughty." And I put an arm around her warm shoulders as she nodded.

"Where to bend?" she asked, and "I expect you wish to beat me in the English way, on my behind..." And there came another glimpse of a disappointment. "But," I countered, "there you chastised yourself anyway." "It was for you I did it that way," she said, and I promised to attend her back on a future occasion though in truth the prospect didn't appeal.

However, I took charge more at that point and tried with a measure of success at the time, I thought, to act the manner of an older and authoritarian father about to strap his daughter's thinly-covered bottom - at least I hoped it WOULD be thinly-covered!

"Raise your dress to your waist!" I commanded. To my relief she obeyed, only to leave in place a dainty white half slip with flowery hem of colours. "Raise your - er - that also" (not sure if she knew the words 'petticoat' or 'slip'). Thankfully she did so and her near nudity from waist downwards came once more into view: she had as the slang has it 'legs right up to her bum' though she was petite, girlish almost in size. Her bottom was round and attractive, ivory-coloured - although not much - where she hadn't tanned whilst wearing a bikini. I continued as the angered parent and commented disapprovingly on the revealing briefs like these.

"Sonia?"

"Yes sir!" she replied, looking down. "Since I have left school I have chosen my own clothes including the underwear. Mama too wears this kind of brief - Oh!" And her hand went to her mouth. "I should not disclose such information, she would be very angry." She giggled. "I am so bad: you will beat me hard, no?... Where shall I bend?"

"Lay down - er - no: take one of your pillows and place it lengthways on the edge of the bed. That's right. Now young lady bend over!"

I flexed the supple leather in my hands.

"I am not," I continued, "aware of why you merit - deserve - this but you will know soon that I am able to give the punishment you say is necessary." Her bottom shifted

11

under my words and the nylon layer gleamed slightly in the afternoon sunlight.

"Now adjust your panties."

"Please sir?"

"Put your hands behind you and tug - er - pull them from the top - well done. Smooth them with your hands - no - from the bottom upwards - yes - smooth them again. Good, you've got it. Move your legs and thighs apart - that's it! How does this compare with positioning back home?" I was curious for detail.

"Sorry?"

"How do you position yourself for correction at home?"

"Oh, for Papa I face the wall and my arms are up above my shoulders. My back is unclothed except for my bra. For my Mother it is the same but she opens my brassiere, unfastens it ... please hurry Will, I am feeling so much better and waiting."

"You will wait 'til I'm ready young lady."

"I am sorry senor."

I had spotted her dressing-table mirror was adjustable and worked it so she and we could have a view of ourselves in its reflection. She was motionless, resting on her forearms and looking ahead within her mind: it made me commence proceedings there and then and I snapped a vertical lozenge of scarlet on to her right chub. It glowed almost at a right angle to one of the paler weals she had placed herself earlier. She stretched her arms out and turned her face to profile with an absent expression but smiling faintly: her eyes widened and began blinking more... This underlining of her acquiescence spurred me I can tell you... I rolled up the right sleeve of my pullover and this she observed with another eye-widening... I stood with feet apart and bent slightly from the waist for I wished to strike effectively, being familiar hitherto with only the giving of a few spankings.

At first I concentrated on her nates individually, thwacking vertical part-divided (the two tongues of leather) rectangles on to her tender convex ivory. She uttered not a sound and I sensed an inadequacy when she turned her head to give its other profile and frowned.

I straightened and began to strike diagonally, the strap swishing a longer arc through the air, and I was rewarded with her giving a small expulsion of breath. She moved fractionally on the pillow. Though I was new to this form of correction I was sensible enough to deliver the strokes leisuredly and I sought and achieved a slow thwacking rhythm.

I paused for short intervals when ostensibly I went to smooth the thin nylon, more to sense her heightened heat rising from beneath it. Her eyes would dart then to the mirror, to me, to elsewhere, her lips curved calmly from some recollection no doubt.

But control of the events passed from her to me slowly but surely as the leather thwacked down steadily. The room was still and somehow prescient, filled only by the swish-thwack of the beating and her sharp intakes of breath and occasional shaky little cries. Her bottom would rise after a stroke and I would hit a nate on the rise causing her to gasp or exclaim brokenly. Then it started to wriggle and move from side to side trying vainly to escape.

I stood next to her right thigh and got the leather lengths to land horizontally: this in effect ensured both her globes were stroked simultaneously, though the left hand had the worst of it as it took the tip of the strap, which smacked there smartly and loudly. She bucked and gasped, the while now emitting little throaty and broken cries: still she did not utter a word.

However, this could not last anyway; many minutes had flown and my limbs ached to an extent that I had to take a real breather. I sat down and watched her arrive at a stasis and some containment of the pain I had given... She shook her damp hair along her back and stared at me via the mirror... I tautened the supple leather between my fists and gazed back as her lips opened and she blinked slowly and lazily. And - one movement only - moved her thighs a bit more apart: quite evidently between them she was wet and a darkness had spread along the layers of material. I tucked the handle of the instrument behind the top of my shorts and stood. Fortunately the looseness of my pullover effectively hid an agitation at the front... Watching her eyes I drew once more close to her her form and her eyes I saw drop to looking at the front of my shorts.

"Well my master" she said, voice clear and unruffled, "maybe there is punishment and pleasure."

"Punishment and pleasure" she murmured and regained a control of our engagement.

I bent to her and fingering the waistband of her briefs started peeling them off: she breathed in sharply but said also "Please, you remove brief all the way." I did so and pink nylon and white cotton left her intimate parts, disclosing a glistening entrance behind a dark bush. "Aah" she sighed. "That is better: my hurt is better." She crooked her knees to help me with the garment: when in my possession I drew its gusset across my fingers and they became moist... She was watching and at that juncture jutted up her bottom and re-parted her thighs. "When my punishment is complete -" she began and squeezed her lips to greater redness.

I undid my shorts under a scrutiny. My freed member, thick and heavy, nodded and bowed to its new friend: her parallel movement was to part her thighs a bit more. I retrieved the instrument and returned to strapping her nates individually and vertically, swish-thwack, swish-thwack, swish-thwack!

At this stage she emitted groans from the depth of her throat and I myself wasn't above expressing one or two sounds of exquisite distress I can tell you. We were at the level of excitement and freedom I for one had never before experienced. My cock waved at her crevice, her crevice become a canyon, the sides of which anon fluttered. Swish-thwack, swish-thwack! Charmingly, her pink button, cossetted in dark fluff, came out, only to nip back in before the aftermath of a stoke; swish-THWACK!

Refreshed, I made the leather length describe perfect arcs through the air to land adamantly where her flesh rose of its own accord and nervy skin twitched with its tracery of red ridges and stripes.

But despite our mutual zenith of excitement I ceased chastising her there and then for fear of breaking her skin, and dropped the strap. Instantly she twisted to see and almost simultaneously jerked up her bottom and stiffened her thighs more apart... Then her button peeped out at the friendly stranger drawing closer to its quivering companion... I noticed her knuckled hands gripping the bedclothes as she cried "Oh, oh, oh, oh!"

She shook as perspiration beaded her smooth body.

My stiffened member shafted into her hot and voracious crevice and she gave out what was little short of an outright shriek and I drove into her 'right up to the hilt' to use a phrase.

If the other Keech households en-mass had rushed into Sonia's room at that moment they could not have stopped us now. My thrusts were piston -like and my belly smacked upon her fiery, ridged bottom. I braced legs and thighs against hers and gripped her shoulders vice-like.

Our initial coupling was a wave which diminished its intensity of sensation on returning to regain its strength and I took the chance to order her to - carefully - bring her thighs some way together. She managed to comply but largely she was elsewhere, close to a drowning... I clasped her trim waist and slowed the shafting strokes and she moved her thighs more together. At the end of one of the more slow thrusts her passage gripped and I must have exclaimed as, with a concentration I cannot describe, I observed her climax her part of the primitive act we had set up with an almost incredible degree of force.

She surrendered, shuddering to her paroxysm of carnality, her head turning from side to side as if she were demented and cries escaped wantonly and uncontrollably from her throat "Aah, aah, aah!"

I collapsed along her sweaty length then rose to gain my orgasm with driving slow thrusts that felt as if no terminus could stop their forward motion. My blood roared in my ears and from my armpits I dripped as, in a crescendo, I gushed into her like a bursting tap - endlessly I thought: would I ever cease? Even when she didn't clench me she fitted snugly and I was drained comprehensively... I was to be sore for days...

We lay there joined for long minutes and I discovered she disliked having neck-bites so I contented with some of the things lovers do after coition; gently stroking her sides for example. Her dark eyes were blurred as if from intoxication and no doubt by correction and coupling she had been intoxicated.

Eventually I took my weight from her and withdrew: as I did so she panted a few times whilst shuddering a little and obviously she sought and obtained enjoyment right to the last of our meeting. Then her clothes veiled the birthplace of her wild abandonment: she shook them to a tidiness about her. Her lustrous dark hair she pulled and caressed from her face and brow: she was extraordinarily pretty now. I watched everything of her fascinated and this she knew of course: she had me - I was hers as effectively then as now, hers to command.

Chapter 2

"You know," I ventured, "your face is shining some-how: love suits you." An obvious thing to say but true nev-ertheless. She did not reply nor did she look at me. She collected our undergarments off the carpet.

"You should not drop clothes on the floor: it spoils appearances. We are not savages."

"Under the circumstances -" I began.

"You like a smoke?" she asked brightly, looking at long last at me. "I know you smoke: I smell tobacco from your quarters a lot - it is ... poof!"

"Is it because I smoke a pipe," I offered.

"A pipe!" she laughed. "Oh Will, how very English. A pipe!"

She put her undergarment into a basket and went to a drawer. "Here," she said, "wear this string. It is cotton and comfortable to your poor fellow: he wants to rest now I think... It is a male string."

I removed my shorts and worked it into place, noticing its strategically-situated zip: "Whose is this?"

"I will tell you all later" she said. Then - surprising me - she knelt and kissed me there through its soft and accom-modating material. "Love," she mused, "is wonderful, very very wonderful. I thought I would die of it today."

Her hands left my hips and bottom and she returned to the drawer and next brought out two pairs of briefs both of fine and expensive cotton: one she hung upon a chair, the second she began to draw on. "I will wash myself later" she said and turned to her dressing-table mirror: the briefs at her knees, she twisted and examined her rear in its reflec-tion.

"Madre!" she exclaimed. "You whipped my behind good and proper. And it is so hot" she continued, cautiously feeling the red and its lines and ridges. "Poor Sonia. Was she so bad she deserved this cruel punishment?"

"Nowhere near cruel punishment" I replied. "But it was coming close to cutting your skin and I desisted."

"Naturally I knew. You do not beat as hard as Mama though: she beats me 'til I weep and there are necklaces on my back."

"Good God Sonia, surely you are never bad enough -"

"Only a couple of small necklaces." She laughed at the concern on my face. "Mama knows me too well I think. It is quite usual back home. If you love someone deep your anger makes you beat them real hard."

I recalled the whip for children in her drawer and still could not forbear from experiencing a frisson.

Her creamy briefs found their home and carefully she smoothed out their thin and semi-transparent material upon her.

"They are sweet," I said. "And they go with your appearance."

"They were very pricey," she said, fingering the pale-blue lacy edgings, touching the flowery embroidering on their front. "I buy them here in London: your underwear is good here. I cannot wear nylon against my stripes: it gets them angrier." She sighed. "You beat me. Then you take me like a dog. Men!"

This was so breathtaking that I was speechless - and also I was willing to let her have her woman's eternal grudge towards the whole of the male tribe. But she must have watched my face because she laughed again: "I will make coffee and we will have a smoke."

The coffee came in dainty cups and was thick and delicious. "These are like Mama's she keeps for guests." She brought cakes that had jam in them and apart from one or two I had myself, she polished off the lot.

"I see a darned good-hiding hasn't spoiled your appetite, young lady."

"Okay" she replied pertly. "I seduce you. I admit it. But I need the punishment also: there was no lie there."

She was sitting on her bed and I watched her, my mouth full of cake, as she lit one of those cigar-tobacco smokes that look like brown-coloured cigarettes.

"You want one?" And I accepted as she blew grey smoke into the air that shortly before had resounded with the swish-thwack of her round bottom being strapped.

She brought a knee up to her chin which rested on it and her eyes on me were lively and mischievous.

"You not a bad swordsman," she commented. "Perhaps you pleasure me again - you want to I think." And her long smooth arms hugged a leg as somehow she fiddled that her dress and underslip fell back a little. She rocked gently from side to side and watched my eyes go to between her thighs, the whiter panel of the lining there contrasting with the other material adjoining it, all suddenly revealed.

"You are a devil, Sonia" I said fondly. "And don't believe desire will allow you to escape punishment."

"I guess randiness deserve punishment too" she offered, gazing quizzically at me through a haze of smoke.

That marvellous first day of our affair had had enough in it - at least for me - to content me for ages, young as I was at the time, but Sonia stood after finishing her cheroot and dispensed with dress and underslip in easy movements: "It is so warm today, I be like you - three pieces of clothing wearing only." She was a picture in her undies and I complemented her. She wandered to the chest of drawers but I expected she would call it a day and we would talk of a future get-together of some sort.

Instead she brought into view the new school-cane: "I not have this administered" she volunteered, turning it over and over, then she swished it through the air. "It means business" she mused. "You ever use one?"

"Never," I answered truthfully. "Spankings - until today they were my limit."

"Spankings?" she said scornfully. "How childish! There is much childishness in this country: the women here they giggle all the time and strut around. They need a good hard shafting - after they have a sound whipping. See here!" she ordered, and having come to stand by me she lay across my lap. I felt the hot skin of her body once more and my hands went to her waist and the twin crowns of her neat bottom. "You are Mama" she commanded. "There is her slipper ready and she is about to chastise me with it. She removes my brief as always - Go on Mama."

I peeled the luxurious undergarment uncertainly.

"To my knees only - there! Ready for my child's punishment. Guess how old I am?"

"Ten?"

"Five. Yes, five years, maybe near six. When I get to ten I get more than the slipper. Spankings!" she concluded contemptuously.

"Well, corporal punishment is not so wide-spread in this country as it used to be," I chuntered, somewhat adrift.

"I not surprised if kiddies' beatings are all what is available." She had the cane still in her possession and examined it carefully, rolling it between her thumbs and forefingers before flexing it and flicking it in front of her: "Here is business though," she commented again.

"How did you come by it Sonia?" My hands moved upon her bottom which of course remained glowing and hot: I travelled there cautiously, mainly with the tips of my fingers.

"Mmm" she went, then "Ouch" and I stopped.

"My ex-boyfriend," she replied eventually. "Only the whip is mine which I bring with me in my luggage when I arrive. But he never got round to using it - the cane, that is. He wield the strap though - but not as skilful as you - Oh there is your saying 'Where there's a will there's a way.'" And she laughed immoderately.

I thought that wasn't half bad for a newcomer but I didn't say so, indeed I drew my palms across some of her little ridges and she squirmed on my thighs. "Oh Will that hurt." She twisted and looked at me reproachfully: "I thought you want just to admire my bottom not torture me. People have loved my bottom - what you say?"

"I say they are right, but also I say it is perfectly designed to receive the bite of the instrument of correction you're holding."

She swished it through the air: the sound was enticing and promising. "Bend over Sonia" she said, deepening her voice to be her Mother's.

An arousal I had stiffened, and she nestled closer into the curve of my body.

"You will tell me all about your ex -" I said. "Or else -"

"Or else?" she enquired, chewing a thumbnail and finishing manoeuvring on my arousal.

In the fullness of the months which followed, she did tell me. And she got her canings too.

Thus was the beginning of our adventure...

She liked IT a lot and I use 'liked' rather than 'wanted' advisedly. She was at least dual-natured: one part of her fierce, unselfconscious, enormously bright - and I don't just mean that she had a brain on her shoulders. Although passive with a child-like mien and subsequently being child-like she could be greedy.

She loved sweets for instance: "Look," she would say. "English chocolates. Have some, they are super." And the packet would go. The range of soft drinks in supermarkets dazzled her. She must have spent a small fortune.

After a coupling she often had at least two, the second accompanied by a smoke which had to be strong French cigarette or - better still - a cheroot: "My cousin Leo, he taught me to smoke. He - how do you say it? - is a fast one." And laughed affectionately. No anaemic fags for Sonia.

And so with our couplings and other play; she devoured them and I was young enough to keep up with her appetite. Punishments obviously were not as frequent though often preceded coupling.

We had to be careful. The first play we were lucky despite the abandon of its actions. Ever after we made sure the house was ours for the day or half-day or, more rarely, found another venue.

Fortunately for me - I was never Swordsman of the Month nor even of the day - her climaxes came speedily: perhaps her age featured here - or she would anyway be happy with other pleasure of coition. It meant of course she desired frequent attention, though not thankfully ever more than say twice in one day - and twice occurred rarely. To this frequency I had to respond by curbing her intentions and managed to get her to a few times per week - as stated I was no champion swordsman. She fell in with this and twice-a-days became rarities; also couplings say two days running.

Nevertheless. quick off the mark she remained and she took her pleasure in all sorts of places and at odd times of the clock. She'd behaved this way before I thought, and I quizzed her: it transpired her last 'ex' - Ralph? Ron? - we shall call him 'R' - had discovered her rushes of desire and willingness to sate them there and then. and so he co-operated. no doubt with a song on his lips.

In her quarters that first day I opened a drawer and 'twas brimful with undies, bras n' briefs, stockings n' suspenders, g-strings. "I shop and I cannot stop myself."

But amongst this cornucopia were items I judged someone else had chosen; "And there?" I showed garments with zips and others with tailored openings in their fronts: "Oh they were presents from R."

"But Sonia, you do not always undress for lovemaking?"

"Not always; sometimes there is not time." And sometimes, quite often in fact, she jolly well liked it that way: "I am ... invaded if dressed. It is play of freedom against the rules you might say." I confessed I was attracted to coupling with clothes on but I was certain she had the best of it when we performed this way. R of course had aided her propensities by getting these garments.

Ruffling in the drawer she said "There is not just English, also much from home" and displayed an assortment including G-strings: "G-strings?" "Oh yes. In my country too we know what they are truly for." And smiled. "R buy the zip-ones. You have strings Will?" "A few plain ones." "R had zip-ones and you should get some for er - how-to-say? - instant readiness."

I did so eventually, from a tiny mean-spirited shop in W1, and never regretted the purchase. Her Philippines undies were racier than their racier European counterparts and suited her nearly perfect form: their colours were superb.

As to the 'instruments of correction' the mysterious R had supervened here also. The junior cane and the strap were contributions towards the sustenance of her responses to pressures of homesickness and masochism.

"Why didn't he take them with him?"

"A farewell gift - and the undergarments."

The straps she relished: easy to tell. "It covers me as well as wakes me... It is comforting, warm - you work it well... It's fire on a dark night."

The cane she was still uncertain about: "It is heartless - pain and suffering?" "If so, it is true punishment after you have been bad." "No, punishment is love and correction. I see it means business: you teach me if it means business only I think?" I thought, yes my little one, where there is ignorance may come enlightenment, and nodded seriously, my mind however veined less heavily.

The whip I had a horror of. It was small, it was for youngsters, yet it gave me the horrors: I associated it with things like the slave-trade or prisoners being flogged. I detested what Sonia was nostalgic about. Reluctantly I used it upon her occasionally. She knew I disliked it but insisted: and I owed her for being my terrific new companion, I acquiesced with distaste.

"Will you are not trying - must I flagellate myself like the day we met?" she protested once, in my place. "I'm sorry Sonia." And laid a sharper stroke above her waist, curling the tip around half her front also. She loved the sensation there particularly.

A defunct gas-pipe jutted above the sink in my living-room and after binding her wrists they were tied to this. She had to stretch and stretching brought the luscious bonus of her bottom protruded by the sink's edge. But I had to perform the abhorrent task of whipping her torso. When she attained a satisfaction I was allowed to finish the occasion by attending to her bottom; my preference of course, if still hankering for a different implement.

"It's horrid Sonia. You're accustomed to it from childhood - I try to understand. However I can't help it, it gives me the creeps."

"It's customary in -" and she named the small country town of her birth. "Our first time together you beat me with

24

R's strap - and how! Yet you hate an instrument for children's punishment... One day I will tell you some things from my schooldays: after you will not shrink from giving whippings - or real stripes in fact."

Chapter 3

We were sitting in Mrs Keech's back garden, which was bushy and secluded. It was an afternoon we both had off work and the house was ours. Sonia, as a preamble to other developments, was yearning for her version of homely correction and was persuading me:

When I was 17 years - 5 years now! - we got a new class teacher - Miss Miriam we will say. She is a secular, not a nun, and she teach English language: also the same time she is over us always.

One day I have no plain panties for wearing for school. Maybe they tear or something, I do not remember. I go to Mama's bedroom, oh so quiet, and take a brief from a drawer there.

They are black pair, very grown up, little lace frills and transparent nylon. I put them on. What can I do? I cannot go to St. Teresa's naked down there. They are fitting well: Mama is little bigger than when I am 17. I feel very grown up and look in her mirror, turning round and round.

When I join with my friends I boast of my new underwear and they say show us and I show, turning round and round, and they clap their hands. But now I guess they knew they were not new and mine truly. You show me I say, it is fair, and one by one they lift their skirts and underskirt if they have one and show me; all plain white panties of cotton or nylon, not transparent. Triumph! And I run into the classroom before the bell rings.

Miss Miriam is there waiting and looks at me SO, and I know she guesses something. Maybe I walk a new way that morning and she guesses I have something new and looks at me all over with a hard look. It is a woman's thing. She guesses either a boy or clothes because nothing happens this part of the term and also there is not news about me in our little town. "Sonia!" she calls. "Come here a moment." I obey. She has blue eyes: they look into mine. Her eyes are intelligent and they looked at me all over. "Is there something that happens?" she asks and I shake my head.

The others enter, sit and watch: they watch and see if I get caught. All of them know about my 'new' brief.

"Is it somebody you see?" Miss Miriam asks. She means boys. "No Senorita, er - Miss." She sees I do not lie. "What is it?" She notices the girls point and whisper. "Silence!" "Please Miss she is not dressed right." This is Juanita, an old enemy. My friends shout at her. "Silence!" Then "Have you forgotten something?" She has looked at me all over. "No Miss." "I must ask you to raise your skirt." I raise my school skirt with the black pleats: lucky I have plain white underskirt on. Unlucky she orders me to raise this also. There are giggles and whispers when everyone sees the sexy brief. St. Teresa's is stern for everything and more stern for two things, boys and uniform - and under our uniform. The oldest pupils, nineteen years, also are ruled.

"So... I have no choice: it is obligation that I must punish you." The class is very silent now: they know what is coming. Miss Miriam goes up on to the little stage where her desk is and opens a drawer. "Come up here Sonia." I obey and she brings out the leather punishment-strap. There is whispering and excitement. Then the silence is deep. I notice Juanita staring, her eyes shining.

"Bend over." It is always over her desk on the stage we get the strap. It is a good view for everybody. I lay over her desk and my bottom is curves on the edge. Miss Miriam tells me pull my skirts above my waist and push them under me to stop them slipping.

I cannot see anything only the class-room door. My position is same for everyone. How I wish I was outside that door! Then I hear a swish and a crack and a line of pain burns across the middle of my bottom. Some of the girls have nerves and I hear their giggles. I hear myself cry out and my voice shakes. The brief is tight on my skin but Miss Miriam orders me to pull them more tight. I reach and do this. After, a second stroke follows and the sound of it fills the class-room. I cannot stop myself and my voice shakes again. A third stroke and the pain grows until I cannot control my bottom, it jerks from side to side.

She beats me three times more and quick before I try to stand and get away from the pain. But she is stopping that and I manage to lay still. The silence is big when she speaks: "Because you move Sonia and are not quiet I will give you two extra strokes - you must not move, you must stay quiet. Prepare yourself." It is a shock and also there are gasps in the room, but I must obey: these are the rules of my school.

With mighty effort I quiet myself and close my teeth hard... There is swish-crack! And the stroke goes criss-cross those previous ones and hurts like hell. It is very loud. I am sweating and gripping the desk which is slippery because of the moisture of my hands. I want to bury my face in my hands but dare not and am willing my legs and thighs not to jerk.

There is a long wait now and my body relaxes after there drains away some of the fierce pain... Then - Craack! Louder and harder of them all and crossing the first stripes and biting me into halves. But I do not move. My teeth are against themselves like they are breaking. I hear Miss Miriam say quick "You may stand now Sonia." She says this quick to tell me the punishment is complete and I may move to try to vamoose some of the fierce pain.

She is expert strapping us disobedient ones and we feel good and respectful after. Some of the teachers hit wild and these we despise.

In truth I had sixteen strokes: her strap split to two tongues of leather towards the end of it. Also I noticed when I watch a correction one tongue hits a fraction more soon before his companion. This is cunning and bad news.

And Miss Miriam is extra expert the way she gets the leather lengths to curl around our curves. These special caresses are bitter to us but we grow to purity and obedience under them.

Then there is one more thing to do. "Remove those briefs Sonia." She puts the strap back into her desk. "You must never wear that sort of brief at St. Teresa's."

I try to imagine what sort she has on under her loose light dress: it is not difficult, the material is thin and we can see the size and shape of any underwear under it. It is briefs all right and I bet sexy colour and material. And there is a dark suspender and dark stockings - stockings this hot day! She turns to the class. "- and that is the same for you all. Is anyone wearing this kind of brief now?" "No Senorita, Miss" they whisper. I am sure one or two are disobeying the rule: I know one who wears a string for games with her boyfriend. None will confess now and they are lucky today.

I reach under my skirts and peel off Mama's brief. It soothes the pain that my bottom becomes bare and I wriggle and rub after I give Miss the brief: she puts them in the drawer where stays the strap, and closes it. I will not have them 'til the end of the term and Mama will seek them. When she cannot find she will guess and ask: when I tell her the events she will beat me and this time I will get the strokes on my bare bottom - what a life!

Chapter 4

Sonia paused and her eyes went unfocused as she smiled at the memory of what she had been saying. I brought her back. "That story cannot make me like the strap. It was horrible and not fair. Why not tell Miss Miriam you had no plain panties?"

"Remember, Will, she asks me before lessons why I am different and I shake my head. I am arrogant and say nothing. I think I will escape this: my attitude is the lie so the correction is for a lie at the end. It was fate."

"Maybe, but still I cannot believe in the strap."

"Wait. I am not finishing. I said there is love and punishment: the punishment is gone, the love remains. Listen, I will tell you the beautiful thing, the great bit of the whole day:

The lesson finish in the afternoon and I am full of fright: I am naked underneath and want to stay indoors or the girls mock me and my friends make me show my stripes. But Miss Miriam comes to me after the bell stops and says kind and quiet - you cannot imagine she is the one who give such awful pain and humiliation - "One moment Sonia please do not leave, I wish to see you."

The others go out looking and whispering. She goes to the door and shuts it, then "Are you better now?"

"I am very sore Miss - and hot. I sit not very easy."

"Show me" she says, and I raise my skirts. But I turn not before I raise them. I know she likes me: she has that look and I am daring so she sees my bush - which is less when I am 17 - and maybe my entrance under the bush. I watch her look there after she examine my stripes. "I am sorry for you but you must obey our rules." I nod and then she breaks a rule: she touch my bottom, on a stripe. "Ouch" I say and I mean it. "Sorry" and "Allow me to help you - and also you will not go home uncovered there. Are you late?"

"No Miss, supper is not 'til seven."

"Come with me then and I will help you."

We walk towards her quarters which is near to the convent where the nuns live. It is a respectable thing: maybe my assignment is poor work and she needs to teach me extra. Our teachers do this and our parents do not pay extra. St. Teresa's is a good school but you must stay within her rules.

It is warm and sunny and when we walk my eyes are on her form which is grown-up and voluptuous. Her garments are few and revealing in the sunshine. She is very desirable and walking by her I understand men's arousal and I tingle. But I remember she beat me and my cheeks go hot. She knows my eyes are on her and gives me hers, dusk-blue and smiling and liking me.

Her little home is tidy, comfortable and feminine. She says "Do sit down Sonia" and puts a cushion on a chair for me. "There, that is better than the wood seats at school."

I sit and make my skirt stick out around me and my bare bottom is direct on the cushion and I wiggle and sigh. She looks at me kind and amuseful: you cannot believe she give me eight good strokes of the punishment-strap.

She brings black coffee in small cups like Mama's special cups for guests: it is strong and sweet, delicious. And there are cakes, jam in them: I eat them all. She laughs and says "The beating spoils not your appetite." But I look at her like a dog and she is decent enough to look down a bit guilty. When I finish she clear the table, and goes to her bathroom I guess, because now there is a white jar in her hand and she says it is for wounds and other things. Also

31

she brings one of her briefs. "These are for you Sonia: you can wear them today. Return them tomorrow."

They are lovely and feminine; cream-colour cotton which is very soft and thin and is half-transparent, they have pale-blue lace on the edges and flower embroidering on the front. "Thank you Miss." And tell her I will return them tomorrow and Mama must not see them. "Why not?" "Because Mama will discover this soon I borrow her brief and she will beat my bare bottom." "But you have your correction!" "I get a second soon or late: she will say 'You go to school out of uniform: you must tell me of this thing and I will phone St. Teresa's and tell them you cannot go. Your arrogance makes you a thief and for theft and arrogance I will punish you'."

"I am sorry Sonia" says Miss Miriam, "but I cannot return your mother's brief 'til the mid term ends: your punishment is record and evidence kept for inspections then." She goes thoughtful. "It is not fair you are punished twice for one offence. I do not want to approach your parents: it is something that is a family matter and the uniform is not the whole of the affair." She looks at me and her eyes very blue and soft. "You have a whipping in the bank my child but if you miss one award at school they will notice and cause questions and dissent... What can happen is an eye for an eye and the affair closes."

She leaves the healing cream and goes to a drawer near: she returns with a small instrument of correction in her hand. It is confusing me. "Will you punish me again miss?"

"No, it is I for punishment: I - or the school - I am debtor to you. Can you not understand?"

Moments pass 'til I understand. Then she offers me the instrument: it is light in my hand and has many strings like shoe-laces but these are leather lashes and at the end of each is a small tip of thin metal, you may squeeze the shape and it is silver colour.

"From France: come when you are ready and begin. It is fair... Or you save it for another time: you have the choice and the bonus."

I look at her and see her same clothes she wears when she straps me and I am vengeful. She likes me but I make my decision.

Nervous I say "You will bend across your table, Miss?"

"Of course." It is the same table where I take her the refreshments. "And will you punish me on the back, the bottom?"

"I think you know the answer."

She reaches to raise her dress but I say "I am teacher now: everything is by my hand." And she stops. I raise her dress which is light for the warm weather: she has no underskirt but has nylon stockings to her thighs and dark like her, plain black suspenders. The stockings are vanity when it is a hot day. This vanity will fuel my right arm and I roll up my sleeve there. She moves a little uneasy because she waits not seeing me. Her brief is pale blue and transparent nylon also: they are tight and sexy, maybe one size under what is right. The furrow is dark between her grown-up's buttocks and it stops where there is white cotton along the gusset.

Still I am angry and it conquers my fear. I grip the handle of the instrument and swing the lashes with a soft swoosh on to her woman's bottom which is pale and seductive: they spread out all over and make many short red lines - they appear quick under the thin nylon.

"If you are angry Sonia, do not forgive me - and I believe a debt must not remain."

This gives me the confidence and I whip her woman's voluptuous bottom. When I strike I am conscious of my bottom also, hot and sore, and I strike with malice. She has no movement but puts her hands by her head which turns to profile: her lips part and her eyes are unfocused - they

33

dream - a suspicion comes to me, and jealousy: I say accusing "You have this play before, then by the hand of your lover?" She awakes with a guilty expression and says "We have a contract: I receive your chastisement because there is a debt to you."

"It is deceit" I say cruel and daring. "You have strategy to get to this stage. Your fiance - it is Daniel? he have you this way and you are missing him these many months and you get me to this play, kind of substitute - Daniel! Confess!"

"Sonia," she protests, "here it is you I love but I owe you, therefore there is this punishment. You must agree -"

"Liar" I say cruel. "And for the lie I will beat you the same." I apply the instrument hard and soon she squirms and jerks and gives little cries "Oh-oh-oh-oh!" I am merciless and whip her bottom 'til my arm works to tiredness: it becomes very tired and rests cannot rouse it.

She is livid there and has no white skin remaining. The instrument is wonderful effective: I hold it respectfully. I lay it on the table before her profile. Cautious, I feel her bottom: it is hot under the nylon and smoothness is gone. She moves against my hands slow and erotic and she breathes and sighs: "Daniel Oh Daniel." Very soft but I hear her alright.

"Very well" I say menacing. "It is your Daniel you want -"

"Sonia I forget -"

"Then it is your Daniel," I spit, "who comes."

I take the waistband of her tight brief and peel them: "No" she say. "No. I have punishment owing but I forget. Sonia you must go not further." I peel them to her right ankle where they hang, tiny screw of blue material. The white cotton leaving her reveals her crevice: it is wet and I watch it, it flickers like a bird wing.

"Sonia," she protests, "this is not decent!"

"You see me in school. It is fair." She shakes her head and wonders but I retain her wonder not long because I go to her mantel-piece where there is a part of a thick candle, thick like the thickness of an altar-candle, and take it by the wood handle. She has this for the power-cuts we have sometimes in our town. And I bring it to between her thighs half-covered with her stockings.

I say "You are without your lover long Miss." And press it to the centre of her crevice which is alive and disturbs her: she cries "Aaah!" And her thighs go apart more. I am not big like her yet I stand above her and look at her body. Her gold hair is crinkly and covers between her shoulders. I touch her body: it is warm and she moves her head saying nothing. It is a wonderful moment when I know I have a power over her: she is adult and seductive and is authority and pride but I am her man she awaits. I need not speak because she knows. She breathes deep when I caress her side and ribs. She murmurs "Daniel" and looks up but not at me. I continue and she is very wet. It is a wonderful moment and her thighs are much apart. I understand her fiance, his desire seeking her hunger there.

She breathes deep and groans soft and moves forward and backward, forward and backward: she plays congress. It is the ghost of it and she waves her hair along her gleaming back. I am Daniel and I have my hard member to her entrance again. Her woman's bottom has the red of the flogging upon it and I sense a power again: I am he who comes to her glistening fissure which is still a bird's wing scared.

The end of the thick candle presses her entrance again. She jerks much and sings low from her throat "Aaah aaah." I say nothing: I do not have her words but I am her silent hungry lover come to her after many miles. We are our joy and cannot wait more: my member enters to the ending of her passage. It is one steady move of my stern hand. She gives a shriek which is long and I feel her jerk and convulse on the length of the stick which I hold hard and with effort.

When she settles I begin to work in-out, in-out, in-out her firm passage and alive crevice. She comes to climax soon because she is away from her lover many months. I leave the stick in when she arrives and her crevice closes around the thickness: I guess her passage clenches the stick hard. She is now wild and distraught and I take up the instrument of correction and hear it whoosh through the air before it whip first her left buttock then right then left then right.

I flog her climax and she jerks and writhes and claws the table. Now she weeps, her eyes shut and squeezing, and her voice gives passionate broken groans. She collapses forward. From under the gold fluff her pink button once came out and I swing the lashes exact centre into her furrow where it lives. Now she cannot self-control more...

But time passes and then she returns and in control: her breast works less and she swallows less. I withdraw the candle and she groans and wriggles. For the last time I am Daniel and tell her be quiet and still or I will beat her again. She rises willy-nilly when she hears this and says "You had no rights to do all these things. And you flagellated my climax: you are a wicked naughty girl, Sonia. I cannot believe how you know these things. What a little minx!"

I do not know what is a minx but I dislike the sound of this name.

She is normal again and I watch her: she draws her brief to their home and her fingers straighten the waistband and then the side-elastics neat on her buttocks. She says "Ouch" and caresses them, smoothing the triangle-shape seat. She is a neat-body for everything. And perhaps this is one of her troubles.

When she finish tidying her clothes I sense she stares at me but I look elsewhere very calm. "You allow me Miss, and you were nuts in your pleasure." I smile when I remember and she notices my smile and becomes angry. Also I say, like a needle, "Maybe your fiance has not this little sweet in the cake?" She is self-conscious, then is furious. Now it is woman's things between us and again I look elsewhere. It is enough: she comes and stands before me and holds my arms hard. "You minx. If I was your mother I beat you until you weep. Look at me you minx, look at my anger you wicked child." I look into her eyes which seem dark because she has temper. There are woman's things between us because of our play.

I blink and become a kid and cute now: it is a trick I use which works often - it works now.

Chapter 5

Sonia was in full flow now. There was no stopping her tale:

Miss changes and her lips part. She looks at mine.

"Kiss me." I say soft. "You like me and I love your beauty which I desire - kiss me."

She loses and covers my mouth: she tastes salt. She is gentle and wants me. "If you do those things again," she says, "I will eat you young lady limb after limb until you have only your toes remain on the floor." We laugh. "There Miss, you are free and can love."

My hands go to her full bottom and rest there. It is wonderful I have this grown-up woman against me. Under her light dress is her smooth brief which I can feel and the elastics which grip her skin. I move my hands slow because I do not want to wake extra pain of her chastisement... She kisses my neck and I go to her long damp hair, she has curls of strong silk... I say "Miss" and she straightens. "Now you are very very pretty." And she is; pale and lovely. "Go to the mirror, your face is shining!"

But I break a spell: she was mother, she is teacher again. She advances, she retreats. I think: she is crazy mixed-up kid this one and I smile.

Always it is my smile which gives me trouble. She becomes extra-teacher. "You are an impudent squirt. I cannot understand how you are this strong in love's domain and where you learn these plays we had today - I tell you, you are lucky you are not my daughter." She leaves my arms and her mouth closes. She walks around the room and she thinks but this cannot solve the puzzle. I sit - careful - on her sofa and say "You are stiff Englishwoman, you fears the freedoms in love and desire; and the games which come from desire."

"I am not English, I am Irish."

"It is the same; the Irish also. You are north Europeans, you are big with wealth and command and these things kill you inside because you fear you may lose them. I know: I meet Europeans of the north before - yes, in our small town. It is Papa's business, his - his contacts."

"I do not know," she says, not wanting to know and disliking my words because I am young and also I make her lose her self-control. This made her more pretty but the lesson here is something my teacher has no wish to learn. Now she craves authority where before she had love and playing.

"You have great possessions and command," I say, "but we are powerful where things are big truly. Take the warning: what you have half-kills you, your race - if you allow, it may kill all."

"I do not know."

"You are teacher and you do not know?" I am daring and it is too far: her mouth goes resentful and she stands by a window and gazes. "When I began at St. Teresa's I disbelieve the punishment-strap and consider it over-severe for you girls. Now I am not sure."

I think I am wise to shut up right now and change the subject pronto. "Oh," I say, "here is the ointment and your cotton brief. It is ages you get them for me. Will I see if they fit?"

"And what of your stripes - you want some healing attention?"

She looks at me odd and I guess there is a plan. If she plays poker she loses always. I do not care. She wants to be boss again but I do not care. These grown-ups with their pride and jealousy, their punishments; they are ridiculous. Sometimes I can manipulate them: occasionally one is a child in my hands. I get from them pain and humiliation but they are weak truly because they dominate from punishment.

She comes and sits next to me on an end of her sofa, which is without arms. She bends a forefinger at me. I rise and walk confident in front of her. "You feel better!" she exclaims and without irony. "Come over my lap and I will make your stripes feel better also." She pulls back her dress and I see again the tops of her stockings and the suspender pressing her thighs... The little hairs on her skin are gold in the sunlight of the evening. I look between her thighs and she watches me, she pulls her dress again and I see part of her brief still dark from wet. Some of her curly bush is visible above the start of the gusset and a few golden hairs peep from the tight layers. What a woman she is! What seductiveness!

She has the jar ready. Then her hot flesh and underwear are against my belly and abdomen. "That is the ticket." She is the brisk proprietress and pats my bottom like it is an old friend.

"Never must we have other upset at school like we have today, Sonia - will you promise?" I promise, but it is empty I think. I consider she guesses I am not honest, but her pride is tough and between us she can sense no defeat of her in the air again.

"This is like when I am a kiddie and I go over Mama's knees for a spanking from her slipper" I say.

"I expect you were a naughty girl a lot... I must say there is no change in you now you are 17: it is possible you get worse." I keep dignity and do not answer. "When you were on Mama's knees you howled and cried?" "Always" I reply and we laugh. "You get it on your bare bottom?" No ointment comes and her dry hands move slow on my globes under her gaze. I think she is very keen to know of this history and I wonder - and then I do not care. "Always," I say. "And it is the same these days. When I am kiddie she pulls off the brief before the action - they are nice ones also, chic, not like the we must wear at St. Teresa's - plain white panties. Ugh

"It is respectable wear for school, Sonia. In your leisure time you can wear what pleases you -"

"I am 17 Miss, a young woman, and St. Teresa's remind me it thinks I am small with ink on my fingers."

"Where there is study and discipline all of us must be children and quiet in all things. Time passes and you will understand." Her voice is soft and low and it charms my whole body. Her voice follows her hands which make my private skin tremble and yield: this is a different ointment.

I move into the curves of her hips more and slow and detect she is wetting again - it is incredible these grown-ups! Is there no end to their hunger? "Miss -" I begin, but I feel something lays on my bottom: it is the leather lashes not long gone from my hand: she has the instrument and wants to use it on that which is defenceless beneath her gaze.

"Oh Miss" I say "you beat me enough this morning." I twist and see her face: the cheeks are pink and eyes unblinking. She shakes the lashes on my bottom and holds my waist firm with her left arm. I bury my face in my hands: it is new to me I realize she has a sadistic kink. "No Sonia, be at ease. Never before I chastise a naked bottom and with this instrument."

"Oh Miss I want your love not extra punishment..." but she cannot stop herself now: I feel the lashes leave then a whoosh and they return with a stinging all over. But it is a few strokes only; ten? I forgot counting. But I catch my breath all right and I take my hands from my face and clutch the material of the sofa. Swoosh, swoosh! And she finishes satisfied. "There," she says and I twist to see her face again. It is pink and triumphant. "I hope you are contrite after

41

your naughtiness and the punishment which it earned - are you my little one?"

I play for her: it is not half of a beating and stings only.

"Yes Miss," I say slow and precise. "Please forgive me."

"Of course; your slate is clean."

What is slate, I think? "Thank you for correcting my bad behaviour."

"It is well done. Now there are your stripes which wait no longer." She begins rubbing the ointment on a stripe: naturally I flinch and she stops... She begins again and soon her ministrations are pleasant: my legs move apart a bit. I remember her wet and my heart is bumping... Gently she attends another weal: it is an end one and low on my bottom... Very daring I say "your Daniel knows you much Miss?" for her voice also is caressing me but everywhere and I am bathed in her tones, their music and seduction, and I feel alive, confident, awaiting movement.

"He pleasures me often Sonia: he is my fiance."

"It is nice the pleasuring Miss? You want it much?"

"It is a hunger unlike any other hunger."

Her finger slips on to my button which goes in willy-nilly before it comes out again cautious. "Oh I am sorry." "On my entrance I like it better," I say daring. She puts her hand along my bush and I feel the warmth. "Tell me Sonia, how is your boyfriend, Roberto?" And she presses my entrance: my brain swims and I giggle. "Tell me if he pleasures you." "We are young miss and I am virgin for my marriage-bed, for my parents and mother Church." "You have fun with Roberto?" And she presses my entrance again. Then she squeezes it... I am losing my voice. "He, he has tricks for me which are nice: we play sometimes... and under my skirts... he attends my breasts."

So this is her plan: it is simple and gives back to her a dominion which suit her pride of her extra years. I am not caring much: she cannot reign long in this development.

Like that Yankee general I say - only to myself - I will return.

"Imagine" - she speaks soft - "Roberto one night comes to your house. He enters and finds the way to your bedroom door. It is a hot night and you are naked under the sheets. He startles you, then you feel fright - you know him but cannot stop the fright because you see he opens one of his garments and his manhood is visible, seeking... you see his manhood before Sonia?"

"Yes Miss: please tell no one." O beg and feel foolish.

"It is a fine size?" she asks, and her voice caresses.

"Yes Miss. He is ample there."

"He comes to your bedside and he wants to pleasure you. His appetite is great. You are scared and speechless because he removes the sheets. He looks down at you... There is enough light in the room and you watch his member thick and stiff advance for duty, and you are powerless and cannot resist... it must take you and pleasure you and Sonia will writhe upon the altar of an urgent copulation... suddenly he spears with a strong whisper: you argue but he is implacable, his hand cradles his stiff member always... You bury your face in your pillow when he slaps your legs apart." Wack, thwack! Miss Miriam's hand lands on each of my thighs and hypnotised I move them apart more... I twist and see, what? She takes a long fruit from a bowl on a table near her. It is yellow and brown, not hard, and she brings it to my entrance. "Moments pass then sudden you feel it."

I cry when the end of the banana presses on my entrance.

"His manhood arrives: his quest is over. He ignores your words and movements and there is start to pleasuring you." I shudder and cry again when Miss Miriam pushes it in.

"To and from, to and from, his manhood like a piston pleasures you from behind." This imitates her words and I cry and shudder on her lap. She also is stern and pleasures my passage 'til I am distraught and lose control; my bottom writhes and my hands tear on the surface of the sofa. My thighs crush against her and she grips my waist with her left arm, hard.

"Eventually -" And I approach orgasm: wild cries fly from my throat. "- his thrusting manhood brings you to your climax. You are beside yourself. There is a crescendo, an unbelievable pulsing which spreads from your passage and makes your body jerk ecstasy before you fall into exhaustion..."

It arrives; a crashing flood and my body rocks and shudders. My feet drum upon the floor. I move my head frantic and claw the sofa. It is not ebbing and I groan low in my throat.

She leaves the fruit in the whole way and gives me strokes with the instrument: she whips my orgasm. My globes move wild but the leather lashes find them and with skill lick them all over.

"There! He pleasured you Sonia - are you content?"

"Yes, yes Miss. Content-ah-content." I am on fire. My heart will burst.

I stop shaking after long moments.

The final sensation is when she withdraws the fruit... I groan and shudder again. "In a perfect world Sonia," she says, turning it over and over, "the bottom is flogged during a shafting... This I do for you and we understand now." Dumb, I nod and tug my skirts and cover the birthplace of my body's abandonment.

I rise all right but am unsteady sometime... She waits. Unlike me her thighs remain with no veiling... I look between them and know she watches me... The white and blue layers are dark where there is extra spreading of wet... She watches me and her low lip pushes - so - it is red and her eyes search. "Come Sonia." I obey because she pleasured me and it was wonderful. She takes my hand and stands. Sudden, she kisses me on the lips. I respond and maybe surprise her: she looks very blue eyes at me, wide.

"It is time we part," she says. "Evening comes." And she is my teacher again and formal. But I kiss her cheek: then she looks those blue eyes at me and I think she loves me... Later I am sure.

She puts the instrument of correction in her drawer. "Daniel bought it in Paris. It was a joke. He said 'It is a good present for a teacher.' In France it is punishment for children."

"You holiday Miss?"

"Yes, two-years ago."

"And he punish you with it?"

She has a guilty expression again and pretends tidying the table which in fact has nothing on it. "Oh yes, a number of occasions." And she smiles weak. I feel malice towards her and say "Before he shaft you over the table, heh?" She is pale and very pretty now and I have recovery after our plays. She pulls her crinkly hair and looks into my face. Her mouth is open a little but she speaks not or cannot. Pink comes on to her pale cheeks. "We part now my dear." I know her feelings are puzzle and hurt: she loves me and I am unkind.

"I see you tomorrow morning Miss Miriam," I say, "and I bring your brief also. Please you launder them because I want not Mama sees them."

"Of course Sonia. I understand. Sleep well and take good care of yourself."

'Take good care of yourself': they are words from a love-song. 'Take good care of yourself, You belong to me.' She chatters and hums the song's tune: her head is light I think.

"Goodbye 'til tomorrow Miss."

I look at her lips which have some colour of the lilac in them: she thinks I am near kissing her there and her eyes are bright and fond of me... But I touch her woman's body

45

which is warm under her dress of blues and grey: I touch where her ribs are. Then I turn and walk to her door but before I go through I raise my skirts and show her I have brief in a new home. "They are sweet on you Sonia," she says with affection. Then my skirts sway against my legs and I walk from her house and consider I will hurt her in the future because today I discover the pleasure of cruelty on a grown-up and want exploration more in this field."

"But Sonia," I said. "This is terrible. She loved you and yet you wanted to hurt her... And also you worshipped her... I can only say youngsters can be heartless."

"You are a man, Will," she said. "You cannot understand: it is things between women, not only between child and adult."

"I am glad I am a man then."

"She has her Daniel who pleasures her womanhood. My lovely Roberto gives me pleasure which is not forbidden. She has what I have not because I am young and not betrothed. I push a balance and make a plan for punishing her."

"So, women are bitches after all."

Chapter 6

Now where was I? - At Mrs Keech's with Sonia home from Miss Miriam's. I asked her what transpired after the day of the classroom punishment. She continued. "So, Will -:

I returned to my parents and am careful to hide Miriam's brief which feel superb and caress my bottom, its welts and marks of the french instrument. The material is soft and clings to me sensual. They are fabulous expensive I guess: mine are poor next hers. the difference also makes me wish to hurt her.

Next day in class quietly she asks "Come to my place after school Sonia?" I nod and when last bell ring stroll to her home: she has got there already and prepares coffee with cakes. "I like you eating and drinking: you are a sweet young animal."

"I am not animal!" I say indignant.

"You are a minx. If I was your mother I beat you every day. You are lucky I am not your mother."

"Your blows are not harder than Mama's." Talking of her I remember Miss' brief and take them from my school-case: "They are lovely and comforting. Are they from Paris?" "London; read the label." And yes it is English underwear. "You may have them as a present." But I remember in time: "I cannot have them, Mama will find them and question me."

"I understand."

"May I see what else?"

She thinks I mean underwear, not all her clothes, and in the bedroom empties a drawer containing underwear only - nylon, cotton and silk. "Silk is nice," she says. "Do you wear silk?" "No Miss I am not old enough." "Of course."

She says 'Of course' a lot: it amuses me. "Of course. 'Tis a pity you can't have something."

"It is all right... There are no G-strings."

"I do not like them."

"And Daniel?"

"He does not wear them." She lacks understanding. "They are great fun Miss, you must try one." "Maybe I will." She is not convinced and I resolve to get her some and she will change her mind. "My Roberto has some." "Oh." She has not understanding, in some ways is innocent and her intelligence here, insignificant. "Why are you laughing?" "It is someone I know." "Oh." And gives me a look like Mama sometimes gives. She puts her nose in the air and stares.

"How are your stripes today, my dear?"

I annoy her but she knows not why.

"They are better: your cream is excellent. You want to see them?"

No answer, so I bend, flip my skirts and pull down my panties. In a mirror I see her stoop and put a hand towards my stripes: it is warm and slow over them... I respond against it and she straightens and tidies her blouse which needs not tidying.

"What is wrong?"

"We must not always be arousing," she says.

"Why not?" And I make her laugh. "With your stripes, Miss, nylon panties are unwise, but you are golden-lady I think." She is pleased but hides it: she is proud of her lustrous hair.

"Will you give me some money?" I ask later.

"Oh Sonia!"; there is surprise and disappointment. "No Miss," I say, "it is not for me." "What is it?" "You will see. give me four dollars - please." "You vex me child. Your poor mother." But she is relieved I do not crave the money for myself.

Next time in her place I tell her to stand then bend with her bottom to me. She hesitates because she is teacher and I am young: she wonders if I am arrogant and if I don't stop before she is humiliated.

"Bend over" I command. I have no instrument of correction nor anything to pleasure her with: she obeys slowly. I push up the material of her long loose dress and tell her to hold it above her waist: she does so. She is not watching in the mirror because she is reluctant and may get to a refusal. Her woman's body is pale and seductive: there are the gold hairs.

Her suspenders this time is classy purple: her undergarments are expensive and superb. Again the stockings are vanity this warm day: they are gloss and light blue, a colour she likes much. The brief is tiny; a small triangle to her front another, bigger, on half her globes. Its silk is blue and black flowery patterns and bending she stretches it like it is painting on her curves.

She is treasure any man desire!

I am silent a while... then I go to the top elastic, black lacy edging. I take it in my fingers. "No Sonia" she says "I am not willing for a play today." "There is no play I promise." She wonders but remains bent. I pull her little brief to her feet and sandals and look at her secret place and know she is proud, for she tosses her hair and her form goes harder.

"Step from them and the sandals," I request. From a pocket of my skirt I bring a new-bought G-string, white but transparent. It is not high quality but will serve its purpose which she will discover.

"Step in this Miss." And she steps realising there is a garment for her. It goes up her legs and thighs to its new home. "Please adjust it for your comfort." She does so and straightens, looking in the mirror. "Oh it is nice." "It is your first string: there is another from the four dollars, scarlet one." "Thank you Sonia, you are thoughtful." And kisses my cheek.

"Well?"

"Mm?"

"You notice anything?"

"Notice anything?"

"On your button."

"Button?" Her hand searches on her blouse. "Oh Miss" I laugh "you are a silly parrot. Walk around, or bend... I mean the button between your bottoms." "Sonia that is quite enough -" she stops and considers: "Yes I understand. There is a stimulation." "Good for lovemaking." "I hope you never use these young lady -" "Good for other pleasures also: Roberto has some we use. There are male strings I can get for your Daniel - they are dearer." And she gives me more dollars. "Yes I think they will be useful for Daniel and I one day."

I have a pang when I see her eyes distant, remembering...

Chapter 7

A week or ten days later Mama discovers her black transparent brief missing: it is through Papa. He favours them and probably asks her to wear them. In the evening he intends to have her after he takes them off.

She knows I am responsible: it has happened before and she is angry. I am doomed but I tell her what went wrong: "You are not old enough to wear that kind whatever the reason. If you have no panties for school you stay here and do homework instead - I arrange." She looks at me through and through: "You showed them - my private underwear - to your friends, yes? I know. You are a bad child again and there is a punishment for continuing badness: go and fetch the whip." It is kept, handle hung on a hook, in the wardrobe in my parents' bedroom. I suspect sometimes it is in Papa's hand at night, but they are very discreet.

I return slowly to Mama's anger, the narrow supple leather dangling by my side.

"Come here," she says and sits on a chair. She flicks back her short skirt and frilly underskirt. The day is hot - so many hot days of late - and her legs are bare. She has not the vanity for stockings always like Miss Miriam. Miss, I think, where are you with your kinder French laces? Reluctantly I surrender the whip, noticing Mama is wearing a yellow brief and predict Papa will be unhappy tonight. Perhaps there occur two whippings in one day.

"Why do you smile Sonia?"

"It is nothing Mama, I remember something."

She gets angrier and orders me to lay over her.

These grown-ups I say to myself, they are wax in the fingers: punishing they kid themselves they are in charge... As I lay there I ask "May I retain my panties Mama?" It is my traditional request; her answer is traditional also. "Certainly not; you are going to feel pain my child with no gloves on." 'Certainly not' she says often. It amuses me always; 'Certainly not.' She sees my expression and gets even angrier: "I will wipe off that silly smile from your face, girl." She is grim, her eyes do not blink and she rolls up the sleeve of her blouse: there is much purpose and I start to tremble.

My skirts are pulled up abruptly and breeze from the open windows and door lingers on my uncovered skin. Then my cotton panties are peeled sharply to an ankle, their elastics chafing and twanging slightly in the descent. Now is extra sense of incoming breezes and I hope no-one outside glances in or enters our doorway: I am conscious of my revealed maidenhood and turn my head about.

Mama grasps my waist and draws me into the angle of her body. It is strange to realize I came from between her thighs seventeen years ago: I was her joy then, now I enrage and she will beat me 'til I weep. Her hands, rough from housework, move upon my bottom: she searches the shadows of the eight welts from Miss Miriam's strapping. Lucky I checked, the lines the French instrument made are gone quicker. "Excellent," she comments. "I need help in this department."

"How can you say that about your poor daughter?" I respond daring. "It is terrible a flogging from someone who is not a relative: it is so cold." She is really furious this time and I think I am growing that she cannot cope the situation lately: "You will be obedient" she shouts. "I will cut your tongue: you do not speak to me like that or I will take the skin off your back you creature - Why am I a mother? God please send me to a prison away from this house."

I have dug my grave with my mouth and the little whip swishes and cracks on to my defencelessness: it swipes centrally across my bottoms and pain starts instant like there are stings from wasps... Mama is practised beating her daughter: this position over her lap I know since I was a small child.

I breathe sharp and a broken cry escapes: I cannot stop it. Already the pain is burning in my flesh awful. "Yes," she says, "this will be a harvest from your insolence and rule-breaking, above all your insolence." Her voice is like the whip: it is harsh and wants to hurt. "Look at me," she says and I twist and look up at her: her face is white and hard and the eyes are dark holes to her deep rage. "I promise you today I make you regret your tongue and attitude Sonia." I go icy from fear, turn back and bury my face in my hands.

The whip swishes again and again. Automatic I count the strokes, four, five, six, seven and onwards... My lips part and surprised I hear my cries; "Oh-oh-oh" I cannot help myself. Swish-crack, swish-crack and the room, the world, all is filled with my flogging. I am uncontrolled and weeping. My body cannot escape the pain as it squirms and jerks under the lashes. Mama's promise was good and I suffer worse than I ever suffer on her knees: I offended her deep and she does not restrain her energy.

Now I perspire with fear and twist to see her, crying urgent "Mama, please, no more; you will kill me, I will die of this beating - please, please." Her severe face assesses my words and she ceases, dropping the instrument on to the floor while I am shuddering, yearning to run anywhere.

Her strong hands are to my waist and side. "Oh Mama, please do not hate me, I am sorry! Please let me stand." I am released but fall. She looks down at me. "I do not hate you Sonia. You are my child and I love you - I will love you always. It was your insolence I punish... You are growing. Do not be a young woman who is arrogant and despises her family. If that happens I warn you I will beat you worse and if you are bigger get everyone round here to assist me: that is my warning - Come!" And gets me to my feet, not steady you can imagine... Careful I touch my bottoms which are on fire: pulses of pain go through them and I weep with self-pity and misery. I recall the counting: it went to sixteen at least - the most I have ever had, I think.

My fingers are sticky: "Blood!" I exclaim. "Oh Mama am I so wicked you want to mutilate me? Oh God -"

"It is one small necklace. Do not be silly. Go to the bathroom and and attend your stripes. It is finished. Tomorrow we will be partners again." She rises and kisses me, pushing my damp hair from my brow. I cling to her: "Oh Mama, I love you. I will be good for ever for you." She speaks softer. "Sufficient unto the day is the evil thereof. Go and get better my cherub... Return the whip and do not forget your panties." These I gather together and after re-hanging upon the the wardrobe-hook, the begetter of my agony, I walk slow to our bathroom.

At the supper-table I realize I am smiling and laughing with my parents, my earlier chastisement almost forgotten.

Chapter 8

It is night although this is meaningless in my state of asleep and dreaming: mother and Miss Miriam meet together friendly only to become hostile and bossy to me when I run into them. Where should be smiles and conversation come unkind expressions and they point accusing and shout into my face. But I am unafraid and give back a few shouts of my own which make them very wild and me pleased.

I am outnumbered and they try to grab me, specially Miss Miriam who clutches at my stomach and pulls me there. "What is this?" I yell. "What goes on?"

And I wake muddled head and frightened in the blackness of the night: "Who is it?" I whisper. Something on my belly moving, a weight... then a small wail: what relief.

"Oh Lima, you scared me. Why are you here?"

He is my tortoiseshell cat though most time he spend in my parents' bedroom. I lure him back with sardines but he does not stay. I am too racy for him now, he is no youngster. But now I caress soft fur between his ears and he purrs comfortable. He is affectionate but not much loyal.

I deduce he quits their place because they are awake and doing and spoil his rest. He rests nearly the whole time everywhere in the house until any disturbance nearby makes him wander away calm and unconcerned.

I listen in the dark which is like a substance and unyielding; nothing. I grope for a match and ignite it: the flare shows Lima alerted and gazing interested at it yet not respectful of something humans can engineer that cats cannot. By my watch it is 2 a.m. The silence sings in my ears and I light my bedside candle.

It is hardly cooler than in the daytime and I have not bothered to wear anything: the air is a warm cloak as I pad to the window and stare out. A crescent moon sails through a cloud-streaked sky, beauteous on its journey. Below me is our courtyard and to the left my parents' quarters lit, a cosy dim yellow: ah, there is Lima's disturbance. I turn to him who has remained on my bed in spite of losing my nice hot stomach.

"Hey Lima, Limmy!"

His head moves idly, then is still.

"See my stripes Lima - you lick them better?" No response; for him, if he notices anyway, I have been in a scrap and have wounds. I tend his after he fights, mine he ignores. "Faithless animal," I murmur. "And typical man."

For once our home is empty of guests and I decide for exploration. I tread light, the house is ancient and there are many creaky spots but my quiet is unhindered and eventually I locate the parental door which is not difficult because it is ajar for ventilation and lamplight within glows through its gaps.

Gently positioning, I peek in.

The tableau there does not contradict my suspicions. The saga of Mama's brief it seems has not yet an ending: she continues it now and as I take in details of the scene I hear a smart snap and a narrow brown band falls away from her behind which is curved on the back of a chair.

I shake my head and sigh soundless as possible. Another snap and falling of a length which in fact is a leather belt for her dresses.

They have their backs to me. Papa's tallness is remarkable and he is distinguished despite having on only pyjama-trousers. His bare right arm formal and measured works the belt's motion, and I reckon he has been administering punishment for a while: Mama's bottom has reddened much with lines and patches. Demure and formal also she has legs and thighs kept together though beneath her bedtime

56

brief which has no lining she shows a tuft of her intimate bush.

I shake my head again for she is otherwise no credit to our sex. She wriggles under the steady strokes giving restrained squeals and uttering such things as 'Oh Ferdinand I am sorry, do forgive me - aah!' And wiggle, wiggle.

Papa rumbles that which I cannot make out and lays on some punishment. I note he does not strike particularly fierce and this is usual for he is a man of kindliness: he dislikes to beat me for example. But he attends Mama's bottom keenly and stings well her silly bottom wriggling. 'Oh Ferdinand - ' and so forth.

Is this the same woman who whip me to distraction only hours earlier? I am exasperated 'til I speculate she may be sacrificial to protect me from his displeasure. Still I consider she reacts silly and I would not behave caught so. Once my cousin Leo he try to be the heavy male and spank me but I kick his shins hard. For a long time I am not able to cadge smokes from him.

Minutes pass and I observe her wifely chastisement. I have watched this her subjection before and it is true that it fascinates, this beating of the woman by a man's stern arm, though I am outraged and vow I will not submit similar for my husband.

Thus the swishes, snaps and squeals unto the hardest snap! of them all and the last and she squeals double and jerks on the chair making it slide and creak; "Uh-ah-aah! Oh Senor, leave me to my sinfulness."

My sinfulness! I tut-tut, but subdued.

Papa drops the belt on to the carpet and moving to her puts his hairy hand upon her glowing crowns. It must cause extra pain but she juts against it and groans: I am suspicious she is being phoney but, whatever, I know what is to happen next. His other hand presses her waist and he strips the thin nylon off her compliant flesh.

He rumbles and with her shortened name 'Bella' in it: otherwise it is not clear, his tones are so low. The seat of his pyjamas tightens meaning he holds their material in front undoing buttons and sure, then I see it, almost side on, Papa's generative member stiff and horizontal, big and powerful where Roberto's is interesting and exciting but lesser.

Mama looks round - a trapped look - and he grasps her waist, takes her off the chair. He pulls her to his strong thighs and she hangs from them like a large doll, arms and hair drooping to the floor. Her body shudders when he drives into her, one slow and practised thrust, she gasps and groans - not phoney now! She begins rhythmic movement as Papa pleasures her, rumbling to her greedy panting and tiny cries.

It is here I decide to leave. I do not find my parents' lovemaking abhorrent as some children do. It is just that I believe it is a sacrament and must contain privacy which I respect. Coincidence there is crackling on my ankles and sensuous fur of Lima: a signal to my feeling and I know he follows me on my return to my room.

Next morning I wake and remember it is school. I yawn and snuggle into the bedclothes but Mama calls "Sonia, Sonia, you are very late. Just shower and coffee and you go straight to St. Teresa's." I yawn again and rise unwilling to do as she bids. You can imagine I seek out cotton to wear upon my weals then descend to the dining-room where she is sitting at table, reading the morning paper.

She has on a dress which is biscuit-coloured and belted with what was across her bottom last night. She has her badge of wifely submission and I bet she put it on slow and significant in front of Papa, approving. 'Bella' 'Oh Ferdinand' etcetera. Tut-tut.

She sees me looking there. "What is it Sonia?" She is quick on the uptake and if you are her daughter you do not upset her or you suffer, so I reply hastily "Oh I am think-

ing: I must have a nice dress for mass on Sunday Mama."
"Yes that is well." Her eye is clear and lively and there is a
hint of make-up. What fools women are for a portion of
love or attention.

She smiles cautious. "And how are you my child?" And
lays down the paper. "I am fine," I say and continue: "Please
Mama it served me right what happened yesterday. I will
be good in the future, believe me."

She smiles cautious again. "You are my beloved child
and I do not chastise you gratuitously. Do not grow away
from me, Sonia, I cannot bear it."

"Oh Mama" I cry, "I love you." And wind my arms
around her neck then her waist still slender. "I promise I
try not to disappoint you in the future."

"I know it, I always did know it. You must forgive my
anger: I fear for you and over-react." "We shall never be
separated, never!" She pats between my shoulders and I
feel her body's warmth, the dull pulse of her heart beneath
her frothy blouse.

Then I am outraged because she lifts the pleats of my
school-skirt, the silkiness of my slip, and regards that which
is under them. "Mama, still you do not trust me!"

"I do trust you. It is your school-friends and your im-
pulses I do not trust. When you are a mother you will understand. I see you are in uniform everywhere and you may
go now. Be good at school my sweet and give my greeting
to your Miss O'Shaughnessy won't you?" Probably I nod
evasive for she says: "There is someone who understands
you also and does not permit your naughtiness, hmm? She
and I must converse one day - please mention this."

Silent, I leave her and enter the sunshine and join my
friends who are laughing, cannot help themselves. They
remark remembering my beating from Miss so many days
ago for it was sensational and they remember and its beget-
ting.

· "Brief today Sonn?" is a remark and I raise my skirts and hear: "Oh she is obedient, there will be no excitement at St. Teresa's." I run and catch them and raise theirs and find they are obedient also and together we run calling and laughing 'til we are inside at last and quiet and submissive under the steady gaze of our beautiful Miss Miriam.

It is a dreary day at lessons and proceeds slowly. We pupils study the clock as much as our books and cannot avoid a show of relief when the bell signals end-of-school. We chatter and clatter from the room, desk-lids banging, 'til suddenly I realise I have not told as I promised to my teacher and special friend of my mother's inevitable correction of me yesterday.

I pause and wander back to her dais on which she sits with our task-books, severe presently and annoyed at what one of us has submitted. She clicks her tongue and murmurs "This is too bad and quite unacceptable" then looks up: "Oh Sonia, I am sorry I did not see you there." She did but I let it pass. "Who's book Miss?" I ask though I can guess: this she ignores and I mount the dais to her desk and recollect her strapping me bent over it, so long ago it seems now!

I feel my face blush and she notices and is very blue-eyed just then as she regards my discomfort calmly. There is a silence and questioningly she lays down her pen and brings her fingers together: she has painted her fingernails! I am shocked and angry at her. This she notices also but squeezes her lips dismissively and says "Well Sonia what can I do for you?" She regards me comprehensive and I pluck my skirts and turn my shoulders self-consciously.

"It has happened Miss. Mama punish me yesterday about her missing brief. You wish to check? The reckonings between us are finished, I think."

She rises, takes my wrist, and re-seated guides me to lie across her thighs. "If anyone comes in I am smacking you for talking without permission. Mind you, if I truly did that you would never be off my knees would you my little one?"

"Oh Miss, am I so disobedient?" And wriggle pleasurable in her familiar curve and warmth.

"Disobedience should be your middle name - What is your middle name?" Her dry warm hand rests unmoving on the skin of my waist, the other is upon my inside left thigh gently stroking. My lips start to tingle and things are pleasant.

"One is Teresa," I say fairly steady, "the others I do not care for."

"Well that is nice isn't it my little one?"

"Yes Miss," I croak.

But again I recollect her beating me here and I shiver. The leather strap she used must be centimetres from me.

Then her fingers are on my panties' waistband and she draws off careful the thin cotton. I feel the breeze from the windows upon my extra bareness. She says: "I thought you are punished on your back usually, Sonia?"

"For this offence my bottom was deemed appropriate."

"Of course."

There is that 'Of course' again and I smile. She gasps: "I do not think I smile if I have what you have: it is a battle-field. And your skin is broken."

"It was my worst ever. I got 16 strokes. She is furious and it is because she thinks she is losing me."

"Ah-ha! Even so it was a fierce punishment - I am so sorry, the whole matter has gone somewhat out of control and my conscience still bothers me about it." Her finger tips dally along a weal which is central and over my cleft and I ouch, not at all theatrically. She stops. "Do you want a cushion for your chair young 'un?"

"Oh no Miss. My friends - and my enemies - will notice and laugh me down. Still," I continue brightly, "it is done with. The coming days promise no clouds and I will work and we will be great friends, kissing friends in fact - Why, Miss, you are gloomy and tense while I am happy and rejoice in the world and its possibilities?"

Gently she pulls the material on to its home and it clings and encourages the hotness from my stripes. I wiggle sensuously as she adjusts my skirt to a correct position, and we both sigh.

I am the trouble-maker of her existence presently and so decide to force her from her low spirit. "If I am here for a pretend-smacking you should not have unclothed my behind: it is a rule protects us poor pupils too you know."

She stiffens. Triumph. She is wax in my hands but forgets her mood. "Do not try to be fast with me young lady." And I bet her shapely nose is in the air. "I am always ten minutes ahead of you. Do not spoil my sympathy." I bite my thumb, smiling. Not in a lot of things I think. "Oh I am sorry, it is only that I do not wish you to get trouble over me Miss," I say innocent.

"It seems to me you are one with a great deal of trouble lately - And I see you are grinning impudently. I can still smack you where you are not beaten. Would you like to walk home through the streets, my finger-marks on your legs, Miss Impudence?"

"No fear, I am sure to meet someone I know."

"Then please rise immediately." And I do so.

She opens a drawer in her desk and brings out Mama's brief and shakes it to its shape. "So much punishment and unpleasantness from one small garment," she sighs again. Oh dear I think, teacher is back. "But Miss," I argue desperate, "sometimes life is thus: you hit a bad patch, it seems unending but eventual sun returns and good does."

She nods absent, next withdraws the punishment-strap, runs its length across the palm of her hand. "Oh!" I exclaim and search her frowning face.

"It is sad; two chastisements in a single term when many terms have had none."

"I was the first, who will be second? - Miriam, what have I done?"

"Nothing, nothing; it is not you. At heart you are a decent child. No. What I hold must pain another, I am afraid. The rule you broke was important but secondary."

"The eight strokes felt primary!"

"Six official. Do not exaggerate."

"Exaggerate! How can I exaggerate what truly landed?" My protest passes her ears.

"You will be glad not to bend beneath this tomorrow."

"Tomorrow - so soon?"

"Perhaps."

"And who?"

"I shall not say beforehand. Time will reveal."

"I know who it is." Or I can give a shrewd guess.

"Probably you do: I wish I didn't. I wish I didn't know anything about it." And, yes, she sighs.

I force her mood again by standing before her, taking the items from her and replacing them. I touch her at her ribs and her expression softens. "Thank you Sonia you are thoughtful, sometimes..." And she examines my eyes.

"You are beautiful, always" I say. And she is. "You are an angel in white but for your stockings. Do you need them this hot weather?" It is her vanity again but she is entitled to it, this one.

"I guess not."

"You are meeting someone Miss?" I ask lazily and stare obviously at her dress which is, how you say, flimsy and requires not much to detect the undergarments, the shape of her woman's voluptuous body.

She laughs. "Oh no, I would not deceive my Daniel."

And I am happy she is cheerful. She has a delicate perfume and I sniff appreciation. "Your clothes are a torment to us in our sensible uniforms: you are a cruel one today."

"Your time at St. Teresa's is ending and soon you discard them for prettier wear that will satisfy you and delight your fiances and husbands... Now, would you care for tea at my place before you go home Sonia?" She shuts her desk, gathers books and her bag and smiles.

I decide here is something, maybe nothing big. "A good suggestion." And, school and its grounds almost empty, we walk peacefully in the sunlight through to her secluded quarters, feminine and cosy, past trees and bushes bearing blossom, birdsong, and the meanderings of vividly coloured insects.

Chapter 9

It is cooler inside her little home. Nothing has altered since my previous invitation. Except she has dainty under-garments drying on rails when outside is a line only half-used by laundry. What is the reason? Aloud I comment, and she goes sombre: "The nuns pass here on their way to chapel. It is not seemly they can see a secular's modern underwear."

"Ridiculous" I say scornful. "They have the same - certainly the younger ones."

"How can you know Sonia?"

"It is not hard to know. They are not secretive about their clothes, why should they be?" I lick my fingers and take a cake. There are two left on the patterned paper disc. I chew contentedly and alas these go too; excellent. She makes them herself with loving care.

"Next time I bake more," she says affectionately, watching me. "You bet." My voice is muffled by cake. "I wish I was a mother," she sighs: she is doing a lot of sighing to-day. "You are delightful, a masterpiece. Your mother must be very proud of you." I splutter with mirth and crumbs land on the polished wood. "Mama, she wise you up. And Papa." I rub my hands on my blouse and take mouthfuls of sweet coffee; delicious.

She smiles. "Monster!" Her face is kind and attractive and I notice her natural beauty spot below her right eye. Her eyes are very blue now, the blue of a winter sky after the sun has gone but no stars gleam yet.

"My appetite is monster... Hey, if you get your fiance to co-operate - and he will, it don't take much encouragement does it Miss for these men to start shafting their women?"

She blinks and exclaims and I apologise. "- you produce your own little Sonia, or perhaps a Roberto pop out instead."

She giggles like a kid, then silence. Her laundry comes back to mind.

"Fr. Pablo," I venture. "He must use the path by your gate to go to the chapel. It is he you do not wish to know what you put on underneath? Today though he could see that anyway if he was in here or visited your classroom.."

I find a mark. Her cheeks are pink and she turns her head with its cascades of gold in the light from without.

"He could not see it wholly Sonia; an important difference. You are a young woman also and should know my meaning."

I assent. "He is your confessor Miss?" I query sly.

"Yes, he is. And yours also I believe? No more of the father please."

Oh-oh I think, here is something. And I resolve to be attentive to anything concerning Miss Miriam relative to that much-discussed priest.

"You find him a good confessor?" I continue dangerously.

"I request you to refrain from mentioning Fr. Pablo. And it is a private matter to trespass upon. Please change the subject."

"He penance you strict Miss? He -"

"Sonia!"

"Sorry." I am not really sorry and wonder how to dig in that ground the priest and the teacher share between them. She clears the tea things and as she stoops to the table I am reminded of our previous play. As she spreads a cloth my hand goes to her left bottom and feels it warm and firm. What a moment! She does not look around and her movements become brisk. "One day Sonia you will communicate like a normal person: What is it?"

Gently I pull the elastic of her brief and she observes: "You are a rude child. Stop it or I will spank your legs."

"It is admiration of you."

"It is rude and childish. 17 years old and you behave like a small boy with a dirty mind."

"What you are and what you have are desirable. I do not forget nor do I have a dirty mind about it." Though she is unmoving in response and says but a small 'sorry' I sense she has become self-conscious and slightly excited.

I rise and stand by her, she keeps her hands flat on the table.

"How sorry are you?" I ask softly. Her face pale is evasive and restlessly she pushes hair from her flawless brow. "I - I -" She swallows. "Your mother's punishment of you should have been condign, no more." What is condign I wonder; something no good for my type of person I suspect. She moistens her lips and glances at me and on her hip slides to and fro the flimsy layers there.

"Yesterday I got excess. It was not right and now Miss I shall flog your bare bottom for an injustice."

"Oh no!" But she stays, bent submissively.

"Afterwards we are even," I say. "But if your love-juices run I return and punish you again and again if required until a flogging is true punishment."

"Please do not remove my brief, Sonia, please."

"All right."

I go to the drawer where is the instrument of correction rested upon pretty colours and softnesses of female garments. She follows every movement: I put it by her. The handle and tipped lashes lay there threateningly: they are made for action and she trembles.

"Phew, it is hot," I say and undo my tie. "You are so angry you bind my wrists behind," she suggests, and I do so, interested in an addition to the play: I secure them tight and they twist uselessly

"You have this before?"

"Occasionally," she replies defensive. "It can be part of a just humiliation. Now give me the hem of my dress." And I bring it to where it is taken by her fingers.

She positions against the edge then bends: below her curving the thighs and legs keep together. A proper Miss and she has the garments to match; dark stockings tugged by plain white suspenders which run beneath and highlight the transparency of her white unfrilled brief. Its lining upon her cleft is immaculate white and she appears chaste and sacrificial.

"Remember, if you have juice you lie here again for punishment that is punishment."

"I understand."

As she turns to see me I administer the first stroke. The sharpness closes her eyes.

"Pain will also make you move," I say louder, and withdraw the narrow lashes from her bottom which reacts not so soon in the play. "Yes," I repeat, "pain will also make you move." And purposefully I roll up my right sleeve. Already her eyelashes glisten. "Sonia I am sad you were whipped excessively."

"Be quiet," I command, and swing the leather lengths on to her woman's tender crowns once, twice, thrice, swish-swish-swish, quick and with strength: they cover her seductive bottom and I am rewarded when red accumulates and agitated wriggling begins.

I flog her soundly and for a good period of time. Nothing is said and the sun-lit room is still, witnessing the rise and fall of the swishing instrument, the writhings of her revealed intimate region, and the hearing of her broken ill-controlled cries.

Eventually I say "I am tempted to unclothe you where this leather beats you yet I must respect your wish. However, gather yourself for the finale of your chastisement."

"Oh little one, do not be so full of vengeance."

That I ignore and bring down the strokes harsh and rhythmic, scarcely a pause between. She is helpless now. Her urgent voice wavers and she can only writhe with the pain I lash on to her curving flesh. The tight brief cannot protect her and her wrists strain ineffective within an implacable bond.

I grow tired and perspire and she sobs from her bosom. There is not a centimetre of unmarked skin to her area of punishment and seeing this I replace the instrument beside her wet and distressed face.

"I congratulate myself," I say cruelly. "We have settlement at last. Open your legs."

"Sonia -"

"There will be no dessert," I state roughly, and scan her gleaming layers: "Very good, Miss. You had a true correction. Let me feel please."

"Be kind Sonia, we finish as friends" she whispers.

This is dumb stuff for my taste, but when I hold her hips and look between them I do have pity for her and impulsively I caress her crowns with my cheek which feels the heat off a surface no longer smooth: "Oof!" she goes, and "Oh don't, don't! I am hurt enough."

I desist. Licking my lips I place a dewy kiss middle of a bottom: "You prefer that?" I ask, casual. "Oh yes." And she smiles despite herself.

I free her wrists and encourage release of the hem. It drops past the fragile underwear and conceals where justice acted fiercely upon her tender flesh.

"So. That was done well." And my finger tips comb the silk of her crinkly hair 'til she stands awkwardly, massaging carefully behind her. "Too well done, and you enjoyed every minute you, you sadist."

"I enjoy we are quits and remind you of your waywardness beforetimes."

Her mouth is crooked and she blinks much not having an answer.

"Come," and unsteady she nears. Her eyes rimmed from weeping are shifty. She bites her lower lip already swollen and, like I have ordered her - maybe some way I have - outstretches her arms: I am in them and kiss her face everywhere 'til she weeps afresh and I say: "You must not love me, I am neither daughter nor fiance, only Sonia."

She hugs me extra and I wait while she calms. "One more thing," I say. "We hate untidiness." I point: "Replace the instrument forthwith. We are not hoboes." She sighs: will I ever do with her sighing this day? And slow and abject replaces it. She sniffs using a handkerchief absurdly tiny, turns and - yes - her nose is higher in a fashion getting familiar.

"I had hope you would be a kinder friend. I suppose love from a youngster is impossible."

"Kind? I am kind. I keep a piglet once and he squeal each time he see me. As for love -"

She bangs the drawer shut and being teacher quite invades her.

"I do not want to hear about love, and as for your flippancy -" she exhibits restraint, then curiosity: "What happened to him?"

"Eh?"

"Your pig."

"Oh, he finish in our dining-room: Papa ate most of him. I could not bring myself to eat -" she is sympathetic "- for pork is heavy to my stomach." Her eyes narrow sudden. "I learn -" I chatter "- the Irish are keen on the world of pigs Miss -"

"I expect the impossible from youth!"

"You should keep a pig, it is a hobby -" And she slaps my face. "Ow, that hurts."

70

"THAT I enjoy: I enjoy stinging your superficiality when I am low-spirited."

"My brain is chiming. What a brutal way of ending an interesting conversation -"

I falter because she stares and her left hand palm outward - not to hit me - is by her knee and I recognize from this stance she is about to state something - how you say? - 'not to my advantage.'

"You should leave now or this talk will break our friendship."

"Miriam, please, you complain I am the hard one."

"I have a diary."

"Oh Miss, how exciting! Is it hot and sensational? Am I in it?"

From a writing-desk in the corner she returns with a maroon volume. She is firm and I can win no exchange in her new mood.

"It is an appointments diary." And riffles the pages. "Let me think. Hmm, eleven days hence, yes that should do it. Yes. The nineteenth, Sonia; when you arrive I will have the school-strap here ready for you. Meantimes if your so-called humour is bridled we can remain friends. Your love for me of course is a non-starter. Well?"

I feel tears of my own begin and murmur: "I let you down, I am sorry." There is a long silence, then we embrace. "I cannot help it," I say. "I am not old enough I guess and you are absent from your Daniel. It became a poor mix."

"Do not be sorry for what you cannot help."

"Did you mean it? A school-beating here, the whole thing?"

"Of course."

"I jolly-well not come."

"Oh you would come: I arrange. So, beware and think to your future." "You will have to drag me."

"Then I fix you in class: I would set you up. You beware of my diary Miss Flippancy." And waving it she returns it to the desk.

Speaking of our class I am reminded of tomorrow.

"St. Teresa's retribution will not check Juanita." I am guessing Juanita. "She is er-recalcitrant that one: she is a tough egg."

"Umm?" Miriam half-listens for she is hungry since her punishment and this overtakes her disappointment at that of my manner she dislikes. "Sit beside me," I say and we get comfortable on the sofa. "We made this sofa famous, you agree?" But flicking my skirts she smacks my thigh. "Ow, you are hitting me again Miriam. You are not fair."

"I am sorry." And she kisses my neck slow with desire, her hands to my belly and right breast. I stroke her gold hair and smell it and dig my chin on to the hardness of the scalp. "It is Juanita Neruda is it not?" I ask, insinuating.

"I must not tell." But she does not deny. "Nothing may happen: I pray nothing happens."

"It is more than a school-rule she break: she -"

"Do not be a sneak Sonia, it does not suit you."

"I am not: she must be saved. You will discover her state. It is St. Rita's chapel for her - as it was for you."

"What do you mean?" She sits upright and clutches my forearm 'til I protest at the pain.

"You know what I mean. But for you there is a difference: you are a woman. She may be a tough egg but the law considers she is uncooked. What you are penanced for she must be double-penanced."

She stands frightened and her eyes I search. I am not hostile and she recovers. "I am foolish to forget you would make a simple deduction but how you know it was by Fr. Pablo, not my priest in Ireland or a priest in France?"

I have trapped her. "I did not know for certainty 'til now." Her face is paler than pale. "You - you terrible child." And she covers her mouth to stop further words.

"It is not so terrible. In - we are aware of St. Rita's, its penances, those that deliver them. Your attendance was not novel: believe me, many have suffered."

"I - I -?"

"I suspect you attended Oh, seventeen days ago? And it was he who penance you? I am right. And the next day I pleasure you Miss, here where I sit."

She links her fingers, walks back and forth biting her lip.

"Unaccountably - to some," I say, "you wear yet a vest. It is pretty and fetching but unnecessary; a puzzlement as the rest of you is not much hidden. But possibly not a puzzlement to you. You want to show me what is beneath? Shall I oil you?"

She halts. "Yes, it was he." And unbuttons 'til the bodice of her dress falls. She removes the vest revealing her back.

"I postponed confession so often that at last I had to go and this was the result:" The band of her brassiere is snowy and contrasts with livid weals above and below and crisscrossing.

"He whip you strong," I observe without satisfaction. "He does it if he fancy you. If not, his tame nun Sr. Consuela punishes. She is as strict. Was she present?"

"Yes," my friend and teacher grimaces. "A witness is obligation and safety, of a sort. Less fun though if another woman is watching: the two of you alone would be something else."

"Sonia, he is a priest!"

"He is a priest and a man. You like him?"

"Enough of stupidity. I have a sacrament I pray need not be repeated. I admire him for that only!"

73

"And Juanita, this is her destiny? I said she must be saved, I wonder now if she can be saved."

"It grows late my little one, and we are having a grim discussion. Let us part to rest for the evening. Tomorrow can take care of itself."

"I agree I assure you... were you scared?"

"More scared than I have ever been in my life."

"Poor Miss. In the aftermath was I of some comfort to you?"

"You are my treasure in this place Sonia."

"Then farewell 'til the morning Miss."

"Farewell Sonia, farewell."

I walk swiftly to my house and am overjoyed to be within its ancient walls and upon its congenial furnishings. My parents notice my lightness of heart and Papa rumbles smiling: "She is to meet her Roberto tomorrow I think." I nod which is a lie for the idea of tomorrow grips horrid in my breast and it is the loveliness of our home I draw from in compensation and which sails my feelings this evening, prior to another's dreadful nemesis.

Chapter 10

"Santa Maria!"

"That is worse than impolite, to use a saint's name in such a manner. You surprise me Will, for you also are of the Faith."

"Apologies; it was disrespectful."

"You have to confess that one I am thinking."

The mid-afternoon sun was at its hottest and my Sonia had unclothed to briefs only. I sweltered and retained but shorts and undergarment.

"Astonishing events Sonia and really I begin to appreciate those patterns of behaviour where you come from and concede they are suitable."

"We are not barbarians: we chastise because we care or enjoy, not for blood-lust or to gain the other's servitude."

"You'll continue your history? You're not bad at relating by the way."

"Thank you, Senor. But I am dry, I wet my throat first. You like a drink?" She stood and I contemplated her form. As desire mingled with admiration conquered me also I became perturbed: "You can't go into the house like that - What if someone's returned?"

"In England I lay on the beach how you say, topless, and no complaints. Where is the difference? And I say all God's children have nipples."

I forbore to mention the nude effect of her sole item of apparel and anxiously counted the moments until she reappeared bearing glasses of iced lemonade. She laughed delightedly at my face, no doubt exhibiting concern. "Everyone saw," she teased. "And the cat put his paws over his eyes. Here, cool yourself and calm your nerves."

"I wish I had your nerve. You realise your bum, and elsewhere, shows you've been beaten?"

"Oh, I am a naughty girl. Should my punishment be a secret?"

"You're incorrigible."

"That had better be complimentary or I do not continue."

"It is not uncomplimentary this time." And I devoured her as she stretched beside me, noisily sucking the lemonade and noisier finished before rolling on to her back: she did not angle her knees and idly touched her small and shapely breasts. An old stirring came to life in my senses.

"I think you are rehearsing a famous idea," she commented.

"Sonia!" And tenderly I stroked her belly.

"You rip off my brief now," and she went big-eyes, "or later you do the deed after! Carefully I watch you peel yours and after you hear more history. What you say?"

"Go ahead my love," I answered encouragingly, remembering things so far told. "I am ears only, for the present."

"It was not just sad happenings subsequent," she offered judiciously. "There were others that should spice up your pecker okay - It is no joke," she said sternly to my grin, "so listen close to the fall of it. You owe me, Mr Collett."

I turned on to my back by hers and gazed at the unclouded sky, nibbling a stem of grass.

Sonia's voice, low-toned, seductive of the male, went again to her narrative like a swimmer's flawless drop into restless but brimming waters:

A roar of a window opening, a thump and a cut-off cry and I wake, heart pounding to full alert: thank goodness night does not greet me. The morning light is brilliant and birdsong has entered my bedroom as has Stella, a best friend,

76

and undignified for she is upside-down, a foot held by the window-sill.

"Help me Sonn, I am - ow!"

"Not likely. You visit without announcing, you help yourself. And you disturb Lima poor fellow: you give him a seizure one day you know."

"Huh." She is disbelieving and indeed he walks leisurely away. He is the gentleman strolling who does not wish to be accosted by a beggar.

"Get dressed," she says urgently. "You will miss school-bell."

"Plenty of time" I soothe and watch her manoeuvre to a conventional stance. "And about dress, you are out of uniform:" she has a scarlet nylon brief. You cannot see through it but it is sexy just the same. "You ask for it if you get caught. Do not forget my licking for that offence."

"Oh Sonn you are in the wars lately. Show me what you got from your mother."

"No. How you know anyway?" A pointless question, living in this town.

"You should not be neighbours of the Juarezs," she giggles. "They spread they hear every lash, and your howls. They -"

"Oh shut up. When I inspect your arse after school you may see my marks then."

"There is no gymnasium today and" - she speaks quieter - "besides our favourite person will occupy everyone's attention."

"Oh please." And I recall yesterday with Miss Miriam. A familiar sinking is in my breast and I change the subject. "Who are you meeting today?" I demand. "He prefers scarlet to white no doubt and ones that reveal more of his Stella than St. Teresa's allows, yes?"

"I will tell you some time I promise."

"I find out pretty quick specially round here."

"Come on Sonia, get up and get ready."

"I am naked and whereas Lima is a gentleman you are not yet a lady." In truth it is I have young breasts while Stella's are nearly a woman's and she is irritatingly proud of them.

"You have nothing I do not see before," she tinkles and goes to my clothes-drawers. "Blouse. No vest, it is very hot outside - when will the heatwave end?"

A storm of clothes lands where I am still beneath a single sheet: it was so humid overnight.

Reluctantly I forsake bed and pad towards my shower-cubicle.

"Wow, that is a beating and a bit. Your mother was real angry yes?" I am silent because of slight shame and bigger embarrassment: why, my age, am I draped across a parent's lap?

"And you got a necklace, wow, shall I fetch a mirror?"

"Certainly not - and do not touch," I add, guessing her mind.

"What about ointment, Sonn. I do it for you?"

"No thanks."

"You are tremendous brave."

"I was not on Monday."

"I have never been whipped," she says smugly.

"You are a model child. It is a privilege to talk with you."

"Oh do not be cold. I did not mean to sound superior. We are best friends, it was private information."

"Be useful and give me the soap." After she passes it she holds my waist and kisses my cheek. "You clown, you will be soaked."

"Would you like to come to an event at luncheon-break?" she whispers.

"What is it? We are to view your bottom unmarked by human hand?"

"Oh you are frost. It is hopeless."

"I am sorry Stella. I am oppressed by this day and wish it was tomorrow."

"You are free of anything. You ARE free of anything?" she probes not unkindly and I shake my head. "So. Why be gloomy?"

"I do not know exactly. It is St. Teresa's: I have foreboding."

"St. Teresa's is a fine school."

"Not the school, the parish."

"The parish? I do not understand. What is wrong with it?"

"Oh, nothing I expect." She is not keen to deduce and watches attentively while I towel myself. "You are - hermm - a feast" she decides.

She ponders where is easier interest: "You go to Miss Miriam's this evening?"

"Maybe. My English progresses and sometimes there is extra tutorial. Tea also!"

"Ah-hah. We think, a fact, we know she likes you a lot. But it is no use Sonia, you cannot marry her, it would not be nice." And she stifles her laugh, becomes silly kiddy: she does this often despite her age.

I assume a stony face and enunciate slowly to my knotting the towel: "You are very funny my child and since uninvited you crashed into my room there is constant entertainment. Now it is time for your reward."

She attends me smiling but is poised and dodges a swing of the knotted towel to her thighs. A chase ensues and I catch her easily for she is too light-of-heart to wish to escape completely. We trip to the carpet in a struggle and yanking her pleats I whack in a few blows.

"Ow! Sonn, stop it: this is savage."

"When you last get some, you good good girl?" I pant. Then, as I raise the towel again, there is knocking on my door. "Sonia. Sonia! Are you prepared for school?"

"Oh God, it is Mama. sssh-sssh." And I scramble to my feet. "Yes Mama! I am sorting my case."

"It is eight-thirty. Hurry please."

"Yes Mama." Breathless we hear her depart.

"Go Stella, go. We meet at luncheon-break." And almost bounding, not noticing Lima's cool stare, she retreats the way she came.

Chapter 11

The Angelus, rung at the convent's chapel, is clear and precise and enters our classroom, windows wide for the clement weather. The sacred notes substitute for our rackety charmless bell at luncheon-time and now we rise, a banging and chattering flock, and flow to the exit.

"Quietly please, quietly," calls Miss Miriam, but for this she is unusually ineffective.

"You coming?"

"To where?"

"To the event I mentioned."

"Stella, you are not convincing about mysteries because where we live there are no mysteries." I turn towards the refectory.

"It will be educational," she says persuading. "Miss refec and share my luncheon: I have rolls and ham, cake and" - voice lower - "beer. Fancy a smoke?"

"What is the matter with you? You are not the rule-breaker."

"Come on." She takes my arm and we leave the school-grounds.

"Where we head for may we find shade please? I am boiling."

"Oh it is shady enough."

Eventually we approach the old railway-line, shut before I was born and you never encounter a person near it. It is sad and unattractive.

"I know," I sniff, "we are to visit the bunny-wunnies frolicking by their burrows. Stella is maternal - I buy her a new doll on her birthday."

"No, that is not the plan and I dislike your tone Sonia. Return if you prefer. I finish the beer and things alone."

"I hate beer." She looses my arm. "There is something about you invites chastisement: it is your lousy humour and deprecating manner. Your whipping was good news. I wish my hand was responsible for your stripes."

I stop. "Look at me Stella."

"No you will not win."

I hold her shoulders, kiss her warm friendly lips. But her expression is wise and unamenable.

"I may smack your face any second."

"I apologize, look at me," I say again.

"Your act of a little girl who is cutie-pie is a waste on me, and your mother: what works for Miss or Roberto does not work for me. We were babies together, yes?"

"Yes. I promise to mend my ways. You will give me a cheroot?"

Then she does look and surprises me with her kiss which is hard and demeaning. "Rest your tongue and we will not quarrel. Here." And she passes a smoke.

"Through you it will bless my nerves. I tell you I am jittery today."

"Your awareness should make your attitude better."

"I am humble Stella, please forgive me."

"Huh. I pity your future husband."

She remains ruffled and I feel depression. The sun is at its zenith and I undo my tie. "Are we near our destination?" I venture. "I collapse soon I reckon."

"We are, and others are here already."

"Oh yes - they are from St. Teresa's. Is it a party? No, there are different ages."

"You might call it that," and she smiles: suddenly she is a stranger.

"Stella," I say with alarm, "we picnic elsewhere, not amongst these kids."

"You goose, there is time for everything." She re-takes my arm and initially I am glad her mood changes, 'til we step round the side of the station's decaying waiting-room.

That which the gathering watches and discusses is upon rabbit-cropped sward hid from distant eyes but is the glaring point for us metres away.

"It is the Neruda woman." And I gasp shocked: "He takes her in front of youngsters."

"Human-biology lesson," she says, puffing coolly but attentive.

"Stella we quit. It is an unworthy spectacle."

"Be sensible Sonn, they are betrothed."

I pull her but she will not move. "You feel horny?" she drawls.

"There," I say triumphant. "It bespeaks cynicism. We quit this horrible place."

"Bespeaks -" And she utters uncharacteristically a swear-word. "It is natural and educational."

"She will sink because of this," I say miserably. "My enemy but I am sorry for her."

"Anyway I judge they nearly finish. It is terrific and nothing horrid."

To my dismay she sits for a closer view.

It is true they are in the final throes of their passion. A woman I am sure can imitate the increasing pleasure but not Juanita now.

He, Mario, pins her, a speared fish and like the fish she gapes. Similarly her eyes are saucers and stare. Dead in the water she rocks and later I bet she will go under though differently from another's action.... Or will she? her toughness is notorious.

They circle and consume the passion locked conventionally, and I cannot ignore her fiance's strong haunches rippling and driving. He has a string tight on his big body for enhancement: its transparency is colourless and most of him where it is is visible. His seed-bags are plump and the pounding motion discloses regularly part of his columnar member ploughing her wet bush-covered fissure as she cries out despite herself. She is wholly dressed and his ardour has merely pushed to one side the narrow band of pink silk along the crevice.

It is wildness these remaining minutes and she drums and digs his broad and sunburnt back. Around them is wrapt silence and I wonder how many notice the pulsing above his bags as, with a primitive and drawn-out growl, he thrusts mightily into her. She senses their issue I decide, the hot flood, and I see her helpless claw his back taut then subsiding upon her spasms then writhing.

Afterwards, because of spectators, they unlink with a degree of haste. Adroitly she returns the silk to its intended home and her skirts also. She fingers hair from her temples, tosses it defiantly. He the full-grown man closets his joy-maker within nylon and clothes both in the denim of his work-trousers.

A clapping and whistles follow. "Show's over," comments Stella. "We arrive earlier next time for the whole action, eh Sonia?"

"I will have the beer after all: my nerves jangle."

"Pretty good congress those two."

"You are gross - as were those two."

"Oh, you are not invited for another show Miss Metal-pants. I keep it secret for myself."

"If there is another."

"'If there is another?' That was a woman under Mario, no frightened schoolgirl. You are not smart, sister."

"Do not be sure. This business is incomplete. She may run with a bridle in a while."

"Neruda is a real rebel, Sonia, where you are an amateur. The instant leather strikes your skin you straighten out. I tell you she is sterner stuff."

"I suspect you are right," I say wearily. "Please, now we sojourn somewhere lonely to rest and lunch."

She is winsome and I follow, reminded of Mama when I am defeated by her, as always in the end I am.

Stella's suzerainty is obviously pleasing her.

Away from the derelict line we are unadventurous and wander to a favourite spot, a bank of the locality's stream. Its water is clear and sparkles in the sunlight. We count the varieties of birds and eat our luncheon.

"Oh, it is paradise," she says. "I would be here for ever. The thought of classroom fills me with nausea. I wish I was nineteen and left school."

"Thought of that classroom fills me with dread," I respond, and appropriately I light a cheroot, my hand shaking.

"You baffle me. Anyone think your neck is the target, and she is your enemy, no?"

"I cannot hate her now."

I look at the bright water flowing past. "The affair is a stone dropped into a pool: rings spread out and return and intersect. That is my fear."

"There are no mysteries and you talk mysteriously." Stella is thoughtful: "What happens affects others. This follows always, we are not islands. Accept the inevitable."

"And if we are fond of someone affected?"

"Your fearfulness will not help them. They need strength. It is Miss Miriam you consider. Remember she has colleagues and plenty power to sustain her."

I agree with Stella to divert from accurate discussion of Miss: this far I do not involve even a best friend.

"Be cheerful," she says, rising. "Really you have no reason to be otherwise. Come and have a dip."

"I am not going in there," I reply emphatically. "Running water is icy."

"Oh you are a home-body, Sonn. You will never finish worrying."

She disrobes, except the little scarlet brief she wears and wades into the swiftness. "Ooch, it is so cold."

"Your brain is made of banana. The hens watch you with horror."

"Come in, it is super, better than a shower." And she splashes happily, aims palmfuls of water at me. Quickly I gather her clothes and hold them above my head: "You cease?"

"You dare! I tell my parents."

"I tell Miss you are not in uniform."

She clambers up the bank spluttering and shivering. "Here you wretch." I back away. "Sonia, please; I am almost naked, give them to me." I drop the clothes between roots of an old tree and position in front of it folding my arms. "Here they are and here I am." Stationary she regards me. "That is some scowl Stella, you practise in the mirror?"

"You shrimp. I smack your face. I let your bottom off."

"Ooh very well I release you." Her body, all of her, is beautiful as urgently she scoops the garments. Her kick to my ankles misses and I sit as she dresses.

"Now you will not smell for your sweetheart."

"He likes to smell me, it excites him."

"You be careful."

"I am always careful and I trust him."

"Trust a man, my lips quiver."

"You trust your Roberto?"

I do not answer, instead tweak her hair, and we roll together laughing. My hand invades beneath her skirt and presses her warm mound: "Do not let him give you one."

"We are sisters in our virtue." And she sits up, drawing the fine hair through her fingers. "Have you a ribbon Sonn?"

"Sorry."

"Mario's was gross was it not?"

"He pleasure her mightily: she was beside herself."

"The width of an altar-candle; he is a lusty fellow. She is lucky respecting that."

"It will be consolation in her misfortune."

"Oh poohf, she will not die of today or whenever she is brought to book."

"Today is likely." And simultaneously we search each other's eyes.

"I reckon we are late, Sonn." In silence we turn towards St Teresa's.

"You should wear suspenders and stockings for your rendezvous, your rendezvous with a MALE." I say it to lighten our mood rather than to be truly helpful. "Oh, he has enough to occupy him." And she laughs almost relievedly.

Chapter 12

Approximately we are five minutes late and Miss Miriam is ratty, partly because she is tense anyway we guess.

"Go to your places fast you two. Any repeat of this, I will punish you." As we obey, the rest of the class still and slightly afraid, she asks: "Have you seen Juanita Neruda?" She uses 'Juanita Neruda' more than 'Juanita,' an ominous sign. "No Miss" we chorus and are glad to reach our desks: she separated us months ago and it was the one occasion I thought Stella might have to bend for a leathering but it did not transpire.

My enemy Juanita's seat is vacant and I glance at the clock; ten minutes after start of afternoon-school. Withdrawing books and papers she to my right murmurs "Spanish lit. Then English; make you content Sonia."

"The next girl who talks I shall punish."

"Oh God."

"You will all continue in the eleventh chapter of Don Quixote 'til I say and" she adds severely, but her voice is not so steady as normal, "in absolute silence." And silence there is bar the initial rustling of pages. A few moments of the immortal de Cervantes and cautious I look up: Miss has not sat as is customary. She paces to and fro or stares through a window. This awful jittery day, I think, and I perspire coldly.

And recommence Don Quixote until, nerves protesting, I hear the classroom door open sharply. Whoever enters has not bothered to knock as required and we know there is but one who behaves thus.

Her tall womanliness advances to its usual place, which adjoins that of another who comically is the class's shortest and, equally funny, they are matey.

"Juanita," says Miss Miriam softly, "you forget to knock and you are very late: no doubt you will apologize for the first and explain the second."

She halts and turns slowly. To me it is like a western where the gunfighter is challenged and the issue is deadly.

Juanita mumbles, not facing her teacher: she is Brando.

"Over here please: what is it you said?" And lackadaisically she walks to Miss, stands arms at sides not behind as we would have them.

"Well? You said something: I suppose it could have been an apology but, again, why are you late?"

"My watch is at home."

"My watch is at home MISS."

No response.

"Very well, you drive this encounter to a conclusion you may not relish young lady."

The room is so quiet one imagines the clock ticks, which is improbable for it is electric.

This far Juanita's offences are small, though if committed often would earn the carpet-slipper thwacked loudly on your bottom whilst, embarrassingly for we senior-girls, laying across teacher's knees, skirts raised. However we are sentient for more than this. If we were not present at her coupling at least we have knowledge of it and therefore judge the sting-making slipper will stay in the drawer.

Familiarly she tosses her hair, a gesture of special defiance this afternoon, and everyone knows why. My teacher must act immediately if she is not to lose control of the clash.

She steps away to address us and her left hand in old fashion is held outward by her knee: there is material coming all right, not to anyone's advantage, and certainly not Juanita's.

"On Thursdays," Miss begins, her expression tense with anger, "there is no gymnasium and I have discovered a few of you consider this an opportunity to wear fashionable underwear." Stella I notice is a statue. "This practise breaks a school-rule and is of course strictly forbidden." Her 'of course' at last and I smile which receives a glare that heats my ears. A hollowness conquers my stomach and I quake she may tackle me but thankfully she continues: "The breaking of any school-rule earns the higher levels of our corporal punishment. Regarding this particular offence you are also aware uniform inspections may be made." And she turns to her troublesome charge who, apparently bored, yawns hugely.

There must have been a temptation to slap an insolence. Instead: "Juanita Neruda, hands on knees."

And thank goodness she complies although slowly. What if she had ignored Miss?

Her skirts are as short as she can possible get away with and so her hands rest on black nylon stockings, seamed, and no-one else has this kind. Miss, now by her, ups the pleats grass-flecked and reveals a slip purple and lacy; forbidden. Revelation of red and frilled suspenders follows. Forbidden! Finally, above and between the nude ivory bottoms, is the pink and dainty ultra-brief: its decorated edgings hardly worth their tailoring. Very forbidden you might say!

"I expected this. And you mingle contempt with fashion-consciousness. You are worse than any I have punished for this offence."

Juanita's legs are together and somehow her unmovingness signals defiance also. Presently her woman's private region is hidden by flesh and by thin silk.

"The school's decision is bespoken and beyond appeal unless it is your time of the month. Well?" The voice is harsh and demanding.

Juanita shifts self-consciously and shakes her head quickly.

"Very well Neruda, you will receive the punishment-strap. Bring it to me."

A rush of whispering excitement. "Silence this instant!" and we subside watching fascinated despite our horror.

Juanita maintains acceptance though she intends to exhibit rebelliousness, and strolls to the dais as if crossing a road at traffic-lights. Returning she proffers the instrument we have all seen and a few have felt.

"By the handle please."

Meanly she stares back. She is taller than Miss Miriam, herself no shorty, and has a fuller figure. It seems incongruous she is to bend, the other to beat.

"You will now bend over my desk."

Negligently Juanita curves against its edge, where occasionally she got leather times past.

"Your award is twelve strokes minimum. Twelve strokes!" Miss calls to indicate commencement of the proceedings.

Twelve! Concerned whispers are rife for a second or two. "Silence please! I will not ask you again." And we simmer to an apprehensive hush. I recall six at most is rarely given although there may be 'extras' as I know personally. Coincident with my thoughts she glances in my direction the strap straight between her hands. And I the minor rebel feel animosity and think, I will pay you for that look Miriam.

She arranges purposefully Juanita's skirts, tidily folding them upon the horizontal of her red suspenders. Below, a generous-sized bottom firm and shapely is virtually nude. It does not tremble but appears terrible exposed, endangered. And what further will work there, and this time to the owner's distress and agony?

Miss moves from her and as intended we see overall the stockinged legs slightly bent, the line of suspender leading to a shiny band of bright pink and the purple and blue nest of the skirts. Juanita avoids our eyes with smirking detachment, but I detect ever and anon she teethes her upper lip.

Miss, gently stroking between thumb and forefinger the supple leather of the strap, addresses us once more: "Honestly I can say this beating will upset all round. I want you to learn from it. The rule about uniform exists to foster a team-spirit."

Juanita yawns again!

We cannot resist smiles and giggles and our teacher pauses to regard her: "I implore your patience Miss Neruda." And waggles significantly a tongue of the strap separate from its companion, which action is noted by a corner of Juanita's eye. "I can assure you I will be with you in a moment." And continues: "The team-spirit encourages lessening of fashion-considerations, obsession with boy-friends and should enable you to concentrate on your studies. It is not designed to make you small or diminish your awakening womanhood." Not much! and I screw my nose. "I ask you please not to succumb to this kind of rule-breaking in the future."

She turns back to the wrongdoer and her lips are squeezed sternly, eyes fixed and unblinking. A frown is on her otherwise smooth white brow and twice, thrice, she flicks downwards the brown length in her delicate right hand.

Now she is almost directly behind Juanita which spot it devolves is worst possible luck for that miscreant. "I apologise my child for trying your patience. Safely I can now promise you diversion henceforward from tedious lack of occupation... Open your thighs and stick up your bottom Neruda," she orders and, again, flick-flick of the strap.

We are sentinel of a hideously long interval 'til sounds an aggressive sniff and the creamy bottoms spread then rise several centimetres. Miss cannot help it and looks to the private area - anyone might in the circumstances - but what she cons makes her alert and us have nervous reactions.

Where we are we do not detect a thing but certainty is our form-mistress discovers what is left from Mario's vigorous crescendo. She lets the leather hang and stoops urgently hissing in her pupils ear: I hear very little only single, muted words - 'foolish', 'why?', 'spoilt', 'inevitable.' She straightens and I swear her eyelids gleam: but if her heart is hurt she recovers speedily. The ritual must not be lost: it is for all, for what is St. Teresa's.

Meanwhile the tall one merely moves her buttocks suggestively and winks at us as they revolve erotically. This is her response to Miss's concern who then resignedly enunciates: "You will count each stroke Juanita. If you move excessively or are noisy additional strokes will be administered. Prepare yourself."

Which she does not do. We shiver and flex ourselves when across that desk. Our heads incline, we breathe deep, we clench our bottoms for a fragment of protection. Maybe we mutter prayer, anticipating the first lash. We lubricate dry mouths and throat.

But Juanita is casual, elbows on the wood, chin cupped. The sorrow for her Miss had is thereby vanquished and the two-tongued length is laid preparatory upon her crowns. She pats her hair unconcernedly when the flawless skin senses the cool leather.

It flickers upwards, a concise whoosh. A whoosh downwards, but the second is punctuated by a swipe resounding centrally upon her nudeness there.

We start, yet remain attentive of everything, also slyly observe each other. We hear a laconic 'one' spoken like a mark given for a poor sports-performance.

Another duo of whooshes stopped by a lashing swipe! and Miss has brought down the strap harder.

Still the laconic verbal receipt and indeed she wiggles sensually adjusting her fore-limbs to help. It is breathtaking! She absorbs the pain nonchalantly whilst displaying sexiness so soon since her fiance's ministrations.

Miss is aggravated. "You moved. Therefore you merit an additional stroke Neruda. I warn you." And a third swingeing stripe is etched on to her insolent bottom. But it does not jerk and 'three' is laconic yet.

Swipe; 'four', swipe; 'five', swipe; 'six'.

We flinch and goggle for every one.

Angled also, the strap lashes in with the efficiency and power we expect from Miss Miriam.

But I become suspicious she is jealous of the other's recent love-making, does she not beat her near where for herself she is presently hungry, she who is far from home, its association of pleasuring?

The chastisement halts; six administered.

When she remembers she allows - how you say? - a 'half-way house.'

This total the brazen Juanita has had before but we wonder can she journey so insouciantly to more?: beyond six-plus 'extras' is unprecedented.

We, the chastised in the past, have a rhyme:

'If Terry's catch you with the six-pack, you will bend for a burning six-max.'

Our angered teacher has concentrated four of the strokes on to the lower part of the buttocks and I bet she desired to remove the pink silk, not for pain's increase - this would be negligible - but to view vengefully the pleasured fissure as skin by it is powerfully strapped.

The intermission ends and, blue eyes glittering unpleasantly, her lovely forearm moves to the brief's waistband; surely not the unpermitted, the stripping off of the ultimate undergarment?

No. Unseen to our rebel, fingers tug suddenly and tautened elastic must bite delectably, hid by reddened convexities.

Juanita bows her head, holds her face then rests chin on linked knuckles whilst Miss apparently introduces an inspection.

The punishment-strap trails on the sensitized skin, roughened also by the lashes. Now it dips into her cleft. A twist of the wrist and a side intrudes and must stimulate where thin silk is a second skin and clings upon a secret place.

The side is drawn along the intimate centimetres and, what we can see, her thighs stiffen.

I consider how well Miss has absorbed our knowledge of playing down there.

Juanita shakes her hair, utters a breathy groan.

Parallel, a swift step backwards, dexterous realignment of the strap and - swipe! - a reverberating diagonal crosses the six already luridly etched.

A startled and struggling gasp. Then; "you are awarded an 'extra', Neruda, for noise. And where is the tally?"

"S - seven."

"Correct." And with eyes darting a new expectancy she treads firm to behind her desk: now she is the wind which will not desist nor give respite.

Our prior relaxation exeunts and the atmosphere is charged about us: we are horridly enthralled by a higher determination which has discovered a fracture of the other's insolent defiance.

Chapter 13

Over the desk, Juanita hints obviously sudden arrival of a trepidation hitherto never familiar.

And her prone form is become a dish served up to her punisher who now can also see her face, profiled.

As for ourselves, some sight is lost of Miss's near-diaphanous grey dress and misty-red stockings. In the fierce sunlight this afternoon even the colour of the brief and suspenders, a rich red less bright than Stella's, is discernable. We are resentful we are nagged and disciplined about our underwears when her choice items often are half-visible: it is not giving a good example and is possibly a malicious tease. Will she some day put on a string of the two I bought her?

I decide she is getting arrogant enough so to do.

Number eight flogs now from the vertical and swipes ringingly the crowns' centrality where No. 1 is already and undoubtedly still burns. That I think is agony, getting leather where it has bitten before.

And indeed the teenager is silent, grips hard the far edge of the desk as her full bottom with a quiver slowly divorces its life from that of its owner.

"Well Neruda?"

"Eigh-eight Miss."

"Thank you, Neruda. And your new-found politeness is pleasing. However, for omitting to count you are awarded another 'extra.'"

Red lines like foreshortened cart-tracks have accumulated and appear over the hill-like crest of her nearest bottom. She moves erotically no more and not only because Miss in present position is less subject to such provocation.

Juanita's whitened knuckles clench a wood cliff

96

I observe Miriam closely: the breasts rise and fall sharply and her tongue agitates between her lips. I judge her feet are apart and she bends from the waist: much of her body will impel the deliveries.

And I conclude sadly and bitterly she gains enjoyment.

Four concluding strokes are administered. Their sound is big and fills the hushed room. For these the strap travels its longest arcs and we gasp at the appalling swipes.

Our rebel's posterior now jerks and writhes and Miss seizes the chance to swing the flashing leather with envigoured energy.

Swipe! 'Nine' Swipe! 'Ten' Swipe! 'Eleven' Swipe! 'Twelve'.

I try to diminish the enslavement of my consciousness and espy the yellow light without beaming on leaf and static branch. A few birds sing and chirrup and nearby towards town a dog barks: that is the Infantes' hound I think. The ignorance or acceptance of the dreadful beating I watch within these walls is simultaneously an enigma and poetry to me.

Wretchedly Juanita chokes the numbers and tries to reach her bottom.

A heavy pause ensues, followed by a crisp announcement, the end of the strap cradled almost with affection:

"The main chastisement is complete. Remaining are extras; six strokes. Resume your original position to receive them."

These are terrible words for Juanita. Wildly she twists to implore of her tormentor but alas only in time to see a now-familiar flick-flack of the dangling strap.

There is a rasping "Nunno-oh-aah!" and, pity on horror, we listen to pat-pat, pitter-patter then drumming of a runnel on to the floor of the dais. As it diminishes to pitter-pat it glitters in sunlight.

The poor terrified creature has voided her bladder and, the desk side dripping, a puddle's darkness grows below her.

Miss is calm. It has happened before even at a slippering. Deftly she produces a towel and gives it to a shaking Juanita.

"Relax," she soothes and her voice is low and caresses like I have heard on happier occasions. And, like then, it works: her charge manages to stare doorwards whilst a defining hand rests where silk bands her waist.

"Only six left young 'un and then the curtain. Why not look this way? You will feel better during their application, yes?"

And amazingly: "Yes Miss" she manages and trustfully obey the encouragement.

As two impact she watches Miss's face, pleading, but the swipes report loud and implacable for her punisher is ruthless in duty.

Very blue-eyed and moist of lip that one engages the other's eyes and: "Juanita," she suggests musically, "you forget the tally, hmm?"

"Yes Miss."

"Thirteen, fourteen," is re-capped, then; swipe! "Fifteen" Swipe! "Sixteen" Swipe! "Seventeen."

She calculates she can rise but is detained by a ram-rodded arm and a voice demoralisingly altered: "your arithmetic like yourself is faulty. Eighteen, had you been attending, you would realize is the true apportionment." And so said the strap with a high-pitched whistle is swung mightily and lashes resoundingly on the jerking encrimsoned bottom.

Then we are assailed by the unimaginable, hitherto: our most troublesome peer weeps. The reverberation of the last lash dies to be replaced by wretched sobbing and groaning intakes of air.

Triumphant, Miss yanks the pleats and pretty underslip. Victory. And high on her cheeks is consummation's glow. Tensing the leather she scans a still-writhing form and devastated whitened profile, the jaw hanging though not now for carnal pleasure so recently attained.

"You may stand Juanita. Your punishment is completed."

Gulping and unsteady eventually the victim is able to do so.

"You will remove your briefs, suspenders and slip. They are confiscated 'til the end of term."

This Juanita does and proffers them to Miss, who on taking them regards particularly the sodden brief and touches it where also it must evidence the fiance's earlier attendance. The glossy stockings are peeled and pushed into a skirt-pocket. Snuffling and awkward Juanita sleeves a nose made peaky, nostrils inflamed.

"Where is your handkerchief?"

"I have a box of tissues Miss."

"You may borrow mine." And passes her silky one no doubt deliciously scented. "Thank you, Miss." We are then astounded: the conquered curtsies to the conqueror, respect indeed admiration in her eyes and veined in her awkward-moving body.

"Please see to your mishap," the other says, kindlier, and watches while the issue from erstwhile frightened pupil is absorbed and taken up.

"Very good. Leave the towel on my desk Juanita. You will now express appreciation of your needful correction."

"Thank you Miss for correction of my disobedience."

"Your gratitude is accepted. This part of the matter is closed. You will return the punishment-strap - neatly - to its accustomed place." And she does so laying it beside its companions, the whip and carpet-slipper. She is careful not to bang the drawer.

"In the next drawer are school-approved panties. You may select a pair for your journey home. You have been unclothed down there sufficiently this afternoon have you not? I recommend you choose cotton, but knowing you Miss Neruda I am sure you will take the black nylon."

And so she does, working them home, covering her vividly-punished bottoms. Their slight transparency is not enough to show redness, where white nylon would certainly have done.

"Leave us and go to Mother Superior to inform her of your misdemeanours of this afternoon. In your absence I shall prepare a report for her. I am sure you realize the seriousness of at least one of your offences and I am afraid your total situation is still unresolved. Go."

We stare hypnotised as stiffly our rebel walks to the door. Gently it closes: she is gone.

Instantly there is hubbub and Miss Miriam's words are lost temporarily. Soon however we hear them clearer and the racket declines.

"Will you be silent! Girls, that is enough. Whoever speaks next will be severely punished: she will be slippered over her desk."

Silence breaks out, you can imagine!

"That is better. You will resume reading of Don Quixote and do so dutifully. There will be a test. You will study in complete peace while I write my report. If anyone disturbs me she will raise her skirt for the leather sole of my slipper. Be advised my right arm is performing excellently today. Now continue."

And the rustling again of pages. She remounts the dais and elegantly occupies her seat. Detached satisfaction she shows, and her eye is bright. Juanita's garments she puts in a drawer. There are many seconds before she shuts it during which she gazes concentratedly at what is now by her.

Yes Miriam, I think, I discern your emotions about this dreadful episode and I suggest your pupil of lesser egregiousness will exact from you something you will not care to give. Even the highest must accept retribution for exercising excessive and perverted authority. But that is me: around me I see my companions doggedly try to digest the meanings of the text in front of them. The air is palpable with shock and outrage.

De Cervantes' deathless prose flows largely unheeded through my consciousness and I frown because instead I picture what I must do when next alone with her, possibly this very evening.

Her price must be paid and quickly, for I fear another or others may confront her before me, we are a proud and vengeful people and their tariff will be devised of penalties less understanding and more distressing than any I plan to impose on her.

Chapter 14

Afternoon-school glides into an English lesson. Miss becomes animated, glances in my direction and I have to pretend reaction. She who is beside me elbows my ribs and I whisper: "Can it you weevil or I will pinch you!"

"Oh Sonia, is it not wonderful we share these delights?" And there is a stifled giggle. "I will trim your ears you lump."

"- it is said therefore," my friend Miss Miriam lectures, "Eliot in an important respect harks back to a previous century in which classicism of expression was in ascendancy. Carmen -" And this one obviously starts from dozing. "Of which Eliot do I speak?"

"Oh-ah, the first Miss."

"Correct. The second Eliot; can you inform us of his initials and the century in which he was famous?"

"Oh-ah, temporary I forget Miss."

"You will write twenty times on the board 'T.S. Eliot was a twentieth-century U.S. poet.' You have no excuse, we discussed him last week."

"Yes Miss, sorry Miss."

"I despair of that memory of yours. Of what were you dreaming?"

"I was thinking of er - Dickens and er -"

"Really? Can you name a novel of his?"

"Er - Martin Tumbleweed Miss."

"Not a bad try. Tomorrow you will come to me with the right title. Now. Were you dreaming of boys, clothes or food?"

"Oh, I would not in lessons, Miss."

"An excellent attitude Carmen," but looks amusedly at her who responds by blushing amidst sniggers.

Juanita returns not and I deduce Mother Superior has sent her home. There is no time to lose in this affair and anxiously I con the clock; hurry, hurry!

"Sonia, please tell us who also wrote novels during the first Eliot's period. The clue is in all your desks and constitutes our further reading, but not today."

"Go on smart-pants give her some grease" whispers she at my side and adds "Oh Miss thank you for asking me it is wonderful -"

"Shut up you louse I will squash you after school"

"It was Hardy Miss and he wrote Under the Greenwood Tree and we will find much in it to enjoy."

"Very good Sonia. I wonder how many of the rest of you had the answer."

"Phew, what a creep."

"Your nose is doomed Batista: I will biff it sideways."

At last the bell rings and we rise as one a mass of mouths and ears, a single topic bubbling. Few salute their teacher who makes as if to join me but Stella comes and covertly I watch Miss Miriam exit dully with a clump of her charges who seem unaware of her.

"You are slow Sonn. Come, we quit this torture-chamber."

"You have your rendezvous," I say, swinging my legs as I sit on a desk; an offence if you are caught. "You are nearest. Tell me when she is on the path home."

"Who?"

"Miss you thick head."

"All right, all right." And leaning from a window; "Wait a bit... Yes, she journeys now. I am sick of that woman. She is turning this class into a - a penal colony: there will be public executions soon. You tea-ing with her this evening?"

"Possible I invite myself."

"Huh, she should be ambulanced, she is crazy, today more than ever."

"She is a mixture certainly."

"A mixture! You are too polite but then you are her favourite, God knows why." And Stella smiles at me but I ignore her cheap wit. "She is not one of us," I say slowly. "You can say that again: for God's sake where is Ireland?" "It is near England you dolt. They are European countries." "Europe can keep her. I am glad to leave next term. I hope I am not flayed alive my final day." Laughing I say: "Oh Stella you will get leather if there is a uniform-inspection." "I will not: it is school stuff only henceforward I swear."

I jump to the floor, push her head and plant a wet kiss on her warm cheek: "I go now." She aims to hit my bottom but remembers not to. "To the dragon's? I hope you choke in a saucer - Why? You are one of us." "To help her." "Help her? Psychiatry might help her." She does not understand. "She is in danger." "I am not surprised. Half of the town will bay for her blood this evening: she overdid authority."

"You have it Stella. But I can save her."

"You are welcome to." Then "Anything I can do?"

"No, thank you. Besides there is your rendezvous. Do not allow him inside your brief."

She sighs: "I wish I had a fiance."

"With a big one?"

"Oh God, it is torment."

"They suffer also."

"Huh, it is only fair. Well I see you tomorrow, Sonn, in this prison-house. Be circumspect for the teacher's affairs: darkness has come into them though I expect she has plenty associates. Goodbye." "Goodbye Stella." And she waves, leaving the room with her familiar light step.

Suddenly I feel horribly alone and want to call her back, but Miriam's jeopardy bears upon me and I conjure a picture of that beautiful woman, reckless of the consequences of her resentment and weakness, perhaps opening cupboards and gathering tea-things while guilelessly chewing a piece of chocolate of which confection she is very fond.

'Oh Miss, Miss, what will happen to you' I wail, and near-running I essay stairs and landings, stumbling and banging my shoulders 'til I am under the radiant sun and its tremendous heat enfolds me. My agitation recedes and I walk after trotting to her bijou dwelling.

In its vicinity I spy no-one of danger but notwithstanding I cannot soothe myself. I rub sweating hands on my blouse and turn the front-door handle; unlocked! She is so careless in these matters I think angrily, and quietly I slip inside setting the bolt after me.

My imagining was accurate: noise of crockery emanates from the kitchen. And, she sings or rather hums: it is 'You are my sunshine my only sunshine,' a Yankee song she taught me and I forget it super quick you can imagine. Where she is is sunlit and probably inspires her to make this rubbishy sound.

I am in the doorway, my chin high and hands behind me.

"Oh!" A plate clatters in the sink. "Sonia. You will give me a heart-attack. I wish you youngsters would knock more. Why, what is it? Why do you stare -"

"Are you mad?"

"What? I do not -"

"I think you lose your sense, Miriam! Do you imagine you can punish like you punished this afternoon and there are no repercussions?"

"Oh, this is the reason for your ill-mannered intrusion young lady -" And if she were Lima her fur would be rising.

"Do not 'young lady' me" I say. "Your moral mark this moment is about zero and if you do not listen to me I will not guarantee your safety."

"'Listen to me?': you have the impertinence of a monkey. What is the meaning of all this? I will complain to your parents. It is breathtaking and inside my own home."

"Go to your bedroom!"

"I do not believe my ears. You are all the same. Firstly the Neruda child and now you. The impertinence in this place is incredible."

"Yes, the Neruda child as you term her. Well she has a fiance and many friends and relatives. It seems I get here first, though. I am in time but maybe only just."

"In time for what Sonia? I cannot continue in this fog of mystery. Explain yourself." Clearly I have introduced a worrying note.

"You are not of this town, indeed country," I try explain to the dolt head. "And you exceeded your authority. Do not -" I stay her mouth opening "- argue. Neruda's people will have your scalp for that beating you gave her."

"She - she was respectful and - and mild afterwards."

"The bully respecting the winner, Miriam. But that will not hold them. I know."

"You exaggerate. I do not believe it."

"No exaggeration. But if I revenge on behalf of our class it may halt them. Go to your bedroom."

She swallows and regards me frightened: "What are you going to do?"

"It should be obvious. And you are ready sufficiently I think": she wears just three items - a vest and bra and the red brief transparent and tight upon her. Dress and stockings off I suppose because of the heat.

"If this is a trick to get me to a game I tell you I am not in the mood."

"I wish it was a trick. Do not delay, we have not time. Come." And I lead her by the arm into her bed-chamber. "Face the wall put your hands against it."

106

Reluctantly she does so, biting her underlip. "The martinet is in its usual drawer," she says neutrally.

"The what?"

"It is called a martinet I discovered."

"Oh, someone told you?"

She has guilt and replies defensively: "you are not the only one who visits."

"I see. Your·kink, which worsens, is exercised on others' behinds."

"It is play: we are not harmed."

"I remember you strapped me excessively and now the Neruda business. After this, these at least must cease."

Her nose rises. "I understand," she condescends. "I will not move while you fetch it."

"The martinet will not be enough for the Neruda tribe." I unfasten my skirt-belt.

"God, you are not serious! What can they do to me? It is ridiculous - ah!" Abruptly I have struck across the backs of her smooth thighs. "You waste time, but you may be safe now I begin." I strike again: her knees buckle. "O Sonia, this - ah!"

I hate the blows but apply them dutifully and fast, seeking impatiently for angry marks to grow. She sways at the wall and whimpers. Tears spring on to her cheeks and she is unable to protest, she is so full of pain her whole being concentrates upon it.

Desperately I apply the leather 'til her knees give and she falls crying and shrinking.

A few more and it is done. "Take your hands away Miriam." The last strokes and I desist thankfully.

"I trust," she quavers, "you were proud of that. What a viper I nourished to have this acted upon me."

"Nonsense; you may soon be grateful."

She pants like a trapped animal and cannot bear to look at me.

And I? I observe her lovely womanliness and recall: "You were not only sadistic, you were a bitch." I shiver at an image of Juanita's near-nudity prone on a desk and jerking beneath another's joy allied with jealousy. I was jealous also, I cannot deny this, it galls me, this jealousy in me. A moment to recompose and I return from the living-room. Startling her, roughly I pull the nylon off her intimacies: "Oh no," she says wearily. "When will I be forgiven?"

"Two meals you had: the first was sweet, the last bitter. Neither was rounded by dessert."

Deftly I bring long fruit to where under russet and gold was hunger enough to beget injustice.

She is half-resistant but the other half welcomes, shuddering with a lost cry and I work 'til I judge her arousal begins abandonment: at which crudely I stop and take it from her.

An anguished pause and in the silence disturbed by her broken breathing I notice my own tears.

Quite still she becomes and then: "You will leave me now." Then; "Please."

I wake out of shallow sleep and panic. I am still there, at her house? Yes, panic ceases. A dignified ticking makes me look about: thankfully merely an hour passes since ... since!

Heart bumping, I see her door is shut - Was it always so as I slept? Trying it, it opens. To my relief she is within - though what is this? She lies yet on the floor where I left her. Again panic and I shake her shoulder; Miriam, Miriam! Relief! She stirs and her forearm tends an averted brow.

"Go away. I am alone in this place. I ask you once more and politely to leave me."

"Why not rest on your bed? I will help you there."

No answer and she is motionless.

"You are not alone - I love you. Do I not show you I care?"

Then, terribly, she weeps.

"Oh please, it is unbearable to hear you. I know, I make coffee - you have some?"

"I - I - I do want you to stay... You will wait for me?"

It is a whispering in the dimmer room of her solitary sleep.

"I will wait, of course I will."

"There Miss, it is your 'of course' and must be grade A, no?"

Faintly come the chimes from the convent mildly signalling the evening-office soon commences and inviting all people.

"I make coffee" I repeat, and gently close the door.

Oh God. And, give me a cheroot Stella, I think.

My ears go back: there are voices. Scarce-breathing I observe from the living-room window two nuns treading the grassy path chapel-wards. One laughs and almost skips and I mutter 'God is good, yes he is good.' But my swelling sentiment is arrested for Fr. Pablo, following them metres behind, halts, then walks towards the cottage, and I retreat hastily to concealment by the sofa.

The priest's face somehow is also tall and dominates where happily I am no more. Awareness of fancy does not diminish its true severity and bound passion and I scream soundlessly when he raps the glass. I pray Miss Miriam does not choose to answer, and after tantalising moments he departs and the mellow evening light reigns where he had menacingly occluded it.

I am able to bring badly-made coffee, guide it to her palms when there is new rapping, louder.

"Sonia what is happening?" she asks feebly, and pitying I kiss her: "It is trouble for sure, but nothing your Sonia cannot handle. You trust me. I grow up beside this heap of rabblement and can cut a hole through the lot. Have your drink in peace." And I shut the door definitively after me.

I set myself to confront our dangerous priest whatever but it is Mario's opulent features occupy the window and he espies me immediately, raising a meaty fist.

"So, here is a reckoning," I murmur but wontedly I am fierce-hearted as I reach the pane and loose the catch. He wrenches it from me and my heart flutters but I am Sonia who knows him well and as his fleshy lips part for crushing import my hand alights upon them and bold and steady with eye ironic and contemptuous I hiss: "You will guard your tongue Mario or I will take it for a bookmark. And if you scare her I will remove your balls for cat's food."

He seizes my wrist away from him painfully but I do not protest, instead say conversationally: "If you do not release me I will kill you, you rats' dung."

His fine dark eyes glint as he discards my hand. "Miss O'Shaughnessy's prize pupil. You were wise to open the window, now open the door."

"You mend your approach or nothing."

"I have no quarrel with you." His body relaxes. "Despite your insulting manner. Let me in."

I ponder the risk then unbolt the door: he enters towering amidst the feminine surroundings which he assesses, even a faint smile appearing.

He looks down at me: "You are not much of an escort vessel. I say you are a corvette with pop-guns. Where is the capital ship you will not be able to defend?"

He has interest in things naval this Mario and I think if his employer, old man Domingo, learns of his fun with his school-bride-to-be earlier today - and he may already have done so - a hammock on a vessel might well be his destiny.

"She recovers and you will not touch her."

"Recovers? Her arm is in a sling after roasting my Juanita's backside?" He gestures impatiently: "She is in there?"

"And your cock is in splints these hours since?" I riposte, barring his progress.

"Why did you watch? I did not invite you, Miss Puritypants."

"I would not miss a comedy-show and I needed a laugh."

"I know. I will kiss you: that will make you jump aside."

Thus saying, his large hands, scarred from labouring in Domingo's wood-yard, clasp my head and his mouth assaults mine.

"Piss off you sod!" I spit subdued, afraid of agitating Miriam metres away. "I will kick your shins you stink-arse."

He catches on my repressed tone and laughs but low: "Your fingers will flick my shins you mean - That was not bad: a fact you are a peach, Sonia Teresa. Now you can clear off."

I move not. "She is in a terrible state: I revenged on her already. I! I did it."

I capture his curiosity: "What is it between you two? You share more than English studies: do you?" He is filled with suspicion.

"My word is enough. For Juanita, for every pupil at Terry's, I have punished her."

"How so?"

"I beat her hard." Fingering the belt of my skirt.

"I see." Then: "Thomas the very saint sought proof his master had wounds." And seeing I come if anything closer he continues, "So get hopping or I will crack your sparrow's bones."

"I will not nor will you pass me." Baring my teeth I shove his rock-like chest.

"Very well. You prefer I hold you upside-down and smack your bum?" And he grasps my waist: my feet lift off the floor.

"Let me go! Falangist! I tell Roberto."

"Roberto is a good fellow. Do not encourage him to become unconscious at the end of my fist."

"Forget the bigger words Mario, your head will fall off." And, inspired; "you must not break the floorboards with your fat head."

I feel his chest jumping with mirth as swung I meet the cushions of the sofa. Tears of rage burn into my eyes.

He pauses: "While you are there I will have a look at your bottom. Two reasons; to see the marks from your mother's whip and because it is very nice anyway."

"Do not come near me you horrible turd," I exclaim but carelessly he wrenches my skirts and frustration hotly wets my face anew.

"Yes, you are indeed blessed," he breathes and I twist fearful. "Do not worry Sonia Teresa, I shall not bite your cherry: I am betrothed - And you might split if I did."

"You disgust me. What can she love about you?"

"Women are smart: they do not ask but certainly they wonder and do not tell me you have not."·

"Yours is no wonder, Mario, I see too much of it this afternoon. Let me get up please."

Ponderously he releases me and I glare at his breast whilst repositioning my clothes. "There are two exits for this cottage: the front is nearest. Choose it and scram."

Oddly this upsets him: "That tongue of yours, I will knot it one day."

"Scram, I said. Are your ears made of bone also?"

"I warn you -" he begins but enunciates hugely no further, instead spins as if shocked into that motion: a door has rattled and she he thirst to apprehend, and more, emerges, engages his vision sharply.

112

Heedless she wanders into the living-room, the female domain he cannot devastate with his presence.

"Oh!" is her simple introduction. And; "Mario you are I believe?" She wrings the bodice of a dress seen before in an equally unhappy circumstance.

He and I gaze at each other: I react quicker.

"Return to your rest Miss I beseech you. We reach a settlement."

"You are a giant who comes to dismember me?"

"At last teacher." And he advances.

A flash and I interpose. "Please Miss show your stripes. On my knees I beg you."

This halts him and I wind my arms around her and, part skill part emotion, bring fresh tears. "After he sees he will go." A pretty picture. I sense they regard one another intently as urgently I push upwards the delicate dress.

"See Mario": I divert his attention. I widen my eyes which no doubt glisten also. Stella would hate me this moment I think.

His weight is such the boards creak whilst, an improbable St. Thomas, he scans my beloved's latest and joyless chastisement.

"It is fair," he concedes with reluctance. "The sparrow has a beak. You can get up Sonia Teresa, you are not being paid by the hour."

My temper flares but I manage restraint. I rise to between them as they regard one another still and hug her, caressing her back: she shrinks and I remember the priest's ministrations but it is not of these her tension is summoned.

Horrified I see his right hand strike her pale and suffering face: Oh it is by her beauty spot and I squeeze her convulsively. She sways but her stance is sure.

"I apologise," she says judiciously. "You have my honest apology, Mario."

"And I apologise for hitting a woman obviously distressed. I leave now but I shall take a parcel with me."

I am silent to this evolution, have an inkling my years betray me. However this is expelled: an arm growing familiar encompasses me.

"About Isobella Casals I can do little which is unfortunate because I suspect with her is the spark initiating a sorry trend. Nevertheless here I have a warm link in the chain -" I squirm hopelessly against the crook of his massive arm "- and know what to do which may muffle a tendency..."

"Your words are gilded," I say surprised. "Where - ?"

"Sonia," she pleads. "Do not give offence. We are past that stage I trust."

Exasperated I contemplate offended what I did for her.

"She wants to believe I am a savage, which, lucky for her, I am not."

"Do not hurt her, she is my friend and very kind."

"My inclination is to be a gentleman though she is ever unconvinced."

He turns and renders me facing Miriam: "Oh Sonia you are a child under her arm." The ghost of a smile is on her and I rejoice. "I hope you will not be late home: your parents will become anxious." She says this for him rather than me.

"I will not delay," he states.

"The big -" I start but she presses a finger to her moving lips. I outspread my hands, shrug my shoulders and blink at her.

Then we are through the doorway, Miss following, waving 'til the winding path removes view of her.

He paces rhythmically along the earth and greenery and I gather my hanging hair 'til a hand free I pick the occasional flower bobbing up to me: one is a poppy of resonant purple and I retain it because I know its colour suits me.

"Mario."

No answer.

"Mario!" And I tug the top of his trousers.

"You stop that," he says socially, "or I will look at your bottom again."

"You - dare!" I amend, courage draining and sulk lip jutted no doubt. "Where are we going? I am tired of this."

"A favoured-spot; you and that Stella-pal of yours."

"You spy on us!"

"I do not, I have better things to do. We notice you go there."

"I opine this town notices too much."

And yes we approach a terrain of friendly features. Now I pluck meadow-grass as I fly above it. What sort of bird would I wish to be if truly I had wings? An eagle with gigantic talons I decide, so that even Mario's rump cringes from them.

"The river runs sweetly this evening," he muses. "And here is a convenient slope to bathe from: I suppose you use it sometimes."

A horrid apprehension forms in my mind. "Oh I do not think I will just now, my supper awaits."

"A few minutes will not spoil it, Sonia Teresa. Are you ready?"

"Oh thank you Mario I must refuse. I am not dressed appropriately."

"I am afraid," he says laughing, "really you have no choice in the matter." And setting me on the grass immediately he arms the hollows of my knees and I become a baby against his bulk as he nears the river's margin.

"I am sorry," he continues, "you are ungrateful. And do not struggle so much or when you hit the water you will swallow it."

"Swine! Bully! Arse-face! You-you-aaah!"

The rushing waters blow-like accept me and I splutter from their surface-chucklings to another laughter powerful and uproarious.

"You cool off now Miss Casals and henceforward cool your catching inclinations also, you know what I mean?"

"I get you you bum-face. I tell my parents -"

"Your vocabulary is in sad decline. You need extra lessons with the O'Shaughnessy woman. But keep them clean this time you hear?"

"I tell everyone you are a bully and assault me. Mama and Papa -"

"It is a shame you are clumsy and fall in Sonia. Lucky I am nearby to rescue you. Ta-ta and take care of your bottom: I want to meet her again."

Gasping I haul on to the bank. My clothes, weed-streaked, are heavy on my body. Meanwhile he departs and erupts into song, an air from opera, another enthusiasm. He thrusts hands in pockets, swaggers off, the old Mario reasserted. Seething and cursing I watch him vanish.

It is so late I may not linger to allow the sun dry me through and hasten by ways where I greet any acquaintance curtly to prevent time-wasting talk. They stare at my state and news of it will be everywhere come nightfall. "This town," I mutter. "What will happen next?"

Almost frantic I bound into our dining-room and my parents are already at soup.

"Heavens above!" She lays down her spoon. "Where have you been, and what -?"

"I am sorry Mama. Papa. I had an accident. May I dine in my dressing-gown?"

"Certainly you will and straight to bed after. Any assignment you rise early tomorrow to finish... If you develop a cold you cope with it: I will not maidservant the result of your naughtiness."

"No Mama - I mean, yes Mama."

116

When I return her look is a needle.

"What were you doing Sonia you drench yourself, hmm?"

"I - and Stella we - we search by the river for a moorhen's nest and - and I fell in."

Papa who is breaking a pile of potatoes suppresses a snort and she regards him: "I do not think Ferdinand this is funny. If her school-clothes are spoilt -"

"Come come my love, leave her be. The child needs her food. We were youngsters once also. In fact I recall we dangered ourselves at the river and not solely for birds' nests neither I remember."

"You do?" she smiles. Her eyes kindle and mouth curves despite a veritable hillock of potato journeying Papa-wards.

"I do my love."

I observe both clinically, thinking 'Oh Ferdinand' 'Bella' Tut-tut.

"It is good she had a bath anyway: school-kids pong dreadful I am sure you notice." And he rumbles 'Haw-haw' to his oversized plate. Papa's humour is pretty poor stuff but he enjoys it.

Mama forsakes 'Bella' and grants me her look altered to sympathy.

Chapter 15

"I got the gist of that," I said with an expressive puff.

"And did you cool off, my little ground-hugging rocket?"

"Sure; I was not boiling anyway, no?"

"Uh-huh." She eased on to her stomach, a lazy feline movement, and nibbled grass-stems too. The renowned bottom boasted its allure and I could not forbear feeling its soft silky curves without or under the sheath of taut tinted nylon.

"Ow, Will, leave my hurt be this once."

"Come on Sonia, that was days ago and hardly lasted a minute."

We had attended mass on Sunday and when returned to an empty house - Mrs Keech herself at church, the Reynolds absent also - I experienced special delight in aligning her Sunday-best for R's strap to engage thwackingly her evading chubs, demurely encased by a chaster undergarment of snowy hue. It was an event made doubly delicious from remembering her in a pew so recently at holy devotions. But it was hastily accomplished because of riskiness.

"I meant, my angel," I recapped, "you and Miriam relinquished or reduced in number, adventures with the martinet."

"I intend to tell further be assured but today we have already told much history." She moved languidly, enjoying against my hand, now stroking considerately.

"What of Mario?"; the same hand strong-travelling to her privatest place.

"Oh Will." And she stretched along the comfortable grass, her glance disturbed. "He - He -"

"Did he lose his job at Domingo's?"

"He -. It was so. He went to sea not in the navy - how you say?"

"The merchant marine," I suggested. "The merchant marine" she repeated carefully as I shifted the layers upon that place. Were they accruing an attractive moistness from my darlingest latino?

"Will," she managed faintly. "I -"

"And I, I balk at the notion he might have... raped you. That evening, Sonia Teresa," I said, voice firm, wet fingers intruding despite nylon and cotton.

She gasped and her unblemished ivory skin sheened with perspiration.

"Raped you!" I said distinctly, pressing.

"Oh uhh, please -" She left my hand by turning on to her side. "I dreamed of it, I confess." She gazed troubled, those violet eyes wide which hesitated to meet mine. "I am a creature of flesh and blood." Her lips parted bestowing a greater innocence to her face. The youngster's breasts, dainty and perfect, evidenced a conquering excitement.

I stripped my shorts, a disrobing made practised by our numerable couplings and saw the violet flickering assess the state of my hard member tightening the transparency of one of R's zipped mini-briefs. Her pretty pink tongue explored her lower lip.

"Yours is as thick," she said suddenly, loud. "How I dreamed that Thursday night. I could not help it: I am only flesh and blood." She stood and waiting enunciated: "You will not rape me, Will Collett." Her hands rested upon her bottoms.

I pursed my mouth, then; "Perhaps not here." At my uncertainty she smiled a superiority: "You are a coward. What is rape if there is no danger?" And surprising me she slapped me fiercely. "Coward. You excuse yourself because you dare not or cannot do it. Worm. And you have not

Mario's reason for abstinence, you flower." She shook her hair, flared her nostrils contemptuously.

The pain and the contempt had their desired effect and angrily I opened R's brief releasing its stiff vengeful prisoner.

"No you will not rape me": and darted in to clasp it. There was a squeezing warmth of her palms, she retreated and sharply I tried to catch her.

She was of course lighter and easily outmanoeuvred me. Her gurgling laughter decorated her taunts: "You old fool. He stands when you want to sit." And: "He does not need a clue where to go but the owner needs a compass."

She surprised me again, this time by advancing nimbly to land a couple of clips round the ears, which blows aggrieved me mightily and no doubt lumberously I accelerated.

The laughter died. Her mouth tightened to an O under alerted eyes. "You hurrying before your bones collapse?"

"I have one will outlive the rest."

"Your balls are tight: I think if you reach me I really get it the whole shebang."

Where she had speed I had wit inflamed with wrath and an inevitability grew closer.

Our fragmented dance to carnality's imperative brought its first casualty: she tripped. It was enough and I was on her and her doomladen cry; "Oh no, no!"

To draw her hands I encircled her slender neck. Then my right free it was instantly at the waistband of her only artificial defence. I let my weight pin her slight and struggling form. Tugging the yielding elastic I growled: "What did you say about ripping your briefs Casals?"

"Get off. Get off me you savage." My response was a snapping and an unmusical tearing of fabric. "No, no."

"Over!" I rasped. But she struggled the greater so I rolled her myself, my body and fingers rigid and forcing her as lust powered my task.

The outer air now alighting upon her most intimate opening must have signalled to her senses a truer vulnerability: she whimpered and tried to close her thighs but I obtruded a knee, all the while uttering names and imprecations. Her 'rape' was about to begin and she burst into tears.

"Well may you weep you hot bitch for wanting cock the width of an altar-candle."

My old comrade and ecstasy-giver found himself amidst the resisting rippling flesh, the wet curls and tangles of her parting sopping portal, and pitched there with ferocious introduction and harsh promise. "You hate I should plough you now Sonia Teresa?" I interrogated deliberately coarsening my voice.

"God, God!" She wrenched the grass, feigned-I knew-shrinking from the attack that drove me into her burning slipperiness. Her wild exclamations sang out but without pause I hauled her waist and dog-like shagged relentlessly. Uh, Uh, Uh, Uh! modified her jerks to my violet rhythmic thrusts.

We addressed God a lot those few moments joined to each other by a bestial coupling. Often she wanted it quick and rough and this certainly was no exception. Her consummation swelled, a devouring monster breaking the surface of a flood and immediately I changed to swinging drawn shaftings along her spasming passage.

She perished or surrendered then and simultaneously as I erupted I swingeingly spanked her sweating bottom: the vivid imprint of my palm and fingers was a witness to the strength of these vindictive smacks.

"Aah. Uhh!" Between hands become claws, her face convulsively pressed the ground.

It was done.

Separating abruptly I stated, in a tone the equivalent of the pitiless spanks: "You behave yourself henceforth Sonia Teresa or you get it again and next time I may not be so kind, you hear?"

She remained still, her body lewdly angled, her chest sucking great lungfuls of air. The episode needed a punctuation-mark: I retrieved the ruined female briefs and threw them beside her discomposed features. I walked round to the front of her and waited until she acknowledged my presence.

At this with fixed and stern expression I zipped shut R's undergarment. Quivering she watched me until I set off for the house.

Once I glanced over my shoulder: she had risen at last. Slowly and gathering her lustrous dark hair to the back of her head, she followed my victorious steps.

Luck had not deserted us: minutes later we heard returnees.

"Get dressed Sonia," I said urgently. "At least put on a bikini or something."

"That would be okay if I was in my quarter you dope."

"Oh well they're unlikely to come up here."

"For a change you make coffee. And cakes on a plate."

Grumbling I acquiesced. Passing I said: "You are quite naked."

"What to expect, you tore my brief you beast."

"Never mind I'll buy you a new pair."

"And you hit my marks; unforgivable."

"You must forgive me, we are lovers."

I brought the coffee, the sugary cakes she had a passion for. "I forgive you," she said, chewing. "Because we are lovers I allow you are not blameworthy for everything: although do not let this lighten your brain."

"Thank you," I said drily. "May I offer your majesty some tobacco?"

"You have no smokes," she complained. "But I smoke one of your pipes." And she was as good as her word, blowing noisily the mouthpiece of a clay I rarely used. "Oh-hoh, it is the old English gentleman but you are no gentleman I am thinking mister rapist." And I received an ancient scrutiny - and a rediscovered resentment.

"At the event," I murmured to it, "you flipped totally, you and Mario." It was the wrong comment.

She hissed a shot of grey smoke. "I hate you. You and your penis. Men!"

"Finish your refreshments," I countered amenably. "And try not to be silly."

"It is you who should be beaten for being a man. You deserve not to rape."

The tenseness receded. She pushed away plate and cup, then was all over me cat-like. I held her warm soft buttocks and she conned my features, her eyes gone heavy, voice sardonic: "What is it -" she began. "Don't venture the question," I asserted agreeably. "I live in the same conundrum. Instead tell me about Juanita, Miss Miriam, what transpired after Mario's departure."

"Sure." But she was losing her mood. "Perhaps. Later." For while she was silent. "It become sad..."

Chapter 16

The brilliant weather did not abate and the weekend inevitably found us in the garden. Floppy-hatted Sonia perused a Spanish-language newspaper she'd discovered whilst shopping in the High Street. Desultorily I attempted to net goldfish in the small motionless pond. "Leave them be, you are cruel." And aimed an apple-core. 'Heh-heh-heh.' "Oh look there is an insect-thing: it is beautiful." It was I think a hornet of vivid blue hovering and I evacuated my position speedily. "Good. Pity he stings not your bum. Come here my naughty boy."

I subsided sweatily beside her, caressed her perfect neck beneath shining hair - which smelt delicious - and carefully bit it in several places.

"I pray I have daughters only," she said, "when I have family."

"You want the human race to come to an end?"

"That is God's decision. Until then I have only daughters."

"If they are as desirable as you -"

"Sit properly, you are a slob Will: what is it with you?" And her paper swatted me.

I tried: "Gosh the sun, this heat's oppressive -"

"Why do you not dress nicely? You are a slob."

"Sometimes you don't dress at all! You're belly-aching a lot: those apples gave you belly-ache."

"I am sorry, maybe it is not your blame you are a jerk."

"Thank you, Sonia."

Her mouth curved warmly on a face radiant with life and love. "I could scrag you now and drop you in the pond: give you 'how you say' a real Mario-ing."

She jumped up holding the fetching straw-hat. "No, do not: these are good clothes. Please."

"Yes why are you wearing elegant clothes today?" Appreciatively I ran my eye over her: even, I saw, flesh-coloured stockings and on so hot a day.

"It is the last of Miriam I tell you today,"

"You dressed specially for the final instalment? Well. I thought at first you'd decided to go on the game."

"What you say?" She clutched my shirt, right hand balled as if wielding a stiletto or whatever it's called; the latino equivalent of a dagger.

"Relax my love. It's my Anglo sense of humour, a mere crack of little importance."

"Your humour not always gets the spot."

"Go on," I urged. "Tell the rest of it: is it sad? Is it exciting? What is so special about it?"

We resumed sitting. I took her hat and fanned her. She snatched it. "If you are frivolous junior I will not say more."

"No, I was trying to cool you. Really." I lay my cheek on hers. "Go on, you misunderstood. Tell me about Miss Miriam."

To my concern I noticed tears and reached to her eyes: she knocked away my hand and went to them herself. She began speaking diffidently and initially without assurance. I pressed my lips to her immaculate cheek for long moments, but she moved impatiently, so I reclined into a defeat as she delineated mourning an end-time of another who'd cherished her:

"Juanita never attended St. Teresa's again. Opinions became news: we heard Mother considered she was not fit to continue presence among us as a schoolgirl. A fact she left - the same time Mario went to take a seaman's job. It was no coincidence and they married, made their home in a distant place. They live there yet. It is in letters I received. We await a day she bears a child."

My thoughts somehow were guessed by Sonia who added: "The parish and the school tackled them not. Neither was much of the church, particularly Mario. She suffered shamefully by Miss and he had retribution by Sr. Domingo."

"By Sr. Domingo?"

"Patience." She shuddered a little. "It is hard for me, but I am on the road, I must reach the end:

The morning after the excitements I go reluctant into school and it is a hive buzzing with rumours and counter-rumours. Of our beautiful and sadistic mistress no sign. Stella and the Batista girl have surely the sensible information: Miss is furloughed that day and for a big interview later.

"They know not I revenged on her?"

"Huh, your brains are in your boots, Sonn. Your pipsqueak punishment, if they hear of it - and better not for your skin - was nursery stuff." Stella smiles fondly: "One day you realize you are not in charge around here - maybe the end of the century."

I ignore her poor wit. "Miriam reacted it was not pipsqueak."

"You stay quiet: you were the second exceed her authority, except you have none Miss Monarchy-boots." She smiles again and Batista sniggers. I resist an impulse to smite her ear. "So what happens today?" I ask mildly and with dignity which irritates them terrifically; my turn for a smile.

"We have Mother the whole day for lessons," says Stella curtly. "Do not be caught chattering on your desk: it is a thing everyone sees you do too much of."

Thus it transpires. Our head-teacher, presides and not once loudens her voice to control, like Miriam used to do.

Early she opens the drawer and Batista elbows my ribs as Juanita's undergarments get inspection and transfer to a holdall.

"The evidence goes."

"Keep your arms you pest or I pull your hair."

Then my heart beats, face is hot: Mother unfolds Mama's brief. "Who wore this?"

Many eyes are upon me and I raise a hand. "Come to me Casals." Perspiring I obey. "Cease trembling, it is not necessary or I hope it is not necessary. Bend over the desk my child." I sense air on my thighs: she lifts my skirts. "Excellent; you are obedient." Stella winks and I dare a scowl to her. "You received the strap?" "Yes Mother," I whisper very doleful while she examines that instrument thoroughly and Stella rotates a fist, mouth hooraying. "The number of strokes?"

"Er - six Mother. And extras."

Stella, nose crinkled, flaps a hand; not enough. I cannot help smiling. "It is an amusing memory?" "Er no Mother, I have nervousness."

"Return to your place and repeat not your offence."

"Yes - I mean no - Mother." Scaley-eyed we notice the strap re-enters the drawer, no relegation to the holdall.

Towards my place I pass Stella's and dexterously push her papers and books on to her lap. Her kick to my ankle is feeble: I sniff derisively. "No noise please" from the dais. "Study in silence."

Ten o'clock the head lays down her pen. "I will be absent one hour. After your morning-break - twenty minutes only - work with your assignments. Victoria Infante is class-supervisor and will give to me the names of any who misbehave."

She departs. The room hums.

"Mad O'Shaughnessy meets her fate," growls Stella and if it was anyone but her I would fall on them with blows.

"Oh Miss," contributes she beside me, "how may I comfort you in your troubles? - Bet you know how eh Sonn?" She is not Stella and instantly I find bare flesh above her stockings and pinch it fiercely.

"Ow!"

"You gate your gob Batista or I fill it with knuckle."

"You sow you are vicious."

"Stop that," says Victoria. She is ineffectual but nice so we subside.

I dream and ponder the hour in which eventually I decide to call at Miriam's when school ends.

Chapter 17

Miriam is paler which accentuates her loveliness. I view hungrily while she strokes my hair as if it was I stroking Lima. I hold her with anger: "I wish you were naked."

"Sonia you are disrespectful."

"I want to hurt you for your stupidity and beauty."

"You are in a strange mood and you forget: 'Call no man fool' - your mood is inappropriate."

"Kiss me," I order unkindly and she inclines her head. "You open your lips when you kiss me" I insist, and she surrenders. I do it as if to degrade her: she exclaims and draws back. "Get off that road or you leave. I ask you, no more of this."

Her eyes are troubled and, yes, disappointed, as I feel her form under the thin clothes. I go to her voluptuous bottoms, tease the soft elastics upon their ripe warmth: "Silk today," I murmur, and feline nuzzle her. Mechanically she caresses mine and I curse my mundane uniform. "Lust and sadism my little one," she says absently. I look at her, step from her. There is loss so I begin conversation: "You are elegant, for your important interview, yes?" My disappointment I hide, thinking I will dance her to my tune.

"For Mother I must," and I hate her relief that we separated. "Thankfully you are not male or you take me, the mood you are in. Come, we sit."

"Show me what I missed first," I command friendly, and she becomes indulgent. "Lustful young man. I change anyhow." And I watch her disrobe even to the dulling weals on her smooth back.

"That is better. It is so hot that any clothes are uncomfortable." She discards the rich purple silk, seeks, puts on one of the strings I bought for her, the white: neatly it films her russet and gold. "I yearn to play the martinet," I comment, but carefully, she is unresponsive therefore I query laconically: "The interview, you are fired?"

"Not so." She lays on the sofa and verily appears half-asleep.

I think: I wake you. You waste not your beauty and power when I am around.

Merely my stay at St. Teresa's is foreshortened - only a bit though."

"You escape punishment?" I am surprised.

"No." Her reticence annoys and I stare hostilely: this is futile and she turns on to her stomach a leg in the air. She regards me idly and I sense she recollects my whipping her bottom, has a satisfaction she disallows such now. I sit by her and her skin there goose-pimples. The straight white vertical between her tender globes tempts and I tug the waistband: anyone might.

"No Sonia, we behave please."

"'No Sonia, never again Sonia?'"

"You are silly."

"'Call no man fool.'"

She sits up, enfolds me in her arms. "I am glad I wear not uniforms"; a pin-prick I ignore, instead moistly my mouth finds a breast, startles her. Then the nipple hardens and very lightly I nip it; a wonderful moment. She gasps: "Oh you impertinent child, that is enough." And pushes me away. "I promise I will thrash your behind. I remind you of my appointments-diary: it serves me well."

"Miriam," I say slowly and lovingly, and rest my palm upon her mound under a stretched transparency. "Are you within?" I sibilate. "You welcome a guest?" She flushes in agitation pulls her crinkly hair.

Delighted I discover an innocence. "You educate your Daniel."

"Stop it." She rises quickly. "Whatever, I must dress."

"You should. You look terrific. It gives ideas."

"I have a visitor soon." She dons trousers of lavender silk and a cherry-red sleeveless blouse. She is barefoot and I calculate again she has on only three items: and the tight thin trousers are a shy presence.

"May I ask who?"

"Of course. One of my own pupils."

My eye is ironic. "It is no business of St. Teresa's," she adds hurriedly.

"I will go: I am sick of lessons."

"It is not lessons, it..." She hesitates and clears her throat. "It is no business of St. Teresa's," she repeats weakly.

I tut-tut and evasively she cons her mantelpiece clock.

"I guess you will flagellate her," I say heavily. "It is a 'her' not a 'him'?" She nods. "You will see."

The waiting is short. After a rap on the window a miscreant appears: Carmen of the 'Martin Tumbleweed' and brightly she greet me. "Hiya Sonn. You not go home yet, you are in uniform?"

The next person mentions my uniform I will scream.

"Are you a bad girl also? Badder than usual I mean." And giggles her Carmen giggle. "Carmen!" interrupts Miriam. "Your attention please."

"Oh yes Miss. Sorry." She hangs her head, hands clasped behind her. The stance is familiar and resignedly I compose myself on the sofa for the inevitable preamble.

"Carmen de Silva -" Carmen looks up and interested notices the teacher's white string, quite apparent for the trousers are near-diaphanous: Miss consequently holds her hips on its horizontal, arms akimbo. The movement signals: I have experience of male pleasuring under this little garment that you noticed. "- you are two assignments short in your studies. You are lazy, worse, disobedient. Your parents pay a considerable sum of money for your personal tuition. In justice I should advise them what you have or rather have not done -"

"No Miss please, they go crazy."

"You choose then: an alternative is I correct you here privately." She glances round. "Do you want Sonia to leave?"

"I see Sonia beaten Miss. Now she watch me get it. I not mind."

"Very well. The penalty is you present your bottom for the slipper, afterwards for a whipping. Collect the martinet and wait in the bedroom."

"Yes Miss."

The teenager undirected finds its home, enlightening me she visits previously for its ministrations. She revolves it respectfully, lower lip full, and paces to the bedroom. Miriam's nose is elevated 'til she realizes she has no right sleeve to roll up. She also attends the drawer, brings forth something new to me, a narrow pretty slipper with supple leather sole which she bends double then pats a palm with it, an air of grim satisfaction.

"Ready Sonia?"

"Sure. I deduce she gets all of this before."

"She is a hopeless case."

"She makes herself hopeless, yes?" Miriam sniffs and is otherwise expressionless. Her eyes sparkle though.

The wrongdoer yet bows her head but covertly she observes the slipper and her tutor positions a chair in front of the wardrobe mirror. I am happy past events in here subsequent to Juanita's suffering are for a time forgot, am content there is an unfolding now to everyone's wish.

Seated, Miriam crooks a forefinger: "Come to me young lady." She obeys, rubbing her haunches nervously.

"Lay over my knees."

"Yes Miss."

She is average build and a comfortable weight. "You use my tie," I suggest. "Thank you," says Miss and binds

132

the wrists. Her flared black skirt is ruffled up and via the mirror I see an excitement gather in her face.

She likes rock and roll this kiddie and yes a pink racy slip she wears which also she takes by her bound hands. Glossy, seamed stockings, also black, are pulled with frilly pink suspenders which run under a lemon-yellow brief whose size and material disclose much. Miriam tightens it upon the healthy round bottom and consequently exposes more skin. Gently she smooths the taut nylon and we hear the girl's breathing.

"There are no secrets when Miss O'Shaughnessy chastises, eh Carmen?"

"N - no Miss" she whispers, twisting her wrists self-consciously. "You remove my briefs?"

"It is hardly worth it." She considers a second or two then does so anyway. "I suppose the boys clap when you twirl on the dance-floor?"

"Oh yes!"

"You deserve a severe thrashing young lady and I am she who will oblige you." The voice is harsh, causes Carmen's jaw to drop and she stares petrified. "Raise your bottom and open your thighs, child."

"Oh please I am sorry. spare me" and commences a long wailing. But inexorably Miss's arm encircles her waist and the sole of the slipper streaks down, reports loudly on her right bottom and sharply she draws in breath.

Without delay Miss slippers each bottom alternatively, blossoms red the soft curves either side of the dark seductive cleft.

She upbraids whilst energetically swishing down the swiping leather: You - Thwack! - will - Thwack! - in future - Thwack! - try to be - Thwack! - a credit - Thwack! - to me and - Thwack! - above all - Thwack! - your parents - Thwack!

Carmen's bottom squirms with the pain. Then the interest is that she becomes near motionless. She emits another wailing, this like a baby's. It disturbs, but not Miss who hits yet harder and quicker and with the sole bridges the cleft where begins the aroused fissure: THWACK - THWACK - THWACK - THWACK!

Arm tired she desists, rests in the chair. I take the instrument - "Thank you Sonia you are considerate" - touch my fingers along its underneath, feel the moisture captured there. Viewing the shifting flesh, its quiverings, reverentially I murmur "Her love-juices flow."

After the bond's release I venture a hand upon her portal, its wet hotness and hear a shocked "Sonn Sonn" as her own hands massage frantically.

"You. Off." And Miriam replaces the jazzy skirts. "You will stand, Carmen and wait for me." Unsteady Carmen complies, holding a corner of the wardrobe thus is her state.

When calmed, arrives a smart order: "Fetch the martinet, Sonia... Good." She turns to Carmen. "Remove your skirt and slip and bend over the back of the chair." The instrument of greater correction points.

Carmen fumbles off the clothes drops them to the floor and turns. Miss is furious: her nostrils arch and she shouts like never before. "Pick up those, you peasant. My home is not a dump. By God you will jump when I get to you girl!" The other rushes, an animal hunted by a wolf, and folds the garments on to the immaculate bed. Her face squeezes her eyes to tears and again she wails.

"Be quiet, you will be noisy enough soon. Now bend over the chair this instant." In panic another rush and she engages the place of punishment so fast it judders a half-metre across the carpet. "Replace it da Silva you oaf."

"Yes Miss." She re-positions pleading via the mirror only to see fearful the lashes characteristically flicked but harder with fury. Miriam steps to a side: her whole form becomes visible in the mirror to the other's eyes darting haplessly yet absorbing as intended every detail of the tableau.

Then there are those flick-clicks of the crowd of brown lengths which wink at their tips in the early-evening light.

An ominous moment and my heart bumps in my chest.

"Stay still. You wait for me." The words cut and on the reddened skin she lays the lashes which promise to strike fiercer. Carmen miserably utters a tiny despairing cry.

Legs braced apart Miriam addresses her woebegone reflection: "You earned this flogging young lady and it is your final chance. Further work-dodging your tuition finishes. You understand?"

"Yes Miss"; a whisper.

"You will improve your performance I think after this painful submission. There will be no 'six of the best': I shall flog you until I am sure you repent from your nose to your heels. Ready?"

"Yes Miss"; almost inaudible. "Head up da Silva: is water in your veins?"

When she obeys, shaking, her tutor a pace leans back on her right leg withdrawing the lashes and I watch them a second - curious conjunction - hang by the priest's stripes before they vanish in a middle-pitched whoosh and arc to the sacrificial curves centrally.

Then flesh jerks against the crisp lash accompanied by an urgent whimper.

She delivers formally, reminding of Papa's technique, and I hear the swishes sounding precisely, regularly and ended by gasps interrupting whimpering.

Methodically Miriam flogs the bottoms jerking beneath the lashing laces, which spread viciously around her two intimatest openings, lash-lash-lash-LASH! 'til the arm tires. Then I go to my terrible angel, wipe her brow with my handkerchief. "Thank you," she pants. "A favour Sonia;

135

take these, they are wet from her slippering and discomfort my skin." Temporary she passes the martinet its handle warmly moist and unbuttons her silken trousers. Eased from them I basket them and return the instrument.

"Am I tidy?" I straighten the vertical and horizontal of the tight string. "You are superb Miriam, you know it." And observe coolly Carmen wriggling, distressfully rubbing her vivid marks.

"Oh and I forgot: please check the main-door bolt while I continue punishing."

I am aghast: "Miss, what foolishness. Anyone might enter at this time."

"I forgot. It should not matter but please check." And preparing continuation, her legs bracing, she relays the tipped leathers between the haunches angled lewdly and upon the scarlet bottoms their little nerves and muscles flickering beneath the roughened skin: this roughening I hate when I get leather.

One backwards glance and swiftly I am through the doorway to re-commencement of further efficient regular swooshes and also re-commencement of hesitant but deepfelt whimpers.

I have relief the bolt is home and run back to the bedroom in the sounds of strokes and cries which register louder when I re-enter to see the arcing rises and falls of the whip silhouetted by the light of the window.

The lovely punisher pauses, breast heaving, and I smother her neck with congratulation: "You are a terror and magnificent." I bite an earlobe breathing hotly thereon.

"I - I burn." She unfastens her blouse, frees her grown woman's breasts. I intend to support them but she requests faintly: "Bring me a chair Sonia so I rest." The punished in this respite moans, writhing slowly.

My beloved relaxes and from behind her I seek the breasts, and cup them, delight at their soft weightiness. My fingers brush the nipples effectively: "Oh - oh you naughty child." She crosses her legs yet I am unsurprised remembering when she uncrosses immediately. So I say insinuatingly: "You flagellate about her pleasure-slit Miriam, she will have her desire, no?"

"You believe? She is strong and I tire. If I had a cane I might summon a flame from the coals. As it is -"

"Give me your whip. I will serve you and do an act of mercy: I will be twice-blessed." I seize it, capture also a distraught assent of Carmen's eyes. She sweats with ultra tension when by her hungering entrance, curiosity, I touch a burning coarsened bottom. I raise the lashes to behind my shoulder. To them she just widens and her waist is sweaty and she tenses as abruptly I strip the sodden layers off the hungering entrance down the stockinged thighs to release from her toes. I feel her hot coarsened left bottom, raise the whip to behind my shoulder as, sensing the outer air, almost instinctively she juts, widens and exposes extra of her choicest intimacies.

The bush matts wetly and there are jet curls which glisten by the lips alive fluttering short of total sensation.

Miriam is entranced and I grip her right shoulder for balance as careful I flagellate each side of the mysterious cleft and fissure. A reward is Carmen strains outwards more and her pink anus attends the proceedings 'til a stinging lace rebukes and it retreats: a whimper becomes a throaty cry.

"Oh God" she manages and her fingers press my ribs convulsively. "Now Miriam," I judge for her and her pupil. "You swish her central and quick."

She snatches the martinet brings it down rapid and rhythmic whilst I squeeze her body, cover her cheek with kisses. I caress her breasts and sense the body's working movements as she beats sharply.

And Carmen evidences a waxing crescendo beyond selfhood and quite abandoned, collapsed over the chair: but suddenly she can rasp it across the carpet and also there is noise of wood tortured. Her fissure parts yearningly and flickers its separate life. Miss halts the whipping and gazes enthralled.

I need no inspiration, regain the martinet and dexterously intrude its handle - rendered more congenial from much use - into a stranger home of flesh: a higher mewing ensues and intensifies when my nails dig the soreness of her left bottom. "Not quite the virgin henceforward kid - I give it you 'til you finish."

She is past reply while with exploring pushes I fuel the ecstasy of her most sacred passage blazing beyond bearing: she welcome the assuaging fountain of a true member now I think.

And in her finale she shudders her nude lashed cheeks to and fro - yes - Yes, Yes! - YES! - sheening the glistening handle her flesh slapping my encircled fist: at her peaking, irregular groans gurgling in her throat, I note there is no clench of the rigid length. Ah-hah, the bold apprentice though bold is apprentice yet.

I time the withdrawal precisely and Miriam invades under my panties stroking there the old weals, which enterprise reciprocating I jam an unstockinged leg to her mound. I turn. Her eyes are shut as I detect moisture escapes nylon and hair and alights upon me.

"If I smoked tobacco I have some now," she hisses through teeth.

"Or we are cockless," I rejoinder, then: "I will soothe your nerves" and return with a hairbrush.

Slow and admiringly I brush the damp gold and we contemplate the ebbings of Carmen's rendezvous with pain and joy.

138

When able she rises, meekly requires her brief which a scrap of materials, soaked, which I proffer.

"You are not my height but are similar size where it counts," her tutor smiles. "You may shower, borrow briefs before leaving."

"Oh no Miss, thank you. I go home as I am." There is an expression of glee animates her face flushed which she touches, disbelieves she exists, she is very high.

"I hope you love and respect your parents," I say a bit pompous.

"That is unworthy Sonn. It is I gain something redresses the imbalance between us: I will savour it when we argue this evening."

It is her longest utterance ever I hear and Miriam wise-looking kisses her. "I expect completion of only one outstanding assignment: this is reasonable and you do it or my diary will summon you."

Far away Carmen surveys the floor, lightly holding her bottom. I ponder suspiciously and Miriam scrutinizes a skirt my parents never allow while I am a schoolgirl.

"And then my arm and leather will rock and roll you again, young lady."

"Yes Miss"; she awakes, spins of that dance and we get a view boys at our town-hall hops await eagerly no doubt. Even the frilly horizontal of her suspenders shows.

"You conceal your chastisement, Carmen?" The question is full of doubt.

"Oh yes; perhaps my sister see. We share a room but she is under my thumb." And giggles her giggle. "'Til Monday Miss, goodbye." She swings her school-case jauntily and vanishes from our presence and concern.

"Well! Once you said 'youth is resilient', Miriam. You were not wrong."

"You children educate your teacher... She will reveal her punishment?"

"Probably," I laugh. "Worry not: her parents give her worse for less and she enjoys her red badge of courage. She will find you again I think."

"I find her 'til there is no slacking... My trousers are dry already: this heat is miraculous." She resumes them, covers inadequately the stain on the gossamer triangle and refastens her blouse. "Your stripes all right Sonia?" she apologizes. "I wanted their feel: I was on a slope when I watched you both."

"Okay." I engage the blue of her eyes. "You liked them? Not yours for a change."

"Mmm. Deserved by anyone's arm I believe you little heart-breaker. You join with me for tea? - Stay there, I will do it."

She is in the kitchen and I listen to the preparations. Idly I lay the martinet across my knees and stroke with thumb and forefinger one of the guileless yet potent thongs. "This is the life," I murmur though add; "'til cock arrives anyway."

"What you say?" above a clashing of crockery.

"Oh nothing Miss; I wonder if your diary is full to its edges."

She reappears with tray-cloth and notices the supine instrument, how I treat it. "Despite what you accuse I am not mad." She sniffs characteristically. "Give me the whip."

"Shall I?" I tease.

She shakes her head impatiently and takes it, hangs it by her leg then points it at me: "You kneel," she orders clearly.

"Only my back have no blemish."

"I will not beat you though you require a beating always." And as I accede I feel it on my shoulder, attend its laces bisect my blouse.

She withdraws them and I watch in bewilderment while she walks around me, bestows a stare. She halts and pushes up my face with it. Sorry Stella I think, and melt into cutie-pie and big eyes.

"You stop that." Miriam smiles faintly, taps my chin.

"Oh Miss now you; everyone discovers my act these days. My years spoil it, yes?"

"Oh yes," she laughs. "You are dreadfully old, Sonia," and resumes the circling thoughtfully.

My knees ache, I droop and sigh noisily. She halts again and frowns. "Straighten yourself. That is better. Hold out your hand child. Palm upwards you silly." And she gives me one lick of the martinet: "Ow, you promised no beating," I protest, blow on my palm then home it into my arm-pit. "That is nothing," she deprecates. "And when you visit Miss O'Shaughnessy you carry yourself correctly and if possible prettily - though for you that is easy."

"You are unfair," I grumble. "You break a promise. Typical adult."

She smiles fondly. "One stroke to your body is a small betrayal. I pray any future betrayal is so trivial. Good. You are correct and very pretty - No swelling of the head please: it is God alone made your looks."

I lose sight of her, twist suspiciously in time to see her loft my skirts by the instrument. "You swish my behind now?" I say cynically. "No" she overrides coolly. "Tidy your panties then you are perfect."

"This is infants' school" and I tug and smooth them. "I am hungry for refreshments only." My words are a signal to the kettle which begins a low roar and bubbling. "Take a seat" and "No slouching" she calls merrily, which brings out my tongue to her journey kitchenwards.

"Eat slower," she commands later and I mumble something like: 'it is kiddies' corner in this teacher's place'.

"And speak clearer. I hate any slovenliness. Carmen appals that way."

She becomes a mother each minute passes and one mother is enough - especially my one - so I say through chocolate cake, she made it and deliciously - "When will she visit again? Not soon after her chastisement. You have other appointments?"

It is an arrow which deflates her bossiness only a bit for she snaps: "Empty your mouth before you speak child."

"Your appetite, Miss, not for food, needs plenty satisfaction. I like a read of your diary."

"I will put your name in it also," she warns.

"Is Batista a private pupil?"

"Take your elbows off the table." I roll my eyes. "You dislike my seating-arrangement Sonia? You prefer Stella by you? You two together end over my desk within the week."

"I will strangle Batista one day, she is a horrible school-mate."

"Sad for you she is St. Teresa's pupil only. Besides most I tutor are fine students."

"I love a read of your diary. Please."

"Of course not... Why the smile?"

"I help with the washing and instead you tell me."

"No need. You relax: impertinence debilitates, yes?"

I disdain her sarcasm and when she is in the kitchen try her writing-desk: locked.

"I lock it Sonia and hide the key," she calls musically and my tongue-tip pokes again.

She returns and I glare which hardens her: she says peremptorily "The other one."

"The other one what?"

"Your hand" and I get a stroke; "Ow, Miss -"

"You have no permission for search of my personal things. Oh and your next tears are genuine: I make sure." I scowl pronto which amuses her and I smile unwillingly at her.

"I will miss you," she says dolefully.

"Why, there are many months 'til you resign, yes?"

"True." Then; "Come to me."

Since Carmen drained most of her sadism she is maternal which state is a surfeit to me. I skip from her and say: "You put down that thing."

"You are young and lack the higher affections." She says it so sad. "I make a big mistake."

I pity her and am unresistant when she pulls me to her.

"Will you remember me with fondness then, Sonia?"

"I will remember you with love, Miss."

A crease of pain is between her eyes foreseeing pain and I whisper: "It is true." I engage her eyes calming. "You see: these tears are genuine."

A bit I cheer her and we languish in music from her record-player: it is lousy songs of her country, no beat you recognize but she is away and I think: good, an unhappiness recedes.

To the brim though I have prurience: imperative I affirm a prediction is future fact and patiently I wait for her interest. Dinner-time nears so I enter my strategy.

We are on the sofa and my movements push my skirts to my waist as casually I kiss and fondle but carefully avoid her privacies. I kiss her neck and ears, touch her bare back and eventually angle across her thighs. "Your weals diminish Miriam," I say kindly. "You think I am similar now?"

It is temptation she accepts and pleasurably I feel her warm dry hands slip under my panties and caress the crowns of my bottom. "They heal to complete smoothness soon. Such disobedience your mama despairs you bad child."

"That is excellent and after Saturday you also will be past a transgression's penalty."

The hands stop. "Yes. This time I go to confession immediately: Mother required it."

"Poor Miss. I suppose your chastisement here, she said it was no deal?" "I - I was very upset: I forgot and we discussed other things."

You want that priest I think. I have much anger about that, too much! as I sit up beside her. "Fr. Pablo he will give you good penance. You ready for it?"

"I expect it will be dire but I am glad there is no delay."

"I will pray for you Saturday," but I am bitter within with the jealousies that itch to be out.

"Thank you Sonia, you are so thoughtful."

Chapter 18

"Dress yourself."

It is Stella uninvited who erupts into my room when I fancy I will read or play not-Miriam music.

"Mind Lima, he is not a floor-mat. You and your big feet."

"No competition to your big mouth." She comes to the bed and slaps my half-nude rear: "Hello sex-pot. If I was Roberto you get the hots? Or Mario," she adds coyly.

"I ask my parents for bars at my window."

"Good idea; they protect the world from you."

"Oh you are funny Stella but not your jokes. Why are you here: you take me to the dance, honey?"

"Huh, you are not my type. No" she says dramatically. "It is mad O'Shaughnessy. I reckon she goes to confession this evening and earn her reward for loony punishments. You know anything?"

"It is so Stella and she is not mad. I will pull your nose."

"I put you in my pocket if you get physical. Dress yourself," she urges, "and come to the church with me."

I hesitate. The priest is an area where I am impotent for Miss and it depresses me. If I see them together it will depress more. And trouble, trouble much. Yet in the aftermath perhaps I help her.

"Okay." And I swing off the bed.

"It continues warm," Stella says with pleasure of companionship and excitement. "You will not need many clothes."

"You are always elegant Stella. I look a frump if I agree with you." And I put on a full ensemble even to stockings, she has that effect on people.

"What a nice white dress. You are the virgin of St. Teresa's," she sniggers.

"It pleases everybody," I say loftily. "You go the the Ritz while I go to church."

"I hope there are no boys about," she says fulsomely. "They will interrupt our journey to a special event."

"Stella, Miriam is my great friend," and this silences her. "I will switch on the radio," and I drop Lima into the corridor who as usual walks away to patronize royalty somewhere.

My parents are busy with guests and we quit the house easily, enter the warm dusk which enwraps sensuously and soothes 'til my companion shrieks and I glare at her: "That was a moth you dunderhead. How old are you?" She shoves me and we wrestle and laugh almost to Miriam's cottage which we find lightless.

"Hurry, the mad teacher this moment maybe has her comeuppance."

"Stella -" I begin.

"Hurry" and she placates: "You are her ally. You comfort her if she suffers." Her hand goes into mine and I abate my anger which is not difficult with her nature despite circumstance.

But when we approach our destination she idles and I face her exasperatedly: "What is it you mutton-head? Firstly we rush, now you are geriatric."

"I suggest we avoid the church. Others will be there for the event." "So? You are not the shy sort."

"Well I mean really we see the penances only, not the before and after. We hide in the convent part of St. Rita's. I know the way. They happen there - if we are not late."

"Not likely; the nuns catch us and it is a licking. And you die if you get one."

"Are you jelly Sonia?"

"I am not."

146

"Surely you have curiosity?"

She persuades me. She wants the spectacle of Miriam's humiliation whereas I am nosey and perhaps support her somehow if nearby.

"How you know the way?" I demand suspiciously.

"From years ago when I got religious: to be a nun was my ambition. Remember?"

"Oh yes Stella I remember. So the layout of the convent is familiar?"

"I visited often with pure joy."

"You were intolerable I remember. Now you are intolerable differently," and I snort with laughter.

"Oh Sonia -" and after a hug she rubs a cheek on mine - "your talk is famously vivid. But will it prevent ladders in stockings?"

"No, please." I spring from her. "They were very pricey."

"Then walk politely mighty mouse or I chastise you."

Where the nuns live and pray is a pleasant old building. Mainly it is empty: there are few vocations these days. Our entry gained tentatively, I follow my best friend along dim corridors 'til she pauses. Out of her sight I am behind her: her hand cautions, accidently presses a breast.

"Not today thank you," I whisper.

"Oh sorry... Quick, we ascend to the gallery. No-one is here." Her form flits through the noiseless chapel which nearly hums its quietude. Some illumination emanates from the sanctuary-lamp or outside of the windows of various colours.

"There," she sighs. "A splendid view."

I hear unwrapping, sucking and a cough-choke.

"I thump your back," I offer coldly. "You will be comfortable when the big picture starts."

"This is better than the cinema. You like a fruit-sweet? They are super: mother made them."

"No thank you Stella. You eat them all for maximum enjoyment, while mad Miriam agonises below us."

I sense her face turns towards me: "I am not callous Sonn. Tonight the spectators are her best friend and HER best friend; not so bad."

"You give cheer; if you have pen and paper we dart that information to her when she arrives."

"Aww, you" and resumes sucking.

The last of dusk declines and the lamp glows a brighter crimson. Birdsong ceases and - surprise - there is a rustle and knock of leaf and branch upon the panes of the chapel. "Hey" I breathe "a breeze comes: the weather changes." But from Stella an inarticulate low gurgle: her mouth is full of sweet. I calculate the evening-office finished long since: it is confessions that delay penance.

My companion is the first complains of discomfort: the whispering interrupts my sombre musing and I rouse and say: "All sweets gone? And you tell an usherette fetch a cushion you bean-pole." She encircles my neck, growls mutely when a door-latch rattles, wood creaks and a shaft of yellow light yawns into the indigo beneath. Framed in the doorway is a young nun with aflame taper which smokes. She advances to the altar, ignites its candles.

Stella forsakes my neck and encircles fearfully my waist: "Oh God please protect us from discovery."

"Your clever idea, we pay for it."

Three more persons enter slow and sober of tread and one is unmistakeably the priest, tall as Mario but a body leaner which is borne like a bow primed. A horror engulfs me and - my turn - I clutch Stella.

Sister Consuela, the mistress, precedes a novice who is demure and humble and links hands I notice upon her most womanly tenderness. Momentarily the light outlines her perfection, evidences her dress is flimsy and there is no underslip: the priest sees while the ancient door shuts and to his words the older nun grates the massive bolt to security.

He spins to the novice but address the Consuela: she gestures imperiously to the novice who billows again into the sanctuary and there falls precipitately on to her knees.

"For your penance," the priest announces harshly - and Stella stiffens - "you will recite the Miserere Mei Deus whilst your mistress lays well upon that sinful envelope of flesh you used unrighteously. Be thankful our boldness aids you in absolution."

"What was her sin?" my friend wonders, then breathes in sharply: Consuela returns into the circles of candlelight, a short slim whip of twine cords in her capable right hand. Imperatives are hers alone now which to our ears are near-inaudible, but an effect is the novice loosens her garb and her naked torso white but opulent gleams moistly by the wavering flames. When she accedes more, holds the top of her head, a roseate nipple with its charmful collar appear.

"Oh she is attractive." Stella's arm re-finds my waist. "She transgressed by the flesh not half I bet and that beast he drinks her see?" This seems true, he is very intent before her 'til his lieutenant mutters quizzically and perforce he nods brusquely.

It is the signal and no further ado the lissom cording leaves from behind the mistress's back and swishes curtly about that, marble-like, of her charge, who sways and gasps yet manages commencement of recitation: "Have mercy upon me O God -"

This Miserere has nineteen verses and each she intones to at least two lashes of the cobra-whip swishing, swishing. Diagonally lengthy red weals intersect over the pale skin hitherto unblemished. A particularly severe lash and Stella's fingertips dig me painfully. A hiatus comes in which the young nun cries despair, succumbs on to her hands and to our sight a single ripe breast depends.

149

Her vain twists under the echoing lashes disarrayed her habit, exposed some of her vigorous haunches and solid bottom on which like a careful coating of pink paint is a modern but opaque sparse brief: the beginning of its intimate lining is quite apparent.

Consuela shoulders the whip and looks to her superior who acknowledges her skill in the art of flagellation with grim satisfaction.

He pronounces: "Sister Monica, your penance nearly ends." He stands in front of her eyes and enunciates drily: "Nearly. However, to save your back and right breast from injury your mistress will complete elsewhere upon you." He nods again and the cording whistles to the main pink and white of the bottom: a small puff of dust rises from the tight material which therefore is cotton I think as the sound of the crack wanes yet heralds a whole series of lash-strokes. The young woman surrenders on to her forearms and buries her face in her hands. The bottom juts up more, writhes and jerks helplessly under the fall of the whip which plies freely where the rough habit absents: criss-crossings redden her thighs also which cringe abjectly and the priest turns to Miriam, staring at her meaningfully.

Miriam! We had hardly noticed her, kneeling humbly in the shadows. Now she rises.

Initially Miriam is modest, gazes downwards and plucks her dress it seems nervously. But then, surprise to me, she hoicks vulgarly the darker brief visible through the light grey material. She brushes languidly where each covers her woman's opening and wantonly - there is no other word for it - returns his stare.

This shocks me: it suits her poorly and is an expression amateurish. Yet he regards steadfastly and, I divine with disgust, considers what he will attain. And in the candlelight her lips are voluptuous scarlet but I know she never uses lipstick.

Consuela ceases her novices flogging, the lash retires and we absorb sight of one; her skin carries a myriad lines which bunch and cross. Scarcely she uttered while these collected and was brave throughout.

"Miss O'Shaughnessy," says the priest. "You have permission for one garment. Only cover your greatest privacy therefore. You will amend your clothes accordingly."

As she unbuttons the delicate dress, eyes evasive, he accepts the whip from his colleague.

"And you, Sister Monica, will stay in position though," he reassures because her face crumples, "your penance here is over."

The grey dress drapes over the sanctuary-rail and he continues: "You will get a whipping below your back which already suffered from previous sinfulness. Use your comrade-in-penance like a cushion and lay across her. I await your obedience this second."

Hurriedly Miriam obeys: her lovely body meets and presses the hot flesh and fresh stripes of the penitent beneath, who keens but with restraint.

He positions before the newcomer's eyes that travel hungrily, his tall form prescient of menace and vengeful power.

He is wordless and the sound now which appals is a lash! which vertically bisects an ivory seductive bottom I recognise well from another time.

The lash-cracks are remorseless in the cavernous chapel, lit eerily, and its shadows crowd the corners and remote ceiling as she writhes on Monica's chastened yet coping flesh.

He pauses: Miriam's agitation is high. He moves forward, grips her neck and some of her gold tresses between his black-clad legs. She whimpers in half-terror and Stella murmurs with genuine regret: "Poor creature, she will really get it now. She will think twice about the school-strap next week I bet."

My lips are dry and tears scald my cheeks, but I am grateful Stella has sympathy and squeeze her waist.

The whip rises descends longer, and harder lashings obscure the tremulous cries that come now from each of the penitents.

Then Miriam's secretest juice darkens the tight materials of the base of her glossy and transparent brief. I watch her thighs open more; one quick movement.

The Priest pauses again, says something to his helpmeet who stoops efficiently, strips away the light blue nylon familiar to me. Is this breaking of his promise? But no, a scarlet thong divides the bottoms, their weals and twitchings.

He releases her, steps aside and whips diagonally her haunches and bottom: the cording like a live thing viciously whistles and cracks into appearance a grid of the angry weals whilst almost she laughs after throaty groans to a distraught but mighty climax.

Ceremonially he tautens the whipcord above her and sternly regards the woman conquered by pain and lust. The erstwhile silky surface on the tender flesh is a ruination by vivid ridges which intersect and heartily I trust the awful flogging is at an end.

Thus it is. Yet quite erotic she shifts herself and wonderingly explores the area he fired.

"Also you examine your conscience," he states formally. "You will find this evening's work cleanses it. Henceforth be loyal to righteousness. Go when calm restores your dignity."

"What a hypocrite!" hisses Stella. "And he whip her beforehand you see? If his nasty black trousers were not on everyone see his cock undermines the nobilities of his tongue -"

It is so and I hate and fear him myself that I begin words of support when my hair crackles on my scalp and I feel fingerbones hurt and detain my shoulder.

"I thought so"; a voice of culture, Consuela's. "Sonia Casals in a delightful white dress, a mistake in any gloom."

I glance hapless at Stella who is mute because she also has detention. "You come with me, you two, and father decide the matter: for this you have no choice."

Stella turns paler then we descend noisily the gallery's wood stairway.

The novice-mistress presents us, but the Priest has impermanent interest and Miriam after one stare to me of deep disapproval rounds and swiftly dresses. The young nun retreats into the dark beyond the candlelight.

"Sister, you dispose of this intrusion apart from our consideration: we are past petty interruption. Meanwhile I thank you sincerely for your assistance with penances this evening." And simply he and the penitents quit St. Rita's, the massy door grinds then plunges the chapel into its prior inkness.

We are for it I think, and scan surreptitiously the nun's mature but handsome features which go severe as the last echoes fade. She speaks and we are all ears I tell you: "One of you snuff the candles: they forgot." And subsequently we detect she beckons: "Follow me you two and if you chatter -" I sense she regards me specially "- I will punish you extra."

She leads to her quarters which are austere, but the lighting is good, and stands behind her desk upon which she plants her hands.

"Well?" she interrogates. "You trespassed. I allow you explanation which I suspect will not convince." And she raises her eyebrows at Stella who appears older than your narrator.

She, the instigator of our expedition, is desperate: has embarrassment and is fearful. "I am sorry sister, we are St. Teresa's pupils and wanted viewing of a meet penance, you understand."

"I understand you violate the enclosure. Well?"

Momentarily Stella's eyes are upon me but I attend fully the nun's stance of accusation and shiver: she is an ace flogger. "I - we - apologise. Penances were public within recent memory," my friend adds hopefully.

"You entered the enclosure without permission, which demands punishment. This is available here and immediately or I ring your parents -" she points to a phone "- and they collect you. Well?"

Stella's lips tremble and I guess she pictures what I picture; Monica's whiteness jerking and perspiring as a lurid tracery etches it in a noise of whipcord lashings.

But the older nun is wise. "It is not punishment for a sacrament," she reassures. "It is a warning. Quickly please, compline approaches." And raps the polished wood.

"I - I accept sister," I say and my best friend glances my way. "Yes sister," she whispers miserably.

"You Sonia Casals -" her eye is lively and intelligent, not without warmth and reluctantly I like her "- have your mother's whipping still." Is nothing unknown in this town? "Take that expression off your face and stand alertly, child." Oh God another Miss at her worst. "It is with some pleasure I think -" she goes on "- I require you return here some hour next Saturday for what is a child's beating therefore not to the back."

I blink vaguely, imitate dumbness as she passes in front of me, mouth pursed at me. She rustles to a cupboard produces a bijou leather strap perhaps forty centimetres length with hand-piece, five width and maybe not a centimetre thick: I observe it with interest, next Saturday in my mind. It is very supple from regular use I judge.

Stella sways and I catch her waist. Already she whines and tears brighten her eyes.

"And you Stella Nattino I heat your behind immediately. Control yourself," she says scornfully. "You are a cowardly creature. You want I lick you properly? I am aware it was probably your scheme the intrusion, you know the inside of the convent. I recall you believed you had a vocation to our order some years ago. I thought you silly then and today you remain silly."

She sets a chair, occupies it and summons imperiously: "Come to my knees Nattino. You are childish and I treat you like a child."

"I am a young woman Sister. In a few months I work in Sr. Domingo's office, his secretary, receive important business-people."

"You test my patience perilously. Casals -"

"Yes sister."

"Persuade her and quickly. Or -"

"Stella," I whisper to her ear, "it will be near to a spanking. Think of your parents: how they will nag you to death."

And from her petrifaction I guide her to the chair, the shiny ebony strap poised by the nun's rough grey habit. "Thank you," acknowledges Consuela drily.

"My last beating was when I was nine years," my friend ventures but meets a contemptuous silence as awkwardly she lays over the lap, its cloth ruffled.

"Remove those ridiculous shoes girl - you kick them away you will really suffer," as a leg crooks. I start forward ease them from her warm stockinged feet and essay a solidarity tickle to an arch. She unnotices, she is very unhappy.

A skilful encirclement of her slim waist, a stripping upwards of the classy beige dress and plain black silk slip, and she boo-hoos instantly.

"Be quiet or I will not respect your privacy and pull down your panties you absurd creature; such foolishness."

Consuela regards stonily the dark-blue suspenders, transparent-black frilly brief which, a second skin, moulds incompletely upon the neat globes.

"You have the fashions of womanhood and the soul of an hysterical child. I like your boyfriends see you now Senorita Nattino." Hell's bells I think, me too: they surely view more than a dollar's worth.

Forthwith she flicks the ebony leather on to the curves evading. It snaps smartly there and Stella's gulps change to squeals without inhibition.

The little strap smacks rapidly and often. It is unfamiliar with its victim's elegant long flanks and trim bottom, but soon enwraps them matily like it knew no other home.

Oh dear, I think, and resignedly watch my friend's wriggling, the legs kicking and tensing to the swishes stings. It is a sad thing: she half-hoped she encounter boys this evening, also enjoy Miriam's penance. And now she is hurt and ludicrous over a nun's knees. Life is a strange thing I muse. 'til a high squeal draws my extra-attention: Stella rolls on to the floor and sobs despairingly with shame. In our country the fairness of her cropped hair is unusual, but now it is untidy spikes and her cheeks burn redly.

Desperately she tugs her skirts to coverage of her underneath but Consuela rages: "Get up Nattino, get up immediately!"

And with a staggering she manages obedience.

The nun's eyes are ice and the lips a straight gash.

"That is it," she grates and my blood chills. "I have enough from you senorita. Bend over my desk - Now! Move yourself!"

And Stella has no alternative.

Then the energetic nun whisks up her skirts peremptorily and the servant leather sings in whilst a rigid arm pinions the victim's waist.

Consuela with fierce indignation now swipes the tender chubs anchored firmly across the wood-edge.

The young flesh glows and spasms from each of the louder impacts which report and beget 'Ah - aaahs' and piteous mewings whilst ineffectually she reaches towards her punished regions. The sound of these harder strokes dominates the room and I tally every dark arcing down to its bisecting sharply, cracklingly the red twitching and ivory sweating under and to the sides of the pathetically meagre taut-diaphanous nylon.

They constitute a substantial number: I use my fingers and thumbs several times.

Thus to a close and you will state she got a message.

Consuela, sniffing contemptuously, releases her, and she weeps utterly, subsides and wriggles violently against the rigid surfaces. Her long pale hands reach urgently to her strapping and clutch the bottoms there.

"Never I encounter this degree of cowardice and resistance, Nattino. I have temptation to get you here again for a genuine whipping but I control it. Adjust your clothes my madam and prepare for your departure. Your behaviour revolts me."

She returns the strap - and if it lives it is content I think - to the cupboard and with temper slams the door.

Poor Stella is motionless now but cries on, her boyish good-looks in profile between her splayed hands. She snuffles, then hiccups: "Please pardon me," she says automatically.

The nun's features soften: "I remind you replace your skirts young lady," she says gently. "Though your chastisement ceases you give an unseemly display."

"Yes sister." And with the black silk and classy dress painfully she veils the bands of red and crimson strapped everywhere on the pretty shape of her behind.

She rises and looks elsewhere from us. Thus is her pride shattered and she is brimful of shame.

"I am sorry in your thirst for diversion and sensation you ignored sacred strictures, perhaps worse your memory failed about them. And you Teresa Casals -"

My lips part with fright when her alive and liquid eyes engage mine. Why I have more and more eyes see into me this manner so frequently? "- I know of you well and suspect you contribute to this evening's events beyond what appears."

I pluck apprehensively my delicate white pleats which movement she follows closely, but no relaxation of sentiment like for Stella.

"Therefore when you attend here next week it will be a child's beating - I break no word - but gladly I have allowance I bare your bottom for it and all of it I administer with vigour."

I am a rabbit hypnotised in torchlight.

"My wrist is strong and Mr Leather is an old colleague. You will bow to him respectfully soon. If you truant," she adds meaningfully, "I inform your mother. Clear to you Miss Casals?"

"Yes sister" I croak.

"Go home without dawdling, night-time comes. Miss Nattino," she concludes grimly, "I am sure will guide you from the enclosure - one last time."

"Come." I dare not use her name, her state is dreadful and when I touch her shoulder intention of soothing she twists away. "I hate you, you saw everything and it is all your fault."

Obscurely I agree with her and attempt I catch her eye; no success.

"I hope that horrible nun beat you to insensibility you trouble-bringer."

"Thanks." I laugh which is a stupid thing I do in the circumstance. The first time since a long time she looks at me and it is a look I prefer I am not the target you will understand. "So, it is very funny. I give you something will have you in fits I think not." She advances and opens a hand raised. But before my fear she relents: "I will not smack you face. Your parents see the red and ask questions." I relax and retreat further. "Instead I will shake your teeth into your throat you shrimp-pot." I retreat again but she is quicker and her strength and size chastise me into giddiness. "Oh please," I say desperately, "we are best friends and I will get my desert next week and harder than yours."

She desists and I stumble, then sit, I am very giddy. She towers over me and grips the collar of my dress. In my new fright I shrink and it tightens in her fingers. "Oh not more Stella you will tear my dress." "That is an idea: your mother whack you for that." And the fine material rips sombrely parallel with my squeal.

There is a death-silence for she has given herself a shock: out of character she damaged deliberately that which to her is a semi-sacred thing. This I play to its fullness, cover my mouth and stare horror at her.

"Oh Sonia!" she sobs, then awkward-running vanishes into the night.

When I return homewards myself luckily I evade my folks, they are yet with guests.

Quietly I ring the Nattino household and her mother picks up their phone: "My daughter is in bed in tears Sonia. If I discover you are at the back of it I will speak to your mother. Good-night." Not twenty words I managed and she cut me off. I ponder whether my friend's whipping comes to light. Her parents are unlikely to add to it, they believe she is a princess and will nag, nag, nag instead.

"What an evening," I sigh later to Lima in my room and: "Is she royalty? You know best, you move in rare circles oh furry one, monarch above this mundane town." But merely he yawns uninterestedly which is a signal to my tiredness and speedily I prepare I retire.

My dreams are not good though this night. I am not the unfortunate subject in any of them.

Chapter 19

I knock the novice-mistress's door, heart bumping, and the young nun who accompanied me departs with "Good luck Sonia, you will need it."

"Enter."

The voice is attractive, its cultivation. Today also it has pleasantness and I conjecture maybe she will cancel the punishment but after reflection I decide no she is not like that.

She looks up, smiles faintly and rests chin on her knuckles joined. Again I like her: her eye is warm and loves. It surprises me a second time.

"You came; a satisfactory start." She scans my outfit which is not special; no Stella with me. "We begin?" she suggests mildly, and a fear perspires where I am secret, usually.

"I recap," and perches on a corner of her desk. "You entered the enclosure without permission last Saturday, a forbidden act. Then I offered you choice. I offer it today: I inform your parents - especially your mother -" and her eyes is wise - "or, because the offence is lesser, administer a child's beating. Well? I have many things need attention: choose quickly."

"The strap, sister." And I sense she conceals a pleasure.

"You know what it is and where it is, Sonia Casals, bring it to me." And carefully she observes my movements.

I open the punishment-cupboard and con its contents for my objective, which rests by a slipper between it and a spank-paddle. I shiver at the whip on a hook and note also a foreign guest, a small slim yellowish cane hangs upon the next coat-hook.

"An instrument for every kind of misdemeanour, Sonia," she flutes. "Yours was not quite minor but definitely you escape the English cane; if you are sensible today that is."

The bijou leather strap is light and the surface slightly clammy to my touch. She accepts it and her face is that of the sphinx, eyes engage with something past my left ear. I go for she jolts out of that superiority, I think.

"It is very supple," I say precisely and quietly. "You thrash with it since last Saturday?"

Eyebrows raised she stares at me and hastily I look along my nose.

"That is the business of the convent I believe," she says haughtily. "Your business is you bend over my desk for a beating of it. If I detect further impertinence I will cane you." She cradles the end of the strap in her palm and waits expectantly.

Dreaded fate greets me and my lips are hot and dry; not my hands though, which I wipe on my ordinary black skirt.

"I remove my skirts?" I croak.

"Unnecessary" she murmurs and casually points the instrument at the wood-surface just by her. "There will do." She folds her arms and watches thoughtfully my bending beside her. The desk's edge nips the top of my thighs, then I am in final position.

"Excellent. Now stretch your hands out ahead of you. I expect my rules are similar to the school's: no touching your bottom while I punish. If you move or holler excessively you get extra strokes and harder. Are you ready?"

I assent and clear my throat fearfully.

"Good. How you feel?" she enquires conversationally and nonchalantly slips off the desk. I hear a couple of practice-swishes and my ears flicker instinctively. "Not good," I whisper. "Soon finished Miss Trespasser, though you will squirm. I am an expert with this little gentleman."

Because of Stella's absence I wear no stockings and the outer air is much on my thighs, cools them as Consuela arranges skirt and cream-silk slip upon my waist. "This is a pretty underslip," she approves. "And was an expensive buy, yes?"

"It was my mother's then a birthday-gift," I manage.

"Ah. Unfortunately your briefs are an inferior complement." She sighs: "But cotton is dearer these days and my novices wear the same." I envisage her, brow corrugated, poring over ledgers and bills. "I fancy they are not wholly virtuous. What will I do in the world of money? Now. I recap again. Your comrade Nattino was a silly goose who die if I take off her briefs. You are hardier stuff. Also normally I allow female privacy down there but this occasion I want your child's strapping be maximum-effective for reasons I told you last week."

She lays the shiny ebony strap by my face deliberately - I think thus I will view it comprehensively. Her hand warm and efficient alights upon my waistline, the other commences peeling my tight skimpy nylon. "They go. And completely off, Miss Trespasser. There. Better and better but not for you shortly." She drops also by my face the scarlet undergarment, it is like one of Stella's though mine you see through if I let you. I contemplate its perky disarray of shape.

A long silence ensues and I wonder. Cautiously I adjust my nude haunches on the uncomfortable wood: she will discern a bit of my pleasure-places I think: enough will interest her? I test if she enjoys herself with this kiddie and, again cautious, essay minimal movements, a slight opening of my thighs is an example.

Ah-hah, her hand returns to my waist, she comes closer and I wink to myself.

"I have the same problem with the novices," she comments calmly. "It is wiser to lay on upon their backs. If they

162

close their bareness it stimulates. If they open it it does likewise."

"Sister!" I try tones of shock.

"I am not entirely naive Miss Casals, and have beaten the unclothed female bottom on many occasions. Doubtless you consider I am a dinosaur with no knowledge?"

"Why no, you are like my mother; an attractive maturity, no dinosaur."

I hope she is not younger than Mama!

"Thank you for the compliment Sonia but I regret it will not diminish the level of your punishment." And my defenceless skin receives the cool touch of smooth leather a she lays upon me for measuring for strokes coming: I wriggle apprehensively and crook a leg. I notice perspiration from my tense fingers marks the polish, the scent of which also suddenly fills my nostrils.

"Keep still," she requests automatically, "or I award additions this early stage... How are you feeling now?" she asks in genuine curiosity but I pretend she needles and respond daring; "So awful and helpless. I bet you enjoy yourself henceforward."

A short pregnant silence then she comments pleasantly: "More impertinence. You earn additions immediately miss and my arm will ply stronger from the start."

"You have all the power," I rejoinder rudely. "I am only a pupil, you do what you like - Aah!" And I gasp sharply: she swish-snapped an unannounced band of stinging expertly across my rear.

"You be quiet, you and your insolence." Her voice gains an excitement. "I remind you of my cane. He is an old gentleman but will take your breath if he forces his attentions despite his age."

Swiftly she delivers two harder swipes of the leather and I gasp again, my fingers paw the desk and my form rams its no-compromise edge.

163

Yet through the pain she is likeable and subsequently in the brief hiatus I 'ow' and 'ouch' a bit louder and wiggle more than necessary, play up the event: I wish it will please her I have become fond of.

"You are a naughty child in a teenager's body." Unmistakeably an affection arrives.

Slowly deliberately she recommences the swipe-snaps of her 'little gentleman' and a broadening hot stinging spreads over my bottoms.

"Stop wriggling about so Sonia," she says keenly. "It is well your boyfriends are elsewhere: they get a bonus if they watch." And astoundingly she simpers.

In truth the pain now controls much of me, and in particular my cringing cheeks rise and squirm when they want.

Consuela however has great experience in the art of physical chastisement and abates somewhat the strength of her strokes. Also she relishes her thoughts again and loves utterance of them. Momentarily she rests the strap across the tops of my crowns which now pulse and burn continuously.

"Your mother's marks clear yet others come, replace them this soon. You will never learn the lesson Sonia like many who bend here."

Then I feel her hand press firmly my waist and urgently I brace for what I know will be resumption of the proper business. My mouth opens wide and I stare unblinkingly through a window, tree leaves and dull sky beyond: the weather changed and how I think and watch a bird of colours travel the sky-scape. My lips tremble and I teeth the lower whilst in panic I claw squeakily her desk: if I only I reach the further side it is so big.

The wish vanishes with a harsh smack of leather that heralds a series which weld my flaming flesh in a tent of agony to the wood. She pins my middle to it and I hear her grunt and pant her satisfactions to every lash she arcs down.

It is the sombre part of what were jollier proceedings and convulsively I twist and look wildly at her with swallowings and I regret whimperings.

She pauses and I am so thankful. I shudder and gulp. She straightens, those eyebrows rise and: "You will say something Sonia?" She engages my eyes with phoney puzzlement which makes my jaw clench, turning 'the little gentleman' over and over within narrow but capable fingers. "Surely child you appreciate punishment will be punishment? I am strict, it is true, but you are I hope no Stella Nattino." She picks imaginary specks off my twitching and soreness then guides with gentle encouragement my left bottom: "Resume position please. There is plenty of milk between the strawberries awaits a reddening."

That cool and amusement of hers flares in my brain and I search it strenuously for a violent ripost when there is a knock and the door rattles ajar. Again in agitation I twist: comes a male visitor? Unlikely. And yes, thankfully, it is our Miss Nin.

She, not like Stella-to-be, is a real secretary at St Teresa's school and doubles for secretarial at the convent. This evening she carries a bundle of papers and waggles her spectacles with surprise at us - not much surprise though, I notice.

"I thought I heard a flogging," she says carelessly.

Composedly, Consuela administers a lesser punctuation stroke and straightens again. Modestly I close my thighs: though female it is an onlooker and there is some embarrassment. I relax my legs and whistle soundlessly.

"I am sorry," the visitor chirrups. "I interrupt a ahem a meeting."

"No matter, Miss Nin: in her we are theocratic therefore without secrets. Please continue your purpose."

She halts and blinks. "Why it is Sonia Casals: I recognize the face also." And laughs gaily. I obtrude my tongue out of view. It is so, rarely I bend in Mother's office when she is around.

"I only bring a few papers and I leave," she says. Why then I think are you stationary at least a minute this far?

"I warrant that stings," she says breathlessly. You touch, I think, and I become a Stella and racket the room to pieces.

She touches.

Sadly I am a worm and bury my resentment.

"The stripes are so hot and - and - rough... What a naughty child you are." Her finger traces one and when I flinch she withdraws but without apology. "I gather you trespassed the enclosure," she says smugly. "You and your friend Stella Nattino. She got her reward last week now you get yours late after your mother's marks fade."

Everyone knows everything in this town, I think angrily.

"You girls these days are so bold," she says wonderingly, and I roll my eyes heavenwards. "Much like your undies," she prattles on and I envisage hers; sensible panties though maybe very frilly, she has a very frilly personality.

She plucks the scarlet nylon from beside me: Oh God in a moment she will sniff them she is so obtuse. She flicks them to their proper or rather improper shape and holds them up: the light from the window accentuates their transparency except for the intimate lining.

"You pop them in your little blouse-pocket," she says coyly, "when you have games with the boys?"

"Miss Nin!" interrupts sister. "You astonish!"

"Oh I am sorry, sister, it slipped out, such is today's wickedness. I spoke without thought." She drops them hastily back, stoops spinsterish and self-conscious adds lamely: "They are handy for everybody, that sort, they wash in a trice."

"And for the novices," I murmur.

"What you say?" darts Consuela distractedly, she is yet uncomfortable from her secretary's gaffe.

"Oh I bless someone's memory sister," I say neutrally.

"I see." She has doubt but: "Where is the punishment-strap?" And spies it revolving in the other's inquisitive hands. "Miss Nin. Please. We delay and Compline approaches."

"Oh, I am sorry." And passes its ebony length reverentially. She catches my sardonic eye: "Now you feel more leather Sonia." She straightens under the nun's impatient glare and continues hurriedly instead. "You modern girls savour wrongdoing, that is the problem."

She sidles to a writing-desk nearby, ostensibly fiddles with papers but covertly watches the recommencement of my beating.

She moistens her lips and narrows her eyes as I get four strokes in quick succession and feel myself jerk painfully to each of them. They swipe crisply, efficiently, their sound fills my ears and heat from soreness congregates intenser. The secretary coughs discreetly but I discern her pale eyes liven with an eagerness. Disdainfully - she is a pathetic creature, I think - I jut my bottom and swing my hair.

It is a pert defiance not lost to Consuela who promptly swells my allotment of torture with two that smack resoundingly and drive me to a slight giddiness in which also I listen to myself cry out brokenly.

"You seculars," she hisses. "I enjoyed those yells. I wish I had an angel's whip to take to your skin, you are disgraceful, your wilfulness."

All this is genuine emotion and I judge I am really for it, tense and cringe against the wood slippery from my sweating, when I sense she stops.

I look round. She sighs and kneads her right arm which I think sarcastically will have fine muscles, you number the targets incessantly it finds. "This duty exhausts me," she complains. Oh sister, how you suffer for righteousness' sake.

"If you want a rest sister, I give her a few spanks," titters Miss Nin creepily.

It is outrageous when Consuela actually accedes: "Yes, colleague why not, for I trust considerateness is among your inclinations also."

And I am speechless while the secretary's horrid damp hand restrains my waist and quite hard the leather smacks in: she hits low on my bottoms too and across my cleft there, the cow.

"I do this before," she says brightly, she is happy. "Long time ago. Mother had arthritis and I deputised one day. If I remember - smack - it was - smack - the Batista child - for - smack - truancy - smack - but she wore decent nice panties: children were better then - smack - you see what she had on underneath yesterday - smack - whereas poor Sonia - smack - is presently - smack - as her parents first saw her - titter, SMACK! There sister, she has tomatoes ripening beautifully."

"Thank you, Miss Nin. I work the documents later and we will discus them."

"No trouble."

Frustrated spinster cow!

"Oh Sonia," she trills from the doorway. I start and scowl at the half-seriousness she adopts. "You are a naughty thing and I will pray you return to virtue."

My sentiments are deep as she departs, but change in the nun's new silence. From the corner of my eye I perceive she is attentive of my nude submission.

I ponder her essential niceness again and readjust suggestively with a throaty moan.

Temptation, and an inhibition fractures: she trails on my left bottom, evidently a place she favours.

"Ow" I protest theatrically.

"Miss Nin has a competent arm. You regret you kept your appointment?"

"It was unfair you allowed her and not Christian justice," I whine boldly and her fingertips leave the sore skin. That is not my desire and I replace them with my own hand, massage in a fashion that at least opens my cleft.

Another silence poses. "I know your thoughts about her and they are cruel. I suggest my permission she hit you was fair because of them despite her weakness... You are an attractive specimen Miss Casals but the spirit within has not yet total beauty, matches its house of flesh and bones." Her voice is warm and mild but I look at her sullenly and she smiles, her eyes soften.

"Our rendezvous is near finishing. My little gentleman -" and with a palm she caresses the underside "- anticipates finale on your biggest tenderness. I will not disappoint him. Brace yourself, Miss Naughtiness." And I feel the leather laid across my crowns for measuring whilst she absorbs leisuredly my naked vulnerability.

"There is left a bit of ivory among the blossoms around your woman's treasure, Sonia. It will surrender to us I promise you. Your face encourages me to contemplate the old gentleman in the cupboard. You go meek please. Or -"

"It is also unfair -" I say pretend-stubborn "- I am on this uncomfortable edge: it is extra to the official punishment. Stella was unappreciative but her licking had no extras - definitely the award-part."

My strategy works: she fetches a chair, sits, says equably: "I apologise for thoughtlessness. Come, we complete an unpleasant duty." So? I think sceptically and: I delay you Consuela-of-the-strap. My skirts I keep at my waist as I walk to her new place of correction and her clear eyes flickeringly glance at my neat and healthy bush: "What a child of pure nature you are, so delectable. If I was a young man I find you irresistible and yearn I plough you pronto."

"Sister!" I rebuke. She shocks me. "Are you a virgin?" she continues imperturbably and in disbelief I gaze at her then blush. "I am glad you are," she laughs. "Not yet a hot stiff guest paces to and fro your room of pleasure." Alas no live one I think, then I mutter "I believe not my ears."

"I surprise you eh? I have had many fiery shaftings for I was a wife before a religious. They were wonderful: my late husband he was a vigorous lover. Sometimes I miss all of that." She sighs. "And I have a daughter, your age nearly, and like you wilful pretty and chastisable. These are not secrets, but I do not bore people with broadcasting of them."

She tidies the skirt of her habit and inclines her head quizzically to one side. "Come child. Now I whip you well. You ask for it and I will oblige," she says briskly and tautens the length of the strap a few times between her hands.

I am full of questions and astonishment but obediently descend on to her lap. There were plenty of rumours but the truth yet astounded.

Remembrance of my scheme returns however and I ensure my thighs are wider than ever as I lay. I give a roll of my body, exclaim "Oh your lap is strange to me! I hold your leg please?" "Why yes if you wish." She is indulgent. "This daughter suit herself if she wants." She abbreviates 'daughter of mother-church' but means other maternally.

Her calf tapers to a perfect ankle and also I get a surprise: "Stockings, you wear stockings sister," and I stroke them wonderingly A pretence hides a different intent. "So you wear them in chapel for the offices after dark: they are chilly devotions then I notice you never attend, child - Oh I forgot, there it is outside of the enclosure."

I ignore the pin-prick. "What else you have on?" I ask conversationally.

"I am a nun Sonia, your curiosity is disrespectful."

"Show my only for interest's sake."

She tsk-tsks: "You seculars are clothes-conscious on the brain." But she complies and there are plain-white suspenders pass under transparent nylon also plain and white before I re-lay on her soft thighs.

"You content Miss Curiosity?" Her arm comfortingly circles my waist and I stretch Lima-like. "My little gentleman will wake you and from profane curiosity to repentance I hope, though with much doubt." I relax my legs and centimetres raise my bottom.

"You like you beat our bare places Consuela?"

She becomes still. "You are a precocious child. A whipping suits you admirably."

"Which you did admirably. I deserve compensation 'ere you recommence." And I bring a thigh forwarder than the other: my woman's entrance beneath its curls will be visible, and trembling of anticipation starts.

Unexpectedly she tweaks the locks my state threatens it will moisten and I ow! indignantly, subside the threat but simultaneously think: this is novel!

She muses: "One day children will come from here if God blesses. Life is odd and fascinating."

"Only if you take your hand away," I snigger.

She slaps the inside of my left thigh: "Ouch!"

"You are a quick cookie Sonia. Pity your wit deserts your sense often or you avoid a leathering. Now I do what you manoeuvred for." And the dry heat of her clasps me and I draw in breath with delight.

But she withdraws it abruptly and raps, "Merely I test whether you enjoy yourself in this punishment. Others I test similarly." She concludes primly and I watch she plucks off the floor the bijou strap and see - and feel - she begins re-application.

I speculate she beats in a frustration and I clench my teeth, grip her ankle as she swipes noisily and my soreness returns to the burning. "You spoiled my mood Sonia therefore you will suffer extra." And I of course I curb not inevitably my humour.

When I labour and sharp tears course, the door re-opens, but now my hurt is very great and I care not who arrives: may be it is the President of the Republic (There I go again). It happens it is Miss Nin.

"Goodness," she twitters. "Here this long under punishment: I warrant she added insolence to disobedience. The Sonia tongue is famous." She hovers where is best view of my latest and hardest humiliation. "Gosh am I thankful my schooldays end." Silly twit and unprecedented since then I think: I flog you on your bloomers if I had the chance. "Your cane sister speed what is necessary. You weary? You want I - ?"

The eager words spur me. I clutch the nun's knees that I go upright with huge indignation but she executes a superb stroke which collapses me to my original angles and grasps my waist firmer. And fortunately she disregards the secretary's blatant craving.

Then any thought draws in my approach to an agony and when the unendurable is at the threshold she ceases: she has fine judgement from experience.

She lifts me to my feet. "I thrash your wickedness ahead of any triumph," she announces and I know the meaning if the Nin creature thinks differently. Probably Consuela treats the novices likewise, thus finally she is a nun eschews true licentiousness.

Therefore respectfully I listen as she passes to me the little strap but only she orders: "Return him to his home. And if ever you bend here in the future Heaven help you, you will meet my old gentleman. Within the charm of your looks is a good brain: use it Sonia."

Then she ignores me totally. "We confer tomorrow-morning colleague: Compline awaits."

The secretary smirks, dangles my lonely brief which I snatch and send her animosity. "Put them in your pocket, or you cook your stripes," she suggests airily. "I warrant you will sleep on your stomach tonight, you bad child, perhaps throughout the week." And titters provocatively. "I escort Miss Casals from the convent sister?"

"Thank you."

Chapter 20

As I follow Miss Nin through the chill stone corridors I
obtrude my tongue to her back with a ferocity I fancy will
unroot it. Her short hair ages and is thin of chocolate-colour
which will complement the green of her pale eyes.

She walks with a gawky swing of the brown pleats of
her mid-calf-length skirt, which typically at its hem reveals
lacy centimetres of an awry cream underslip. Her ankles
are thicker than Miriam's but within similar mist-blue nylon. Occasionally she turns, ensures I follow dog-like, and
I see her large round specs reflect gormlessly the minimal
gleam from the lamps in the passage-ways.

Though I struggle I am helpless. A powerful anger builds
and I bite my lips or I will execrate vindictively.

Outside a breeze wafts her hair darker from fitful moonlight emitted between irregular small clouds that race. The
air is balmy despite its journeying.

She regards me, speaks lingeringly, her mouth moist
with daring pleasure: "You better Sonia? The welts relent a
bit? You hear yourself, you surprise yourself. It was well
sister cupboarded her cane. I watched she use it when -
Ooh!"

Firstly I enrage by the creaseless skin of her face, no
trouble marks, then I exasperate at her full breasts, bra-less
I note, and hang like they wait for babies, and convex the
coarser cotton of her duty-blouse. My hand electrical seizes
the left, its hot ripe softness, and she gapes paralysed.

There flashes in my mind I doom myself, I do this yet I
care not, I have fury at this spinster-woman, want revenge
on her self-indulgence, her cosy kink.

"I teach you teachers secretary Euphrasia -" that is her
unbelievable name "- Nin. You enjoy you watch the pun-

ishments? You have one you mull over when you bed tonight after you remove your pink bloomers?" And I imprecate and spitefully push my face to hers while I squeeze, squeeze.

She is mute utterly, tries retreats a step but I am quicker, hook behind her ankles, then she finds hopeless voice for she falls gracelessly to the grassy earth.

I am upon her half-a-second and deaf to her squawkings, intrude a knee to the mound begins her bifurcation its writhing. Urgent squeaks replace the squawks and fingers flap white birds uselessly to my chest: the right set I capture and my blood sings joyously as I slap her smooth cheek hard not brutal. A squeak extends to wailing and she blinks rapidly.

"You little animal," she manages breathlessly and thereupon I impose my knee firmer. She moans swooningly: "Oh God, Mother will flog you for this. I pray I am there I see your flogging." I impose more firm and my skin detects she wets through that which surely is silk. Her wrists I grasp and her expression alters to fearful excitement as I press her hot mound for seconds go to a minute.

When I feel she surrenders I stand with satisfaction over her: she is strangely still and I wait 'til impatient I make I leave. This triggers and a fist smites painfully my thigh. "There," she crows childishly.

"Okay" I say and stoop to her sensible skirt. Her innocent idea of retribution is she tries for my hair but I swing it away. "Okay Miss Nin, you have another lesson," and squeaking recommences whilst I roll and shove her skirts, "which is I confiscate your drawers and send you home without them."

And yes they are silk, plain-white panties and not easily off, for she gains an excitement as I strip them along her legs and off her feet. "You tear my stockings," she protests

175

feebly, then looks guilty at me out of her desire kindled: "What you do to me now you savage?"

"Why nothing," I reply cooly, "except this" - and I palm her bush also silky. She cries yearningly: broken like a seagull's and I glance anxiously towards the dim lights of the convent. Luckily they are many metres distant. There is a tearing of grass and a low choke-sob. "Put them on," I say kinder. I wipe her moisture on my sleeve and watch she steps into them, stretches the luxury fabric on her globes, covers self-consciously her woman's place aroused. Truly she is edible: a man peck her mightily if she allows and at my smile all anger drains. Her cheeks are high-pink, and guileless her face.

She sniffs and produces a silly Miriam-handkerchief.

"I suppose you quit now," she pronounces without the slightest twitter. "It is well for I hear someone. If you stay they arrest you for indecent assault and I cheer."

It is so, there are voices, young men, and I hiss "Run for the convent, Miss Nin. It is the night of the dance and maybe they are outsiders."

"I lose my shoe," she maunders maddeningly. "Help me find it."

Despicably I run myself, the voices louden and I carry an image of her face turned towards my flight with ingenuous puzzlement.

Nearby is dense shrubbery which hides me and therefrom I see as my breast bumps she locates the wretched shoe, sits and works it on.

"Go, go, Miss Nin," I whisper, then stamp the ground impotently for the voices owners appear, two of them, one tall, beefy, the other lesser. The breeze brings their words clearly and they accost her immediately.

"Hey sweetheart, need a hand with your footwear?"

She freezes, replies nothing, places her hands flat on the earth and stares.

"Come. she is your mother. Her bones will crack your jaws."

"Not so old," says Beefy, arms akimbo - he dresses for the dance which will liven up later and thus I think for instant shafting if he gets some - he stares back for a rude long time.

She bows her head, plucks the grass and I wonder if she remembers. She returns his stare. Her wordlessness and near-immobility encourage, he makes his move: he bends, takes her shoulders and kisses roughly her mouth below her wide dispassionate eyes which flicker and narrow. "Aw come, she studies the nightingale," says Lesser, and I notice they are careful they use not their names. But Beefy takes her hand, her mouth opens, she wipes her lips.

He guides its limpness to the obvious bulge that is his manhood under tight thin slacks: she has non-resistance, a fact assesses what swells menacingly against her palm and fingers. Then she blinks fortissimo.

Oh God I think, he will impregnate her, she is fertile it is in her face and a babby will hang from those breasts unhaltered.

Beefy gestures to Lesser: "You have a go: you warm her for my entering, hombre." And after hesitating, the other complies: he parts the front of his trousers and by moonlight a competent fat member glows whitely.

She touches her hair, tongues her lips again, and slowly extends fingertips that caress a side of its potent length, which stiffens reactively. She holds her cheeks and her adams-apple rises and falls.

"Phew-ee."

Confidently he flicks up the hems of her skirts, reveals the plain-biscuit colour of her wider sensible suspenders bisect her tender flanks. She accepts his abrupt uncovering her intimate undergarments and tentatively opens her thighs.

"Phew she is wet already the hot bitch." Beefy grunts approval.

"You want it rape-mode honey? You warmed darn quick."

She answers not, instead subsides on to her elbows. It is answer enough. He kneels: it is not for prayer I think and jump when he exposes violently - I hear cotton rips - her breasts which rise and dip in agitation. He has stubble on his chin which he draws across the dark nipples and she sibilates something for he straightens. Her eyes fix upon his thick horizontal rod then her left hand encircles its weight, slides to and fro the unmoving length.

He works her ribs and sides mainly and she groans despairingly. To her flanks he goes and her knees jut if anything further upward and outward. The taut band of white silk below reflects in the moonlight and he has more than mere permission for penetration of her woman's secretest pleasure-slit.

He wrenches the fine fabric but her body's angles preclude his peeling down of it. Therefore with both hands he assaults the sensuous double-layer that is her last inanimate defence: another tearing and elastics, stitchings and material disperse. His rigid cock advances to the wet furry portal, indeed halts and presses thereon. She is beside herself, twists her neck swiftly that she stares jaw hanging to my direction. Broken mewings issue from her which intensify when dexterously he hooks her knees that her legs drape over his shoulders. The slightest pause and she drops to whimpering then, perhaps theatrically, he growls and I see his smooth pale cylinder plough relentlessly into the yielding darkness betwixt the sodden pieces of silk.

She utters one desolate cry but he is precipitate, jab-thrusts voraciously which rocks and jerks her submissive body. Her head hangs backwards, the mouth gapes and while she gargles incoherently she spreads her arms right out for intense purchase on the tufts of grass.

His initial passion abates, which Beefy heeds casually and rests hands on the buttocks' slow-pumping: "You come up for air now," and smacks a rotundity. This he does eases from her fissure his rod reddened which glistens. "She fits snugly, you she will pull beautifully," he pants.

"It is she is childless, a virgin, who knows?"

"She knows. Hat your prick and keep guard."

Beefy stands before her, unzips businesslike, the black string strains upon his flesh and muscles. I breathe deeply, his penis is formidable: though not Mario-size it is noticeably larger than Lesser's. I confess my juice trickles at the sight and along my inner thighs. The residual soreness and pulsing of my thrashing I finger lasciviously and relish certain sensations which shoot meltingly through my core. This is the life.

Meanwhile Miss Nin ventures to him on her knees and, caressing his solid working-man's bottom, worshipfully kisses the face of his erect cock. "Save your congratulations for later," he laughs. "Turn around my sweet, go on to your forearms." She uncomprehends and he waggles her chin that she smiles. "I enter under your arsehole. For women it is a way of shafting cuckoos their brains to heaven and I fancy a change."

After she turns he, macho-man, throws her skirts along her back shaking and noisily tears more ingress of her panties. He cradles skilfully her breasts and she exclaims her pleasure. When his monster knocks once for entry she becomes very silent which is her woman's assent, she endorses with a submissive widening of thighs and obtruding upwards of her haunches. She learns fast, I think drily.

She bows her head and shrieks raggedly when he cleaves the firing flesh inside, the soft flowers of flame within: a single drive of him covers to the hilt of his primordial hard

179

generator and jet, curl engages curl. He sighs profoundly and she shudders, the fierce guest of him is unbearable joy. She fists the ground, begins a spiralling into wild distraction, and he forsakes the slippery breasts, seizes her waist and savagely orders she re-close a measure her thighs.

Then I watch he shags her out of her wildness and to a passion a degree rhythmic: he plays her like a virtuoso plays a violin. When she judders ecstatically upon his thick pole he begins faster thrusts 'til finally he rams into her his entire length and erupts into her convulsive climax.

"Bravo, bravo," his friend claps and the evening air witnesses the lovers' rasping breathing 'til these recede and reluctantly their bodies unlock.

"I like I poke that": Lesser regards the secretary's semi-nude bottom which yet upturns lewdly, trembles and perspires. But he who mightily pleasured her reforms her skirts and she rolls on to her side.

"She is full. It will be rape if you take her now. We return to the dance. One there owes me a favour: she will drain you if I ask. Give me my trousers."

He attends considerately her he ploughed, and she sits within his broad arm. "We damaged your pants and stockings: here are dollars, buy replacements. You okay?" She nods dazedly and he helps her to her feet. "I want you to be here this time next Saturday: we loved and I wish we will meet again, you understand?" He removes her specs kisses her eyes and elsewhere on her face. She searches his: he is a map of a new country. "Possibly," she murmurs. "I have duties."

"Where you live?"

She points to the convent's lights.

"Go straight there," he urges. "I look for you next week remember?" He delays 'til slowly she starts off towards where - it seems days ago - she to me essayed another and obliquer art of the carnal flesh.

When I am sure the men depart totally I join with her and she stops. I pull her into my arms and hug her.

"I am sorry I attack you, Miss Nin." I am not able I speak her impossible Christian-name whatever the circumstance. "I deserve you punish me: I remain after school an evening and you use Miss O'Shaughnessy's strap on me, okay?"

"No matter, Sonia. Nor you will pay for my stockings." She smiles crookedly as she reveals crumpled dollar-bills. A heavy pause ensues.

"You meet him Miss and get his name and things: he impregnate you."

"What? How is that? He is not my husband."

I gaze at her with astonishment. "Lift your skirts," I command and we view where two flows intermingle, one clear the other opaque: "Here," I say incredulous at her opinion, "is his seed brims from your woman's place. Believe me, it will do the trick and make a baby if you are in wedlock or not. You savvy surely?"

"I suppose," she replies wearily, then delicately touches her triangle there. I do likewise and she releases her skirts; "Only for him," she says dreamily.

It is I exist not and this remarkable creature steps complacently into the shadows within the convent and, terminal clatter of bolts and latch, shuts out my wondering non-existence.

Chapter 21

I had dozed a little perhaps. I intended a reminder of a plan Sonia had expressed sooner or later to visit her home. All was quiet: I filled a glass generously with light wine and passed it to her.

"Oh Will," she exclaimed and her mouth quivered that she couldn't continue. Hurriedly I lit one of her cheroots and one for myself. They were good; not too short a smoke and quite a narcotic.

I aimed white puffs at gambling insects and decided against touching her: my instinct cautioned me she was in a wood of dark and pitiful sentiments and instead I closed my eyes, dropped into appreciation of tobacco, and pondered I might doze a while. This stately afternoon I had heard what seemed her longest narrative and a snooze under the hot sun held a charm.

But my lover, a Goddess, was spritely mistress of her gloomy woodland yet and a brief pain pinched my elbow. "You are rotten and undependable," she accused. "I give you me then you fall away when I need you."

"No don't stop Sonia, I drifted a bit that's all. Consider for me it's double-history lesson at St. Teresa's - though much better than that of course," I added quickly and meant it in fact. "Of course."

"'Of course'" she quoted reflectively and teased the material of my shirt. A more lost expression gathered in her face until she said, "I save the rest for the evening if you prefer."

"Nonsense," I countered briskly. "You will forgive my shortcomings and carry on. You can forgive, can't you?"

"Sometimes I think that is the final accolade from any event and all we finish with," she stated simply and solemnly.

"Go on," I said. "Get it out and don't hurry, it's ages to supper-time. And cheer up: you'll have a splendid feed when you've done." She smiled, pulled at the grass, then her brow evidenced comfortless thought and she forgave and began again:

When Miss Nin was gone I stood long seconds motionless, ears twitched for any noises from the ones coming to attend this evening's weekly dance; thankfully nothing. I cursed my white dress appears a sheet of paper to a blackboard in the dark. Stella prompted me I wear it then tears it. While my sentiments mix a warm rain hisses mildly, pitters and clicks on leaves and shrubbery about me. Inspiration; if Mama see the dress I say I flee from the weather and spoil it on brambles.

Also I escape a soak if I shelter at Miriam's nearby which idea has a deeper impulse I confess. Fervently I hope she has no company, especially of him I fear and hate. Surely she will not be so weak and foolish? My heavy doubt lingers. Yet I desire I meet her subsequent to her pain and hunger: there was not my comforting of her in the chapel, maybe I help now.

The silence of our countryside is palpable and, when I disturb an animal on the path, sound of its flight is big under a starless sky that weeps softly.

I have relief Miriam closes her curtains, an anxiety it is for an unusual purpose. There are thin bars of yellow light and I peep but detect merely a portion of a familiar interior. I step back tidy my hair and clothes, try her door; unlocked and I fume again.

She is visible immediately, lies face downwards I note on the sofa of our past pleasures, toys with a glass of wine that glows richly from her main lamp. I deduce she is alone and imbibes uncharacteristically out of a bottle of booze. Well, she need it she had an experience you will say.

"Why you not lock your door Miriam? Our town-hall hops attract strangers. You expect someone?" A horrid apprehension hollows my chest.

She looks not upon me but turns her head sufficiently I see her lips are purple with the wine stain which disfigures them and obliterates the scarlet our priest's attentions engendered.

"You never knock Sonia and you are sharp about another's business. You are sharp generally," she giggles surprisingly. "Have a drink Miss Sharp-edge."

"Who is perfect? What wine is this? Ugh, Domingo's grapes; the worst around here."

"It is not bad and the price reasonable."

"You have not vineyards in England I guess."

"In Ireland we have black beer."

"BLACK beer! You mean it contains dead blood?"

She laughs. "It is good for the blood. If you dislike his wine I will finish it. I hate waste."

"You throw it on the ground, not near flowers." I notice before dollars stick to her pocket. "Besides you are tiddly now."

"I drink double whiskies in my home if I wish," she says, and at last looks at me from those middle-blue eyes, so very novel, even her fair hair. Stella has not such. She plays obstinacy and her nose tightens. I sense she feels her chastisement and another look triumphs: he did it, not Sonia Casals. Her moods change swiftly: a charm that is lovable but exasperates. You understand how she stimulates sadism and chastising of her is alluring.

Okay Miss O'Shaughnessy, I think. "I leave you drink yourself into silliness."

She sits painfully. "Oh no." She observes me covertly and touches her mouth. "Please stay. I drink for my poor appetite this evening." I sit and cross my legs carelessly. "You dress prettily this evening, Sonia. Why, you wear stockings, that is strange."

"Because of Stella. Her company has that effect."

"Oh." Then she remembers: "You broke their enclosure that was the trouble. I expect your pal howled the ceiling down." Undeniably true. "If you like I repair your collar," she says. "It is ugly that state. A boy tore it?"

"Not so" I reply indignantly. "Anyway, you are unsteady you prick yourself."

"Of course not. I rescue it for now. You bring it tomorrow say tea-time I will repair it properly." She fetches sewing-things. "Take it off, I am ready."

"It is colder this Saturday," I grumble.

"The young specialize in ingratitude," she murmurs whilst begins the task, "sit by me for warmth," which invitation I accept.

"I stroke your breasts Miriam?"

"You imagine incorrectly you are entertainment, child. This dress is delightful and except your shoes and suspenders you are all in white: it suits your appearance but not your character I am sorry I say." She concentrates with needle and thread. "Are you sorry?" I teeth the warm neck and my hands press her. "Stop that," she says mildly, "you will create marks and people will talk."

"People will talk anyway: they want they excite themselves." Instead I venture upon her breasts and she seizes a wrist. "I told you." Her stare is hostile.

"It is not his hand," I say sullenly and gasp: she slaps my cheek a real Mama-slap. My gaze to her depth of feeling is one of horror and she bows her head: "Oh it is unbearable," and her lips tremble.

I stand. "I see clearly enough it was so for ages you want that Priest not only for what is under his nasty black trousers. You are crazy, Miriam, the way he used you in the chapel. I say he is affectionless and you will drown when merely they remove him to elsewhere. You follow him, you are that mad?"

"I follow no-one in this place, least of all children," she exclaims and my ears burn.

"Very well. Give me my dress and I go."

But she moves not. "It needs more stitches or you will be scruffy."

"You are the tramp, not I. A tramp for love." It was cruel but I am not a child.

"Yes. It is best you go." Clumsily she pours wine. "I requested so once in the past you recall, but this time you are truly excessive."

"No doubt," I respond stonily. "And if you wish you enjoy the evening to the limit I recommend - excessively - you ease off the booze."

"Get out," she whispers and I take up my dress. I dare I touch her chin: revulsion and hurt consume her face.

"You are not cheap, Miriam. Have a shower and change your clothes. Seduce him not yourself: that is the extent of his worth."

"You are jealous. Never come here again, never."

"I have not jealousy," I say, my eyes hot and full. "Only sorrow."

"It is over. I love you," she says.

Chapter 22

Always afterwards I call that evening the evening of the
betrayals. What I did haunts me. Yet chastity is one of a
priest's imperatives and loyalty a fiancée's journey to joyous wifehood. I console myself neither suffered much in
this life consequence of their liaison, for each gained quiet
settlement of the affair, and worse scandals arose in the
town in times that have followed.

Picture me where rain slants stronger but it is warm
and I suck it from my lips while I watch sadly my beautiful
teacher - for how long ? - draws wider her curtains and
anxiously squints into the blanket-darkness. That is expectancy I think dully, and yes, soon after I hear the crack of
vegetation under footfalls and the height of one I loathe
looms so I step back into a leafy seclusion.

His iron sureness never fails him and in arrogance he
merely taps her window with a nail of his forefinger before
swiftly he receives admittance.

There is closure of only her front-curtains and through
side-windows all that unfolds is clear to my heavy eye.

Firstly you see she is hungry for a man's affection and it
disgusts me she supplicates and clings to him who is impatient of anything bar power and sexual lust. She offers him
wine and he drains it in a swallow: the little amusement of
their adventure is he grimaces at Domingo's rough harvest
and I smile ironically.

He twirls off his priest's cloak and servant-like she bears
it to a hook. Thereafter she is to his tall form, entwines his
torso with pale and urgent arms, such arms a man will dream
of! Yet he is rigid and impervious 'til his hat goes and she
dares, she strokes his thick black hair, and Oh very tenta-
tive and experimental, places a light kiss on his cheek where

it meets unshavenness. Then he stirs and caresses her neck though his face remains without expression. But his eyes, those eyes! They are slits of liquid blackness and he blinks lazily. He speaks at last: because I am by a window ajar I shudder at the timbre of his man's worldly voice.

"So senorita. This far the day's events satisfy you not far enough. I am no maker of poetry yet I understand there is recapitulation here and now will greater conclude that which you began utterance of in St. Rita's."

Her response is she tones wordlessly, grips his back fiercer.

"You listen to me, woman. Tonight you personify a wickedness undriven from you. I will finally drive it from you and after quench your demon's embers with my holy seed. You understand you are possessed?"

"P-please Father, some tenderness... tenderness," she croons.

He forces her from him, holds her wrists massively. "You understand I named you trollop," he enunciates savagely.

She hangs her head and I wonder if she regrets her refound acquaintanceship with one of peculiar detestability I think, but no she straightens, raises eyes of heaven-blue, and stares to his, impenetrable. This once he falters within their magnetism and his hold slackens. She decides. She escapes. She turns and opens a familiar drawer from whence withdraws an also familiar medium of corporal punishment. Her movements slow, the martinet dangles, winks by her calf and she leans provocatively and negligently against that she opened. Outlines and shades of her dainty undergarments become apparent, the light-grey dress is so flimsy.

She is loveliest now. His voice floods her and she blushes. Everything of him she absorbs and her eyes plead widely.

"You creature of Babylon, your desserts await."

She watches his lips move and smiles faintly. That is a trigger possibly she will regret, he seizes her arm that carries the whip: she cries the pain, "please, please," and half-bends from him, placatingly invites he strikes her with it but he snatches.

He is not truly precipitate, it is not his manner and I chill when he says precisely: "You are fortunate I came, I save you now or never."

"Yes Father."

"I flog Satan's guest within you."

"Yes."

Lengths of her gold hair wind around his fingers. She nuzzles and kisses whilst steadily he pulls her to a chair. "Present yourself here," he orders. "Hold the seat." She indicates a dressing-mirror. "I –" she dares not say 'we' "– put it in front of the mirror, sir. It is meet I view my just fate."

"Indeed! Make haste!" and jerks the leathers impatiently.

As she positions subserviently over its back, quickly she glances behind her, a moment scrutinizes where hides prominently beneath dark cloth strains his rising manhood. She turns to her image, shakes the gold tresses and moistens her lips expectantly.

It was a brief attention, its import you bet he noticed, for he passes the implement to her and she puzzles but stays, she bends obediently: she has – she wants also – no choice.

Then her form shivers delicately: please Miriam you do nothing coarse I think, while with easy unbuttonings he releases his penis. It is stark white by the blackness round it and a competent thick pole has its circumcision like an incomplete face, taut pink-mauve concludes, the good length menaces: the whole erects harder as they watch in the reflection.

She permits a tiny helpless 'Oh' of fright, part-genuine I think, but the nether region opens: I tell by her ankles in misty nylon separate.

He retrieves the martinet from her forgetful hands and this time there is 'Ah-ooh!' He smooths the two thin layers upon her, seductive bottom, which yet retains the hot pain of the fierce chapel whipping.

"You begin well huzzy, and you will sing better or my beating of you has no moral warrant: that I fancy is not the case." As I flinch he lashes a stroke that curls sharply across her buttocks which wriggle immediately.

He lashes and lashes, she regains the fever of excitement she had in St Rita's, cries deep in her throat, and subjects the chair to problems - it protests, threatens to break. To each hard rhythmic descent of the lashes also she pants, glares hungrily at him and his in the glass. She is beyond agony, her haunches upthrust display abandonment of modesty over the wood-horizontal: she craves terribly the male rock-piston that will drive fatefully until her secretest sweet flesh yields in burning.

But abruptly he stops the flogging. With bafflement she commences "Please-please-please..." and gyrates her head desperately.

She has a necklace. And another.

Thus he pauses, decides he beats no more.

The life-scarlet stains its line insinuate through the innocent pretty material while he delays there 'til eventually he speaks: "You wound, Miss O'Shaughnessy. Stand when you are able."

The words despair her. She drags hair off her face, perspires. Her eyes beseech and when she stands a powerful signal of distressful desire bespeaks he will respond or receive a high hysteria.

She has no need of anxiety, he lifts her into his arms, carries her easily, I observe despondently, to the sofa of our past delights.

The dress he gathers to her hips. Together they scrabble the slight bunching of the brief down her thighs and legs. She shrieks, arches her bottom's agony from the cushions, and he lances into her without problem of the red string:

merely he tugs its fragile triangle downwards, invades his column further, and on it instantly she convulses.

I delay sufficiently, I see between her thighs he works his eruption in the apex of them which judder ecstatically.

I will I see nothing extra and detach from the spectacle of an apostate who fires erotically a traitor.

The night-rain now is denser and bonds clothes to my body in flight. The flight and the rain involve naturally my being which welcomes them while with sentiment and distraction I sense a dreadful liaison takes on distance and darkness supervenes. But there are minutes 'til my cheeks bathe tepidly and not with scalding.

The convent's telephone number produces only a gadget records messages. It is late that the secretary also quits the office. I speak my betrayal with a cloth in my mouth: "The priest of St. Teresa's, he breaks his vows at the Irish teacher's house. You ask her, she will confess, lying is beyond her."

I replace the instrument with a terminal mute clunk. The deed is done.

"Come Lima." I hear my voice reveals my upset. His fur crackles on the nylon upon my ankles and he weaves sympathetically around them. Astoundingly he mews which is rare he is not a cat who talks. I kneel and smooth the coat by his ear in appreciation. "Come old friend," I murmur sadly. "Lead me to the arms of Morpheus." Wretchedly, I know not how, I ascend to my room and away from the world, but its hideous event yet squeezes my heart with remembrance.

The Sunday, the church; the mass, the people, all are the same like any Sunday before this one. The grey weather abates and sunlight, great planes of it, illumine St Teresa's interior, heighten the congregation's many colours they wear and are.

Abominably the father, in white and gold for Our Lady, preaches and ministers to God's people. Among them I see Miriam who is very noticeable with her English fairness and its pale skin. She has the dress she had yesterday: I disbelieve the depravity, I think, associates. She is I hope unaware or cares not. Or is it horribly she relishes?

"What is the matter Sonia?" asks my mother accusingly. "Oh, it is nothing Mama; a little unwell, I recover soon."

"You hold out 'til the dismissal?" she suggests anxiously.

"Oh yes it is nothing."

Miriam moves not to the sacrament at the sanctuary-rail I observe thankfully. In the circumstance it is the least that she is with those without absolution. I ponder my words wait inside a machine not far from where I sit, their discovery and what will come of them.

Sparrows in the tracery of leaves outside a window filters some of the bright sunshine. I start when with a throaty roar the gathering dips and rises its assent in the joyous finale of the mass.

Chapter 23

School on Monday is similar, there seems little change from the normal.

I effort I mend things with dearest Stella who is dark under the eyes in a pallor I worry about if I was a parent. I deduce she wept much over her humiliation from Consuela's capable hand and had restless nights also. She is very quiet which adds to her gentle beauty.

"Go home Stella," I urge, but not forcefully. "Tell Miss it is your time of the month. You are unready for this dire place this early in the week." We smile at each other; friends again. We were never not friends, even when she tore my dress.

"Your dress -" she begins, perhaps she tunes into my thought.

"It is okay. Instead you think of your health, you spare flannel," and I make her she laughs and she says chirpier "I am not all wet or I run from Casals at sight always." We continue in this way 'til Miriam arrives whereupon a hush falls immediately.

It is a hush of unusual sort and easy to see why: our dishy teacher wears a flowery dress conceals the least of her body ever. The near transparency discloses decorative bands of the black nylons tops tugged by purple suspenders also decorative which pass beneath a frilly white brief, likely see-through also.

If she stoops or tightens the dress upon her bottom probably we detect the marks the priest etched there. Quaintly she has the pretty vest yet covers her earliest chastisement but also has no bra: the round healthy breasts are prominent with the shape of their nipples evident. She glows, her lips pulse red and I know why. This morning her display is

the sexist she commits and there are whisperings of excitement. "No talking please," she chimes confidently. While
we watch she puts a cushion on her chair: all connect the
action.

We are dowdy chickens, we attend our books and papers but secretly wait for when she will walk up and down,
specially within the sunlight by the window. I puzzle she
bothers with the vest yet has no underslip. Maybe she wants
a thrill of sexy showing but conceding something to de-
cency supports conscience.

We are alert as she opens the drawer contains the pun-
ishment-implements, selects one and places it conspicuously
on her desk; the narrow attractive slipper. In her home it
adorns one of those small feet she is inordinately proud of,
and which she applied splendidly to Carmen's behind. I
glance at Da Silva, she blushes modestly.

Oh yes our teacher craves and I wonder whom she will
descend on; likely not me for reasons and not once she looks
at me since her entry.

A familiar Miriam-lecturette commences: I sink resignedly further into my seat.

"This week you children will be extra-diligent and obedient." She pauses, points severely at the slipper. "During
the weekend I studied your previous week's assignments -"
So? I think bitterly. You are a magician with time Miriam.
"- and simply they are not good enough. Slackness is abroad
and you chance Miss O'Shaughnessy is soft in the fine
weather so pull wool over her eyes." Not slackness everywhere I think savagely. "Think again, work yourselves
harder or you will bend and feel the sole of this slipper."

She picks it up, folds its length doubly which demon-
strates the suppleness menacingly, then swishes it once,
twice. Some of us roll big eyes to each other: the old Miriam
remains. If she was plain and unloving we not tolerate her
kink and certainly there will be no repeat of Juanita's de-

gree of beating. "Now to Spanish history and I expect quick answers out of sound knowledge." She rises, reads from a text, and we make notes.

The appalling Batista creature whispers: "She is tough today Sonia, you not pull the chain or what?" I bite my lip against reply.

"You talk again, Assumpta, I punish you," says Miriam.

But more comment is Batista's weakness and she falls when the delightful woman steps into a plane of bright sunshine: "Phew we see her fanny in a moment."

"What is it now Batista?"

"Oh I - I admire your fashions Miss."

"Thank you you are complimentary," Miriam responds ominously. "You are also disobedient. Go and wait by my desk."

My loin stirs when the schoolgirl form gets up, grates her chair. A victim captured, yet I cheer inwardly it is the horrid Batista who replaces Neruda in enmity.

The reading concludes, the book snaps shut with a play of anger and she I lost ascends the dais. She resumes sitting with an elegant twirl of the fragile dress. I bet delicious scent surrounds her and we devour every sound and movement of her.

She taps the slipper in her palm. "Scarcely ten": she glances at the tiny watch upon a slender wrist. "And only the beginning of the week. You seek a citation for earliest punishment of all or perhaps mention in the Guinness Book of Records?" The other reacts not. "I said expressly obedience and what is your response? Disobedience. You earn punishment for that and you will get punishment: two days stay after lessons and write an essay, or a slippering. Which?"

She is always just despite her proclivity.

Batista is surly but like many of us has impatience of school. She is eighteen. She detests the possibility of extra hours on its premises. Consequently, though with dismay, she speaks the traditional formula: "A slippering, Miss, if you will."

"Agreed. Bend over my desk."

We settle and relax: entertainment comes and my loin re-anticipates. If it were another we sympathise, but she is little popular and we are content we witness her beating.

"Not there. Over the front of the desk."

Miriam arrives without slipper as the youngster positions her bottom toward us. The different place means an initial hand-spanking and we are pleased there will be two stages.

When the school-skirt folds back - there is no underskirt - we buzz momentarily, for clearer appear discoloration and lines on our teacher's womanly buttocks specially each side of the filmy brief. "Quiet! Anyone I catch chattering bends here also. You will attend this exemplary punishment in silence."

She smoothes the pupil's snow-white panties with usual care for detail: even the maker's shiny label she tweaks upwards that it is not awry under the waist-elastic. Batista enjoy the smoothing if not the spankings I think: she is not much one of us, we experience interesting twinges and more from chastisements.

Then a pull on the waist-elastic, a tightening of what is already tight over the comely curves: the panties are a couple of measures undersize and she tries with some success they are close to a brief. We aim for this for our boyfriends we meet after school. The dogs.

Miriam surprises, she adjusts through the negligible dress her own modern brief like I saw when she was in St Rita's but this is the first time in class - and possibly the last, I gloom. My sombre thought halts for the competent loud smack of her beginning-spank. She stoops slightly as she spanks and I scrutinize the priest's familiar handwork that she exhibits. My compatriots conclude only she bore penance the same others have.

I return to an enemy's creamy pink behind as it reddens visibly under the fine thin cotton, revealing also a strong hint of her dark secretive cleft terminating at the horizontal of the lining. A procession of regular crisp smacks, their effectiveness I recall myself, impact relentlessly. Part of Miriam's method is she opens her fingers and somehow ultra-flicks the blows on to you, they sting extra than you expect. That feminine hand appears incapable it will deliver that level of pain.

Thus the miscreant is prepared. She shifts uneasily while her soft bottoms jiggle and she breathes sharply with a fear subsequent to each uncompromising smite landed.

Miss straightens, passes her punishing-wrist across her brow, then unfolds Batista's skirt, retrieves the slipper that promises next will be the best bit, and we wait for view of the schoolgirl's face. "Stand," Miss orderers musically. It is a mask of Batista that woodenly regards the floor: she has a thick skin and rarely shames. However, will her manner survive the wicked little slipper, its leather tongue that cobra-licks?

"Now you are warm and ready Batista you will bend over Victoria's desk." This is in the first row. Miss flexes the instrument jauntily and metaphorically we salivate. "No, the end of the desk." A forgetting the spectators have a whole vision of the proceedings. The redirection causes sullenness and she lays before our form-prefect whose place is appropriate for a punishing. Miriam notes the alteration of demeanour and grimly, almost roughly, folds back again the blue pleats. The white-stretch, inadequate cover of the dull red blotches on the tender surface, reappears. My physical pleasure intensifies and my heart bumps greater.

"I am unhappy Miss Batista whether you repent of your disobedience and your attitude displeases. Unfortunately the panties stay up for female privacy but there is something I will do legally. Open your legs." She hooks the elastic, works much of the immaculate cotton into the dip between the seductive crowns which now reveal angry markings starkly in the sunlight.

My loins stirs stronger and specially when the teacher's intimate bush partially we discern while she balances for stage two of the beating. Though we rejoice at Batista's subjection some of us regret we witnessed not Miriam's harsh whipping.

Energy with annoyance accompanies enjoyment. Miss swipes down the supple length of leather. The strokes impact loudly and each begets from Batista a high yelp of astonishment that she suffers so. You will say she is in the centre of action all right and amazes at her painful involvement. I whistle quietly like the others no doubt.

It is an angry long slippering and eventually with a panicky wavering cry Batista attempts, Miss reaches the bottom's twitching and weaving.

"Victoria."

"Yes Miss?"

"Take her wrists please."

The thrashing recommences vigorously: there will be bruises you bet. The dainty slipper flashes many times and the reports echo rhythmically.

At last the youthful bottom writhes and ripples to a state where lurks the unendurable and abruptly Miriam ceases the strict punishment. Silence hangs heavily in the room for some seconds until tentatively then recklessly Batista keens and sobs.

"Yes, that is the reward for disobedience and a bad attitude young lady. You will stay like that 'til the break. Victoria -"

"Yes Miss?"

"Keep her hands off her behind. You have permission you spank her if the hands stray."

"Yes Miss."

When more authority devolves to one who really is only a fellow-student Assumpta Batista's temper, not sweet at ordinary time, flares hugely and very so as Victoria's palm-curve rests and measures ready for use on the sore right chub.

"You sow. Bitch." She spits venomously.

In the awful stillness follow I fancy Juanita's ghost enters the classroom, chuckles and nods approvingly.

Miriam disbelieves her ears like the rest of us at the dreadful insolence. She stares mouth ajar - the flies find home. She recovers soon however. The mouth purses and the heaven-blue eyes half close to ice.

"Come out here in front of the class," she whispers fiercely. Uh-oh. The offender is lightly on to her feet and almost skips to what will be surely a final killing-ground. She tilts her nose, casually links fingers.

"I see!" concludes Miriam with a deadly look, turns, steps up to the drawer of all drawers. It rattle, then she grips the official school-strap, a brown snake dangles and sways. Batista rubs her nose carelessly.

"Take off your skirt, Senorita."

For a moment the heart stops, impressions she will not. Then, careless yet, she obeys.

"Bend over."

She tidies her ankle-socks like she thinks of a separate matter: her chastiser has admirable restraint.

"Touch your toes."

"No problem teacher-baby."

Nervous giggles greet the latest impertinence and Miriam's own temper frays: "Be quiet!" she shouts. Outrageously Batista twists, presses a forefinger to her lips: "Sssh."

"Very well you little bastard, you will get it now." And we shock at the swear-word. "Put your legs together."

Batista' positioning completes even to fingertips on toes. Miss strips the blouse along her back and crudely - she is so furious she forgets her passion for care in everything - tugs the panties waistband that a bit more of the bottom exposes. The teenager stumbles off her heels from the unkind pull but regains the stance required. We note she says nothing more, instead anxiously and awkwardly looks round, which is coincident with the teacher characteristically flick-flicks the leather double-tongue. She turns her head back quickly, no frivolity now.

She sees not as Miriam steps back two paces but hears the duty-strap whistles its familiar whistle through a complete arcing and feels it lash crackingly across the centre of the semi-nude bottoms which jerk captively. 'Aah-aaah' she agonises and rocks forward from the force of the blow.

Satisfaction pouts the teacher's lips and she grunts it also. "Good," she murmurs. "I think you will regret you insult me, Batista. You will not sit comfortably this week. Ready?"

She tenses the leather, judges weight and length, measures distance then lofts the limpness of the implement I felt bite myself - was it months ago? - above her right shoulder.

"I said 'Ready?' Batista."

"Yes Miss," she wrenches out from a mouth howls soundlessly beneath eyes squeeze shut.

The next vengeful stroke lashes hungrily the tops of her creamy thighs: she cries piteously and the knees buckle. 'Aaah -aaah!'

A vivid bank strengthens its lurid redness and Miriam smiles subtly, teases sensuously the malleable thrashing-stripes.

Then the smile departs. "Now you will apologize formally."

The teenager straightens painfully and wet sticks her blouse to where the pale-pink skin begins. It sweats.

"Who said you rise?" And; "Well?" as she resumes bending with a brief moan.

Silence interminable in which amazingly, perhaps admirably, she digs forth more stubbornness.

"Very well Batista, I administer the maximum." And the official strap practice-swooshes menacingly. "Go and fetch my chair. You will need it for support I promise you my child."

An instant buzz circulates which despite her suffering this far is not in the culprit's favour. We decide she deserves plenty off our beautiful teacher, antagonised disgracefully, and eyes shine, there are appreciative sighs.

She brandishes the chair like she wants she lioness-tames Miriam but senses the general mood and Miriam's iron no-compromise. Instead with ill temper almost she throws herself over its back.

Another tug of the waistband then a squeal; Miss pushes outwards the welt-sensitive crowns that the damp thin cotton pinches further down charming declivities and on to a secret opening that maybe withdraws reactively.

She discards sandals, stands apart her feet, and announces to a fingering of the dark leather: "Four strokes plus two you stood up and there is excessive noise."

Number three swipes immediately, a diagonal reacquaints the implement efficiently with its earlier result on Batista's bottom. It surprises her mightily - 'Aaaah!' - she expected a longer preamble, her rebellion is so great. The flesh jerks under the lash and convulsively she clenches the wood edge of the seat. Her hair's descent conceals her face but we imagine its workings whilst her curves upthrust lewdly cope with agony.

It is a moment I regret I savour: in perspiration beneath my uniform I caress my thighs. Awkwardly because of the desk, I cross them and squeeze: a dauntless pleasure flows with which I mingle a sharp hotness - a sensual peeing liberated curtly.

My chin trembles. I glance quickly around: Carmen's stance is similar. She smiles at me, imitates she rubs an erect penis and winks.

Miriam though she is front-on the class notices nothing, her task is all. She pauses quite at leisure. There are thirty minutes to break. She kneads her right arm and regards the senior girl 'til some semblance comes of self-control before stroke number four.

Then swooshes that one in the sunny area of the beating, it cracks across legs welted already. The hard swipe seems it nails their owner to the guileless chair and we hear a hopeless low moan.

The fifth swings likewise to its companions, swipes a higher moan and her slippery knees knock in uncontrolled agitation.

"You show these to your boyfriend or parents Miss Insolence, I not mind."

Likely she will show them at the swimming lesson on Thursday at the town hall pool, and even Batista's temperament go self-conscious amongst the crowd.

Miriam diverts my concentration and incidentally I notice the punisher's nipples now jut. And yes the base is darker than the rest of her bush. I dart eyes to the floor by her shapely small feet black-stockinged: yes a few significant drips splashed there.

What a woman! Exemplary duty combines with erotic joy in a high tableau of retribution.

Unblinking, mouth shut firm, she senses victory and plies six and seven in a fast succession with effortful grunts and, I see, a brief cascade of more drips. You delicious, I breathe lovingly.

The harsh swipings traverse the lowest portions of the youngster's bottom where ridges and mottling are least and the mysterious pleasure slit will begin generously. Those are for thinking of your boyfriend I snigger in my mind also, whilst digest happily each welting curls around the buttocks, falls away from them that consequently cringe rise and spasm whatever Batista's distraught intention.

My cheeks burn that Miriam delays then goes on to her toes and administers swingeingly from the vertical the number eight and last. My hand squeaks on my desk lid thence brush my breasts, and my rear and summer-thin panties unmeld from my sticky chair seat. I rise up slightly as the strap swipes resoundingly the hapless crowns dead centre. The victim's own moisture - mainly fear dew for nothing rally wets her lining - flies in tiny droplets which catch the sunlight in an echo dies away.

Alone of the tally it was nearly a Juanita stroke and she pants like an animal trapped. Miss's chair grates, creaks protest against Batista's body squirms, and braces to the explosive pain.

It was some licking she have but in our country we are hardy people, despise anything with less severity and lacks colourful drama.

Meanwhile our star of the morning pads to before her student's head, which circles desperately to pain's fire.

"Look at me" she commands, and tautens the leather between her fists. The other does so slowly, sweeps hair off her brow. The eyelids flicker and animosity freezes the face when she espies the wet-dark base of her teacher's bush.

"I repeat: now you will apologize formally."

No answer beyond the panting. You hear a gnat fart in the deathly hush.

"I remind you Assumpta Batista if there is not apology I take you to Mother. She will flog you in school-assembly. Well?"

It chokes her throat but she capitulates: "I apologize Miss O'Shaughnessy I called you bad names."

"Thank you... And what else?"

It devolves she forgets what happened at the beginning of the affair but our beautiful boss never forgets the whole boiling. "Obedience Batista," pronounces Miriam staunchly while recognises the genuine failure. We roll our eyes ceilingwards: we do a lot of that since she arrived on us.

"Oh. I - I thank you for er - for your needful correction of my disobedience, Miss."

"My pleasure"; without I think cynicism and she relaxes. "When you are ready return my chair. No, leave the arrangement of your underwear, you lay over Victoria's desk 'til break and we view your indignity you merited today." She passes the duty strap to the offender: "Before you replace it there is a cloth in the drawer and you wipe it nice and dry."

"Yes Miss."

Lessons re-start and our classmate wends to where the prefect sits and bends in a newer obedience.

"Victoria."

"Yes Miss."

"She has permission she soothe herself and copies your notes during break time."

"Yes Miss."

Batista shivers yet, though the skin dried. Cautiously she explores her bottoms and we smile slyly at each other, regard with satisfaction the configurations there made clear by daylight. If you ask us we will say we are content we attend justice's enactment via leather upon a true wrongdoer's obduracy within flesh.

Chapter 24

Tuesday enters the lists but will not fight. This event-less day, I think angrily, I blame on that absurd secretary Miss Nin, she neglects her work that my message lies mute or perhaps, I fume, she breaks the recording-gadget.

Wednesday. And I believe I will see my Miss no more: her absence lengthens and first Mother teaches then a trainee. My heart crushes that steeled my betrayal and pangs of mourning I never experienced 'til today constrict my throat.

Thursday. In the luncheon hours Stella is my companion. She enquires through lumps of pilchards and bread: "Where is Mad O'Shaughnessy? Oh sorry, Miriam O'Shaughnessy. I miss the thwack of leather on helpless kids' bums, how about you?"

"Your sarcasm is low grade stuff, Stella, even by your standards." She chews on imperturbable. "Perhaps we persuade Victoria gets to strapping; holy retribution etc. The trainee's a dimbo at punishments."

"Or ask Sister Consuela substitutes for punishment duty," I add meanly. She swallows, and pales, looks reproachfully at me.

"I am sorry Stella," I say quickly.

"Is she unwell?" she offers, our mutual courtesies restored. It is not that, she knows it, but this strikes one fell blow, splits my heart.

"Sonia!" she horrors at my face distressed. "You hide something?" She tries to humour me out of my misery: "Tell or I shake you your shrimp's tail drops off."

"Oh Stella!" I choke and in my turn I run into darkness though the mighty sun dwells in his dome of blue.

"What ails the child?" asks Papa, who leads strings of meat from his teeth. "She eats nothing or I say it's the substance this house calls food."

"If you dislike my kitchen Ferdinand -"

"The kitchen is fine my love, it is the terrible deeds committed in it retch my stomach."

She dismisses him. "You expect a guest menu every day you stump up for a guest menu every day." Then her eye assesss me and I shrink. "You go without meals Sonia you will be ill and I will not servant you in your bed. What is it?" she says softer. "I am your mother."

"I - I am surfeit of the heat Mama, it returns endlessly. Please -" and my eyes fill.

"If Roberto upset you I will ring his parents."

"Oh no it is not that," I say, specially weak and am thankful then she takes the bait. "I will ring his parents," she repeats like she says: I will wring his neck.

The path of old I walk again and although my spirit is heavy I name the flowers about it in profusion. It is so hot this timeless summer and dully I regard the dust hangs in the still air my shoes scoop up. A blackbird and his mate sentinel my slow progression and I whistle to them but of course they are unresponsive, I am a phoney.

'Of course.'

I will travel the empty plain whereon I had my joy whatever the wound tears from throat to belly.

The wood of her gate is warm in the sunshine and swings from my hand, obeys my sad impulse.

"Oh Miss where are you? I am sorry that I die in pieces this dreadful week."

"You little Judas!" she says.

And she is there, grave of face, unsurprised.

I hold my cheeks. "Oh Miriam." It is odd, I half-annoy, her presence vanquishes my exquisite mood.

"You little Judas! You have the nerve you come here after what you did. The arrogance of your race -"

Relief overwhelms me and I weep copiously which she mistakes I repent and darts a slap, its quality informs me will be one of several if I allow. I sink to my knees and cover the sting.

"Oh please Miriam I overjoy you get through things. I am so happy, please relent."

"You ruin my career in this country and -"

"Is he with you?" I ask fearfully, but she is contemptuous of answering instead continues: "- if I was irreligious I kill you Sonia Casals" and she towers over me in a waft of perfume - is it of gentians? - strikes my body that I sway, go into a foetal ball. "Get up" she says pitilessly. "Stand up you little traitor I will chastise you, I make you fall." She hauls me 'til my feet purchase clumsily the ground and in deep fright I hypnotise to her eyes, which are lakes of blue fire, they want they consume me.

But she hesitates. She turns away.

"Pablo is in... he sees his bishop. The trouble you cause," she says in a dead voice.

I dare I speak she will really hurt me but I will speak.

"It happens before. They will send him elsewhere only. Please Miriam you are betrothed to someone much worthier, yes?"

There is a silence you cut with scissors and I observe her profile warily, is it she ponders she will wolf me?

"I am a great sinner, I deserve all this." She regards me dolefully then, my joy, smiles gently.

"You make that tea stuff you like you drink?" I dare further, and she smiles again.

"Your skirt is very short," she comments neutrally. "If I was your mother I punish you for that."

"This moment," I reply bolder and with cheerfulness invades mutually "you are my mother" and she takes my

207

wrist, we walk the cottage path. I am a bit behind her and devour her form moves beneath her delicate dress drifts.

We cross her threshold and I receive appreciatively the familiar air of her feminine interior and, where there are not yet sheets, sight of the pretty furnishings.

"Saturday I go to the convent for a beating," I say over the top of my cup and hope I impress, she is not alone in misfortunes. "Oh yes, the enclosure business"; unimpressed. "What of your offence against me?"

The cup raps in its saucer. "It was right your liaison comes to light and if you are sane you avoid that megalomaniac in the future." The crockery rattles.

"You have small experience in these matters yet you betrayed, and one who loved you." Her lips tremble and terribly for me, she looks without where all is green and yellow sunshine.

"Here are both my wrists if you like," I say quietly. And, such is the vanity of youth and my sex, I admire their slim daintiness.

She comes back resentful and examines my face. "It is hardly recompense," she says bitterly, but pulls from her gold hair a pale blue ribbon. "I will give you the whip Sonia 'til it discovers the conscience even of a callous child."

"My conscience falters at the act of betrayal, nothing else," and I unbutton my blouse. "To me you punish that. To yourself you feel better." I unclip and uncover my breasts, they loose free: I have pride, although not quite womanly they complement well. Then I attend her carefully and solemn while she binds me neatly.

"You are lovely naked to the waist like that," she says ingenuously. "Does your hair tickles your back? - delicious sensation." I gaze wider at her. But good: I make her she forgets anger and reverses.

She gestures to a coat-hook on the front door: "Go there, Sonia Casals, and wait for me."

Over my shoulder I observe she opens the residential drawer, withdraws her objective: Oh it is a spider thing almost, the dark long insect limbs they will claw the bare innocent skin! Quickly I turn, study a paint surface, and my toes squeeze the carpet.

"You will get the martinet from your shoulders to your knees," she announces, and I sense she flicks the leathers with anticipation. "Why are you not ready?"

Slowly I engage the tight ribbon to the hook. "I remind you Miriam of Saturday's appointment," I say anxiously.

"I understand, but I unclothe you anyway. It is meet for a final occasion."

And I endure while she strips me even the ultimate undergarment which disapprovingly she drops to the floor.

"Your underwear is a disgrace."

"You wear the same."

"I am an adult, there is the difference. And change the expression please: you children do that in class, it is impertinent."

I think: you will never see us again roll big eyes.

Hot tears splash my breasts.

"Oh Miss," I choke.

She strikes formally and I gasp. "You are silly and I beat your silliness. What else is there one does with it?" I twist. Her voice is loving and warm. I want I see her face but the next stroke partially stings my right breast which agitates me wonderfully although to pain.

"Keep still. Treachery demands punishment, not torture."

The lashes swish regularly and I gasp every time. There is no agony, yet my flesh smarts sharply enough.

Eventually she pulls tiny whimperings from me 'til I sag and the ribbon bites my wrists. At this point she stops.

Her body's glow I feel encompasses mine while she guides my head round. I regard her: I am very careful I avoid any hint of cutie-pie. "That corrected nothing: the pure child will betray another's sin. But you were right, I feel better."

"I feel like somebody's small dog," I reproach as she unties. "Ooh" she laughs, detains a wrist. "Come." She sits on our sofa invitingly gathers back her dress which discloses the woman's seductive thighs and thin expensive triangle glosses upon the secretest lips beneath.

"Consuela -"

"I will not dismay our redoubtable nun I assure you."

That I descend to paradise is exaggeration yet description fails when I resume over the valley and tender plateaus of my beloved teacher whom once I taught.

"I will give you primrose, no cherries, fear not... You win the nobel prize for bottomry, Sonia. When I leave perhaps I luggage it, it stays with me always."

"What an indecent idea," I say wonderingly, and ouch she delivers the first. "Please Miriam, close your fingers."

"Of course."

Her arm locks me: I settle to the stingings and pleasurable sensation. She pauses, covers and presses my portal: a little broken cry and my juice runs extra for special time.

She spanks harder, though under her Batista strength.

I hear the sharp contacts and breathe bigger, work the sofa's cushioning, and moan greedily as pleasure spasms wider.

She ceases. "You have me now," she states. She is dignity despite the face flushes.

A realignment and I think: Please please Miss henceforward you avoid that hideous priest.

She expects me between her thighs and there I go obediently, reminded of the dog I felt after the whipping. She unclothes her breasts. I pang at their maturity then engage them, their nipples with lips and careful teeth.

She slips from dignity, clasps my hair, and I prepare.

"Miss," I remember, "your brief."

"Too late." She manages like she is a bit drunk. "It is silk anyway." And true the ultra thinness moulds along her fissure sensually you will know.

Ecstasy invades, we coalesce. "Oh Miriam I wish I die into you."

She smacks a bottom like she really drive me into her. I hear she catches breath. "Miss," I encourage: whisper in an ear burns. "I am glad you thrash Batista 'til your juices gushed." And I impose firmer and her entrance yields. She utters raggedly.

Our hot flows intermingle. Simultaneous I kiss savagely, I feel her teeth's edges. My wealed back protests, her nails tense and scrabble there.

When the wave recedes, trails the consummation, she spanks conclusively. I kiss her mouth, softer caress the ribs bathed in sweat. I am like I am vulnerable to the gods ravish me everywhere for I am vulnerable everywhere.

Then I also tumble into the wave of it diminuendos and I swim a knowledge, but believe me not entirely as a pupil.

By my side suddenly she tickles my lips with a forefinger and I attend her, which is what she wanted. She takes my hands, counts off their fingers, then says "I will write to you: we are not lost to one another."

"When is your going?" I ask dully. "Tomorrow." And my heart is lead, I bear not I look at her.

"So soon?"

"It is best. Also a confession in this parish is abhorrent to me."

"You do that before!" I accuse and she hangs her head. "True. Be kind to a failing, Sonia."

"I despair of you and at you" I say angrily.

"See here." She delves into a dress pocket. "I brought bonbons. They are good; currant flavour."

"I am not so childish" I say sullenly.

"Oh but I am. Open your mouth." And she pops one in. Reluctantly I smile at her smiling.

"It is cooler now" she comments, hooks my arm and pats. "We circuit the garden a last time."

"Oh do not" I anguish. "Shush-shush. I have something for you: what will it be?"

We pace slowly to a part where is a crowd of flowers she grew. A funeral pace I muse; how appropriate.

She halts. "Well?" "Loads of flowers" I reply ungraciously. If you ever see her gardens she is beautiful a green blossom amidst courtiers.

"Violets," she announces, stoops and picks. "Here." And I receive it, put it to my nose for the scent. Self-consciously I engage her eye. "Suits you: you know that of course."

"Suits you also, Miriam. These grow in England?"

"Ireland. And in Ireland we grow plenty of potatoes."

"They are not very attractive flowers." I sense a suspicious glance.

"In your Bible in the old testament I forget where you will find my name -" A desperation invades me. "You listen to me?" "Yes - yes I am sorry." "On the page you lay the violet." "I will" I whisper miserably. "A memento."

I have it there to this day.

"And here is another": her lips brush my cheek becomes wet so late. "Execrate sorrow Sonia or he is an unwelcome guest will call often."

We link hands and continue, she thoughtful I silent with foreboding 'til she remembers almost brightly: "My sofa! Our sofa." She startles me from my mood. "It is yours, you collect it Saturday. I pin a note to that effect."

I flash a vision of Papa, shirt sleeves and grumbles, helps manoeuvres the piece through her front door.

She assumes my lack of words signifies unwillingness. "It was not cheap though not new" she persuades warmly and I nod in distraction, feel she speaks incongruous.

"Where is your tongue child? I learned had blades for most suggestions?"

Our stage of furniture occupies a corner of my room yet. Now it is a rest place for Lima and you request permission you share whereupon he acquiesces grudgingly moves his shoulders. "Oh you again."

Sometimes in peace and recollections that wrench I rise from the cushions emptied of my first love and stare witlessly on to our courtyard. At night bars of deep cosy yellow trap the gloom. In the day time homely sounds echo across its expanse freed to the sky. Either, the one of gold hair never traverses it in decision she seeks me.

The gate no more has the heat of the sun declines and I toy its weight 'til her hand, dry yet living flesh, lays upon mine. It is the end.

She says anxiously: "I study my watch two minutes then I wave to you."

"O Miss I -"

"Sonia. Sonia we correspond. Who knows what arrangements come in the future?"

I pray no-one enter the kind of void opens that moment within me.

Speechless I dare not utter, I pace in nightmare away from a citadel whose ruination I made myself.

When the madness of my sensations is unable it fills further, terribly I turn once.

And discern the distant fluttering of a silly feminine handkerchief.

Then the convent path curves familiarly and by bushes

I fall - no other word describe my motion. Dust trickles through my fingers, and some I thrust into my mouth exclaims desolation.

'I suppose love from a youngster is impossible.'
I never saw her again."

Chapter 25

In London's summer evening a slight breeze sprang up and my quiet-voiced companion wound drifting strands from her contemplative face. I noticed the sun lower in the polished turquoise heavens and decided I would risk touching her, which dare met with her relief and indeed mine: "Will. Thank God I am not alone."

"Come come," I murmured inadequately. "That was a long reminiscence and it saddened you dreadfully. Time for some healing supper I think. Where's your hat?"

We were near enough to the house for me to carry her there: happily she surrendered to this with a girlish shriek and protests. "My skirts, Will, you pick me up all wrong, it shows underneath."

"Casals the little puritan; that's unusual."

"What is 'puritan'?"

"Oh, I'll tell you later. Much later. Perhaps not at all."

Indoors rapidly I set to preparing meals and generally being a medico to her injured morale.

"Omelettes?" No response. "Omelettes it is then, my angel. Fried tomatoes?" This was a crafty move, she had a weakness for fried tomatoes. "Oh yes please." "Here you are, have some more wine. And a smoke." The flaring match illumined her expression, becoming cheerier by the second, and man was I restored myself.

"Although you are a handful, Will, you are good for me."

We ate handsomely then to mutual sighs relaxed with tobacco and drinks.

I was loth to resurrect the ghost of Miriam, so-to-speak, but I had to because ideas were buzzing about in my head which I thought might mitigate her entrenched distress.

"Sonia," I began carefully.

"Yes Will? You look serious. I make it you are clean out of tomatoes."

"Oh no," I responded innocently. "I've got so many I have to sleep on the floor," and brought her laugh: "you goon. The boy has a real sense of humour. That is the propaganda anyway."

"Do you," I continued slowly, and took the plunge: "Do you get letters... from Miriam?"

She swallowed and stared down at the carpet, "Yes. Yes I do", then looked pathetically at me, which clinched what was forming in my mind.

"But they are in-inconsequential," she pleaded and I waited. "Miriam, she is not in her letters: she is all in her life. I lose her twice over."

To my horror her voice quivered. Quickly I captured her hands. "Where does she live?"

"Um?"

"What is her address Sonia?"

"Oh. It is in France, she teaches English and English literature."

"Is she married?"

"I think not, and she never mentions Daniel many years since."

"Well whatever. France is next door. If you like I'll take you over there. Are you game?"

"But -"

"But me no buts. It'll be an arrangement she mentioned remember?"

"Will -"

"You don't have to call on her: even if she has someone you can fix a meeting in a cafe or something. I'll keep in the background. We'll book a couple of nights in a local hotel. I bet she'll want to see what you look like after oh six years, yes?"

I had struck a chord, her silence told me so.

"Don't decide now: let me know tomorrow or whenever, okay?"

"I think I have a decision Will, and you are a light the saints switched on."

EXTRACTS

Allan Aldiss: The Barbary Series. There now four in this series, Barbary Slavemaster, Slavegirl, Enslavement and Pasha. These are all self-contained, to be read in any order. This is the opening of Slavemaster:

I stretched out on my back with my legs apart and my hands behind my head on the soft pillows of the couch, and snapped my fingers. Immediately a soft little wet tongue was joined by the tips of delicate fingers.

I could feel the girl struggling to get higher so that she could show me her face, but the short chain is intended to prevent just that. A man did not want to be bothered with a girl's identity during his siesta - he just wanted to feel her gently pleasing him. If he desired more active sport he could always ring for another girl, one on a long chain.

ISBN 1-897809-01-8 Barbary Slavemaster
ISBN 1-897809-03-4 Barbary Slavegirl
ISBN 1-897809-08-5 Barbary Pasha
ISBN 1-897809-14-X Barbary Enslavement

Rex Saviour: Erica, Property of Rex, is one of our most popular titles. It begins like this:

Paint was peeling from the woodwork of the dingy inner-city terrace house at the end of the pathetic strip of unkempt garden. The family might well have gone away after all that publicity: neighbours get very militant when youngsters are abused, even in this foulest of London slums.

The front door was ajar. I thought I heard crying from inside, or perhaps this was an abandoned kitten. Nobody answered my knock. The noise that had disturbed me stopped abruptly, that was all

I pushed open the creaking door. It led to a bare narrow uncarpeted passage. In front I could see into a cheerless kitchen with unwashed dishes piled high in a sink with a dripping tap. A door was half open on my left. I went in, and there she was, lying naked on her stomach on a shabby green couch.

She turned over and sat up in alarm, an extremely pretty girl, obviously the one I was seeking, the one mentioned in those titillating press reports I had brooded over all this time. She tried to cover herself with the only protection she had, a very small cushion. For a moment big bewildered blue eyes peeped through long reddish-auburn hair which hung over her face in a haze, then she jumped to her feet and scampered to a corner as far away from me as she could get, turning to face me shyly, shaking her head so that the hair swung behind her. She was holding the cushion to her loins, but it could not conceal the fact that she had a perfect little figure, slim but nicely rounded. She stood very erect, which drew attention to those budding breasts, so high and firm.

There was no heating or comfort in that bare room, apparently no one else in the house.

"Are you Erica?" I asked.

"Yes." It was almost a whisper. She was shrinking into the corner. She had the wide sort of mouth that so easily shows the upper teeth, and hers were good, regular and very white.

"Where's your step-Mother?"

"G-gone to the pub."

"Does she always leave you like this, no clothes?"

"Oh no, but I mustn't go out because -"

"Because what?"

"Because, well you see, Uncle Willie is coming to - to punish me."

That troubled me, of course. In fact I had been troubled about 'Erica' ever since that first newspaper story - I have changed all names, for obvious reasons. As she cowered in the corner my eyes dwelt on her skin, so very smooth, a beautiful light brown, maybe olive, verging on golden, inviting the fingers to slide over it, all over it, to explore its shyness and secret recesses ...

I licked my lips. "I think I'll wait for your step-mother. Will she be long?"

"They'll be back any minute!"

"And your Uncle Willie is coming to punish you?" It seemed incredible. "What do you mean, punish?"

She hesitated, biting her full lower lip. "He - he'll beat me, I think. With the belt, I expect, the leather one that hangs by my bed."

The sequel to Erica is BALIKPAN 1. This is 'harder' and published by another company, but may be ordered along with our titles. Here is a glimpse of Balikpan, where the religion is Sahdism, worship of The Marquis:-

... as usual, Oi stood on tiptoe a pace or two behind Sir Stephen.

Her slender wrists were crossed and secured high behind her back: I had never seen her otherwise. Today, the thin chain that ran from them between her legs to the ring set in the peak of her sex seemed even tighter than before, tight enough to straighten her back a little more than usual and thrust even higher the firmness of her perfectly formed breasts with their delightful little nipple bells. The links of the chain gleamed golden in the bright lights and the way she had been shaved and circumcised made her seem more naked than the mere absence of clothing.

The stiff gem-encrusted collar with his name embroidered on it lifted her delicate chin in a charming fashion, and her lightly rouged lips were parted and moist as he required.

Her elfin face really appealed to me as much as her cruelly displayed body, and once again it struck me that never before had I seen anything more erotic than this poor unfortunate plaything of a sadist.

1-897809-02-6 ERICA PROPERTY OF REX
BALIKPAN 1 (£10, mail order only)

Rex Saviour also contributed a novelette - Robin, Property of Ogoun - to Bound For Good, our 3-in-1 special. The other contributors are A.Darrener - Teacher's Pets, end of term and Mr Robinson is having trouble with two over-nubile school leavers, but fortunately these young vixens turn out to relish the punishment they have earned.' Darrener is well known but under a different name and we are hoping for a full length novel from him in due course. The title novel by Gord, foremost in his field as many of you will know, is surely the ultimate bondage novel of all time:

... Sam began by dressing her in an all over leather suit, fashioned in a thin pliable leather that hugged her body like a second skin; the smell of that leather was divine.

With Sam's help she steadily eased the skin over her naked form, noticing as she did so the plethora of buckles running right across the reinforced shoulders.

Now from Robin, Property of Ogoun:

"There is no need to go back to HIM," he said. "You could come with me."

"Oh?"

"You are very pretty."

"How I wish I were not!"

"I would not beat you as hard as that monster would."

She looked at him, head on one side, a sad little smile on her seductive lips. "But you would beat me?"

He did not answer. She had had warning enough. "You are hungry?" he asked.

"Yes, I am hungry."

"Very hungry?"

"Yes, I am very hungry. The reason I order nothing is that I cannot pay."

He took a deep breath. This would put his fantasy on the line, almost certainly destroy his slender hopes. "I shall pay," he said. "If you pay me - with your bra."

She looked at him hard and for a long time, her dark brown eyes questioning.

"Well, I must eat. So yes, I would obey, if that is what amuses you. But I am not wearing a bra."

"Your stockings then."

"Did you not notice that my legs are bare?"

"Of course. I just forgot." And very enticing they were too, the dress so short. He licked his lips and clenched his fists for resolution. "Your knickers then. It will have to be your knickers, if that is all you have."

Tears came to her eyes, running over and tipping the long lashes. Then she stood up silently and went towards the ladies, her walk outstandingly graceful. When she came back he had his travelling case open on the table and at his gesture she dropped her knickers into it.

ISBN 1-897809-05-0 BOUND FOR GOOD: A 3-in-1 Special

Lia Anderssen, Biker's Girl, Biker's Girl On The Run, The Training of Samantha and The Hunted Aristocrat, all separate and complete and to be read in any order, but surely in a class of their own! From Biker's Girl:

The leader of the group, the one she had heard called Perce by the others, spoke to her.

"Wanna eat?"

She shook her head, gazing down at the ground in front of her.

He grabbed her by the chin, pulling her face to his. "Answer me. Wanna eat?"

"Not in there," she muttered. The diner was crowded.

"Then you'll just have to come in and watch us." He reached down and undid the locks that were holding her ankles bound to the bike, then released the cuffs from the ring on the bike seat, leaving her hands still fastened behind her.

Lia felt the panic rising in her. "But you can't make me go in there like this!"

He smiled. "Like what?"

She lowered her eyes again. "You know!"

He grinned, his eyes piercing hers. "Tell me."

She hesitated. "I'm stark naked," she said quietly, blushing at having to say so.

"What?" he asked, pretending to cup his ear.

Lia's face reddened more deeply. "I'm stark naked," she repeated, this time a little later.

"Sorry, I can't seem to hear you, better tell me when we're inside," he said, shoving her from behind.

Inside there were plastic topped tables, each with salt and pepper and sauce, fluorescent lighting that cast a flat glare over the whole place. At the far end was a bar with half empty liquor bottles lining the shelf behind it. The floor was covered with linoleum, dirty and faded and scarred with the burn marks of a thousand cigarettes.

The room was about half full. At the tables sat men in dirty overalls, smoking and picking at grease-covered plates. In one corner was another group of bikers, drinking beer and and laughing noisily. At one or two of the tables men nudged one another and pointed, grinning. In vain she searched the faces for one that offered solace from her plight.

Perce nudged her in the ribs. "What was you about to tell me?"

When she hesitated, he started to undo her belt. She didn't want to be beaten again ... just in front of her, on a pillar, was a full-length mirror, placed there in better days to allow the clients to adjust their clothing before leaving. Now it reflected her body, and she studied in momentarily. She saw a slim, willowy figure, dark hair draped across her shoulders, the breasts not over large but firm and jutting forward proudly, the dark nipples prominent and upturned, her belly dark with downy pubic hair kept trimmed short so that the lips of her sex were clearly visible, her long shapely legs tapering gracefully beneath. She was probably the most beautiful woman that these louts would ever see clothed, let alone as she was.

She took heart from that.

"I'm stark naked!" she said, in a loud clear voice, proud of her beauty and, to her amazement, getting an undoubted thrill from the situation.

Then, in the silence that followed, her brief moment of courage deserted her, but the arousal grew as the full enormity of her vulnerability sank home. Not only were her charms openly on display before all these uncouth men, but with her hands fastened behind her as they still were, she had no means of covering herself.

There was no mercy or compassion here.

Then an eye caught hers. The man sat with the another group of bikers. Like them he was clad in leather, his jacket open to the waist revealing a mass of blond curls on his chest. His eyes were deep blue and compassionate, his face was somehow kind, framed in long blond tresses of hair that hung to his shoulders.

To Lia he appeared like the prince she had always imagined in the fairy tales she had read as a child ...

ISBN 1-897809-04-2 BIKER'S GIRL
ISBN 1-897809-17-4 BIKER'S GIRL ON THE RUN
ISBN 1-897809-07-7 THE TRAINING OF SAMANTHA
ISBN 1-897809-11-5 THE HUNTED ARISTOCRAT

Janey Jones. Circus of Slaves and Caravan of Slaves, two erotic fantasies. Our extract is from 'Circus':-

Mr Columbus ushered Jasmine into the dark interior of the caravan and turned to shut the door. She felt elated, and found herself stifling back a sudden girlish giggle of delight at the excitement of having him accept so quickly her clumsily-put offer.

She didn't want him to think that she wasn't serious, because she was, she really was. Something inside had told her what she wanted the moment she had set eyes on this man. It wasn't just a physical affair, not his fierce eyes that burned into you - though they had made her shiver with pleasure - or his magnificent whiskers, or even his mouth, so ... so sybaritic. (Was that the right word, she wondered? She had a weakness for rich words). No, the truth was she had recognised him. She couldn't have explained what she meant by 'recognised' to the others. They wouldn't have understood what she meant, she knew that. It probably belonged to that oriental part of her psyche which Westerners didn't understand. Mr Columbus and she were kindred spirits. Perhaps they had met in some previous existence.

Slowly her large dusky eyes became accustomed to the dim light and she gazed in wonder at her surroundings. A bulky mahogany desk filled one corner of the caravan, but the rest of the interior sent a tingle of delight down her spine. A huge leather settee stretched the length of one wall, dotted with cushions covered in brilliant silks. Amethyst, ochre, and azure - lovely words - came to her mind. Gorgeous Persian rugs were spread over the floor and lay at every angle. Some, more costly, even hung from the walls. To one side stood a low table covered with brass vessels of almost barbaric form and decoration, which glittered in the sunlight filtering in through the slats of the window blinds to create an atmosphere which, to her mind, simply oozed softness and sensuality.

She turned round, sighing with delight. She had heard that Romanies lived in great luxury, but this was beyond her dreams. This is a caravanserai, she thought, not caring whether it was the right word, it was the expressive one! This was a scene from the Arabian Nights, and she was about to become part of it. Her heart swelled with joy.

She noticed a sweet odour about the place, not unpleasant, but unusual. For a moment she wondered if this might be the smell of a hookah-pipe. That would certainly complete the impression. Her eyes glittered with pleasure and she strained to look into the dark corners of the caravan.

Her inquisitive gaze froze and a gasp escaped her throat. She instantly became aware that a third person was present within the enveloping luxuriousness. Jasmine stiffened like a surprised cat. In a dim corner there knelt, perfectly still, a small, dark haired female figure, head bent forward, legs spread, hands palm upwards on naked thighs, her wrists connected by fine silver chain. A helmet of shiny brown hair hung over her elfin face and her pale, naked breasts shone like alabaster in the soft morning light.

Mr Columbus had turned and stood back, eyeing Jasmine closely from beneath his bushy eyebrows. Her slim delicate body swayed slightly in the warm closeness of the caravan and a nervous shiver ran through her tense body.

"Let me introduce you to Tina, my personal assistant," he said.

ISBN 1-897809-10-7 CIRCUS OF SLAVES
ISBN 1-897809-20-4 CARAVAN OF SLAVES

Ray Arneson, Rorig's Dawn. At last we have a writer in the manner of Gor, sci-fi fantasy from our special angle:

Rorig was puzzled, his recollections hazy and unsure, but at least he had a woman, it seemed.

He kicked the girl awake, though he suspected that she was already conscious and just trying not to attract attention. He rolled her over, quickly snapping thongs to her elbows and securing them to the tent pegs either side of where she lay. As a chattel, she slept outside the tent.

Her hands and legs were still bound, as they had been all through her fitful sleeping. A Warrior with little but a tent and his weapons does not allow any possibility that a girl might escape. A girl is a disposable asset, however poor a price he may get for her.

She whimpered, and tried to hunch up into a ball. He concentrated on looping more thongs to the posts he had driven into the ground last night, feeling nothing but contempt for her - as if she was to blame for his predicament. His movements though skilled were angry, quick. The slightest inaccuracy in his swift work brought a curse; the faster he went, the more frequent his errors. He knew it. Still, the anger released made him feel better.

The posts were about level with her feet, if she had stretched out straight from the collar chain clamped to the main tent post. Two arm spans apart, they had but one purpose, that she was about to be put to. Part of the reason that she hunched up was to keep well away from the posts.

Rorig grabbed one of her ankles and pulled her out, taut, wrapping the thong about it as he did so. She struggled, but Rorig was a Warrior and the girl was tethered to his tent. It was not a serious contest. He freed her knee and ankle straps then, that she had slept in.

The other ankle was wrenched wide, out to the other post. Soon it too was fastened. She was ready; a relative term, since the girl did not wish any of this, and especially what he was about to do to her, but she had no choice, no defence. The scrap of rag around her waist was no hindrance. She wore nothing else.

ISBN 1-897809-16-6 RORIG'S DAWN

NOW ABOUT SILVER MINK - Our Silver Mink imprint treats similar themes, but is intended to be more suitable for women - they are more subtle, but it doesn't seem to put off our male clients from reading them.

1-897809-09-3 WHEN THE MASTER SPEAKS by Josephine Scott:

EXTRACTS

July 1869, My dear Sister,

Sister, I have felt rage from Papa before, when I broke the fine china dish that was his mother's wedding present to him, when I did stand knee deep in the river and search for fish, my skirts held up in a shameful and wanton fashion (so Papa said) and I felt then the terrible force of his rage and the terrible sting of the strap.

... but stay, let me not think of the strap for a brief moment, though the whistle of its falling echoes loud within my head. Perhaps that is why I write this letter to you, to purge such thoughts and also in the hope nay the prayer that one way I will be free to send it to you! and you will know what became of your sister Clarisse after I ran away -

Let me speak first of London town where it is fine and warm. Let me tell you here in London there are people - so many people! You would not begin to believe how many people could live in one City, for sure it makes our local towns look so provincial. And people smile when they hear my voice for I speak with the voice of a country girl and I hate it.

Ah Sister, I can see you disapprove of me even as I write these lines! You always said we should be proud of what we are, country people, the salt of the earth. But who knows, it may be you will never see these words. They are to ease my mind as much as they are to be read by you one fine day.

Sophie, I can delay no more, I must tell you what happened before I left...

[her father caught her with a man]

...Well! I have seen Papa in many a rage, but sister, I have never felt anything like this! Peter James hustled out, fled the church even as Papa roared after him that his Master would be told and retribution rained down on him. And I stood, skirts awry and blouse awry for he had sought and I gave a breast into his warm sunny hand. I must have been a sight, stood with hair atumble and my eyes aflame with the feelings I had. I know my bosom heaved with breaths so deep it was as if I would take into myself the whole atmosphere of the church and breathe it out suffused with life!

And Papa looked at me and I saw in his eyes the truth.

He lusted after me.

He seethed in his anger and rage at his own feelings and what I was about to do before the high altar, and he the Vicar of this church too! I knew my time had come. That this would be a punishment not to equal any other I had ever had.

1-897809-13-1 AMELIA by Josephine Oliva:

Amelia falls under the sway of a 'Country Gentleman' whose attitude towards women was learned among the slave owners on an American Plantation of the 1850's.

He submits her to deeper and deeper discipline and degradation, until at last the tables are turned ... and, as Mistress, Amelia knows exactly how to exercise her new won powers.

A robust tale of punishment and retribution that begins like this:

I think what affected me most was the shock that welled up in those dark eyes as the frightened young black girl realised what the auctioneer had pushed up her arse, the coarse way he handled her, the laughter of the bidders as they mocked her squirming as it grew more and more frantic. Certainly the remembrance of her dark beauty and shaven nakedness, and the knowledge of the many beatings she had undoubtedly had, haunted me for many years.

All that and brooding on the way the bully who bought her unbuckled his belt as he dragged her away and the thought of what would follow may have twisted my whole personality and eventually determined the cruelty of my actions when Amelia fell so defenceless into my hands ...

1-897809-15-8 The Darker Side: a collection of short stories by Larry Stern. Here is an extract from one of them:

The spacious, high ceilinged room is brightly lit. The large windows, almost the full height of the room, give out onto a view of an extensive parkland where people stroll and an occasional horseback rider passes. There are many such rooms in the civilised world. In New York the view would have been over Central Park, in Paris over the Bois de Boulogne, but here, in London, we are overlooking Hyde Park. Despite the headlong rush of the traffic outside no noise of the busy world penetrates to the room; all is deeply, forebodingly silent.

A young woman, hardly out of girlhood, sits with head bowed at a piano. It is a full size concert grand piano. She is formally dressed as if for a recital performance. A long black skirt reaching down to her feet covers her legs while a chaste, high necked, white blouse, a crisp ruffle at the front, completes her outfit. Her long chestnut hair, well brushed to shine in the intense light, frames a pretty, oval face which is marred only by the blemish of a distinct look of apprehension.

To all outward appearance there is no abnormality here - just a pretty and talented, albeit somewhat nervous, concert pianist at practice, preparing for her next engagement. The knowledgeable eye will, however, notice that her skirts are arranged after the fashion of Roissy, draped over the stool on which the young woman sits rather than gathered beneath her bottom. Indeed, after the fashion of Roissy, this demurely pretty creature wears no undergarments and the bare flesh of her bottom is in direct contact with the cool, smooth leather of the piano stool.

Beside her, as she sits upright at the piano, her body held almost unnaturally stiffly erect, there stands a man. A man very obviously in late middle age. He stoops a little and his hair is streaked with grey. He is elegantly, yet austerely dressed.

The room is full of atmospheres. The air is distinctly chill despite the warm summer sunshine that filters through the tightly sealed window panes. This feeling of coldness is enhanced by the stark whiteness of the room's interior and by the virtual lack of any furnishing save the piano and a heavy leather armchair. Then, too, there is the almost palpable feeling of fear and apprehension that emanates from the young pianist.

1-897809-19-0 The Training Of Annie Corran by Terry Smith

The Ford Escort pulled into the kerb and, leaving the engine running, the young man at the wheel jumped out and went round to open the passenger door. The blonde girl inside looked at him in alarm.

"What are you doing, Jamie? Why are we stopping here?"

Without replying the man took her arm and pulled her out of her seat. She was not prepared for his action and she quickly put one foot on to the kerb to steady herself. Then she tried to resist him, but with one violent tug, he wrenched her free from the car. She squealed then and looked at him in amazement.

"If you want to go home you can bloody well walk," he said.

"On one shoe?" she replied, giving a little laugh and trying her best to calm the situation down.

"On your knees for all I care!" He slammed the door and moved quickly round the car.

"Jamie!" she shouted. "Jamie you can't, you can't!" She was devastated by the realisation that he really intended to abandon her where she was.

The car roared off with the engine racing and the tyres squealing, leaving the girl to look after it with an open mouth. As it accelerated up through the gears her lips moved, but no words emerged, and as it turned the corner and its sound started to fade, she looked round at the dark alien street. She stumbled back on her single high heel, slowly becoming aware of her situation and her potential danger.

Most of the terraced houses had lights shining in their windows and the corners of one or two curtains had already been pulled back to show staring faces. Soon the front doors would start to open. She bent down and, removing her remaining shoe, held it in her hand as if she intended to use it as a club. As she straightened up she felt a tiny hand slipped inside hers and looking down she saw the pity and compassion shining from the saucer-like eyes of a little girl.

"Hello, who are you?" she said smiling, already feeling comforted by the touch of another caring human being.

Before the girl could reply they were joined by an equally small boy.

"Are you in trouble? 'cos we gotta phone," he said proudly.

The girl looked round the street once more, to see that many of the front doors were open now, with predominantly young men standing at them, observing her plight. It didn't take her long to decide that she wanted to be off the street and she let the children lead her to a nearby house. The door was immediately opened by a handsome woman in her early twenties who gave her a beaming smile.

"Come in, go straight through," she said pleasantly, holding the door wide for her.

The blonde girl walked ahead of her down a short passage, talking to her over her shoulder. "This is very good of you. I'm ever so sorry to be a trouble."

"No trouble, no trouble at all," the other woman replied, ushering her towards the open door to a dimly lit room.

Then she heard a booming laugh that filled the room with its authority. "Come in, little girlie, we are all friends here, though I can't guarantee that no one is going to eat you!" The deep male voice was as assured as the great laugh had been.

She had walked into a large oblong shaped room containing several people. They were all laughing as if the speaker had made a huge joke. In the dim light she could make out at least six men, two women and some children. And like everyone else she had seen since leaving the car, they were all black.

EXTRACTS

The men ranged in age between early twenties and late thirties she guessed, except one middle aged man in his forties, who she took to be the owner of the voice she had heard. He was a large man, over six feet tall and heavily built with solid looking muscle. He was dressed in a double breasted, two piece suit and a trilby hat and sat in a large leather arm chair which he filled to over-flowing. The way that the chair was positioned to dominate the long narrow room made him appear like a king on a thrown surrounded by his courtiers.

"Scat you kids, give the lady some room," he said.

There was a babble of talk in patois as the men took the opportunity to discus her appreciatively, but it died away immediately when the older man began to speak again.

"My name is Stig. What's your's, honey?"

"Clare," she replied shyly.

"That's a beautiful name for a beautiful young lady. It suits you just fine. Would you take a drink with us, Clare?"

"I- I don't need anything, thank you. If I could just phone -"

"No need to be shy. I know it's scary when you first meet new people, but we are your friends, sister. Taking a drink when it's offered helps break the ice. I have something in mind that I think you will find just to your taste. Something so good that you will drink it all down and beg for more."

"No nothing special please. Perhaps just a Coke then, if you've got one. Thank you."

"That's better, girl. More friendly isn't it?"

She nodded her head and he gave his big booming laugh again. He looked her up and down, undressing her with his eyes and liking what he saw. He felt the excitement of the chase rising within him and he was instantly in the mood to take advantage of the situation the fates had presented him with. He looked at her flushed face with the wide staring blue eyes which he held with his own deep brown ones like a mouse hypnotised by a snake. The room was fading from his consciousness now and this was a battle of wills just between the two of them. His audience was watching and waiting for the master to perform. He wanted to go for the kill straight away.

"How old are you, girl?"

"Sixteen."

"Sweet sixteen. You wouldn't lie to me would you, girl?" he asked and Clare shook her head.

"Don't just shake your head at me, girl. God gave you a voice and two beautiful lips and a heavenly little pink tongue. And he gave me two great big elephant's ears. So let's not waste his gifts." He cupped his hands behind his ears, pulling them forward.

His words and tone had the effect he wanted. She was not used to being treated this way, or verbally attacked by a complete stranger for no reason. She was immediately on the defensive, almost believing that she might have appeared rude.

"No. I am sixteen, honestly," she hastened to assure him.

"I know you wouldn't lie to me, girl. You have proper respect for your elders, don't you?"

Clare nodded her head, but then remembered what he had said. "Yes," she said, dutifully.

"You know why sixteen's sweet?" he asked.

"No."

"Now you're lying, just a little bit, aren't you? You know that when a girl's sixteen that's sweet for a man, don't you?"

"Yes." She nodded and lowered her eyes.

Stig gave his big booming laugh again. "It's also sweet for a girl when she is sixteen isn't it. Do you know why that is, girl?"

"No." Again Clare shook her head.

"When a girl is sixteen, she's a woman, right?"

"Yes."

"She has a woman's body."

Clare didn't say anything. Her cheeks went bright red and she dropped her gaze from his.

"Have you got a woman's body, Clare?"

She didn't answer. She tried to look at him defiantly, but after a moment her gaze dropped again.

"Show me!" he said.